teas & tribulations

A Cozy Fantasy

Tales from the Broken Claw
Book Four

don jones

donjones.com

also by don jones

stories of witchkind®

<u>Age of the Adherents</u>:

Daniel Scratch • Master of the Tower • The Fifth Axis

<u>The Order</u>:

The Order of Some • The Conspiracy of One • The Truth of All

———

Clara Thorn

Clara Thorn, the witch that was found

Clara Thorn, the witch that fought

Clara Thorn, the witch that won

———

Endless Sky®

Truthsayer • New Worlds

———

Tales from the Broken Claw

Pubs & Pegasi • Anvils & Avatars

Volumes & Villainesses • Teas & Tribulations

———

The Never: A Tale of Peter and the Fae

Bob Constantine (no relation)

———

Find more at DonJones.com, including a free fantasy trilogy, a free superhero duology, two collections of short stories, and even more short stories and flash fiction. You can even listen to free music inspired by the books!

contents

Urwald
North Pointe Common Towne
Gray Foal Pass
The Mistral Mountains
Strongfast
Celestrum
Elgindam
Lake Evendim
Smallhaven
Scintas
Westhold
Demonbane Range
Lake Midton
Holderdown
Magefell
Skyreach Range
Stormport
Kithwellen
Salten Sea
Flameheight Range
Lake Trenton
Trenton
The Mountedives
Dunereach
Shorehaven
Highseat
Farreach
Darkehame Darkestore Forrest
Bright Islands
The Forbidden Continent
Amber Sea
N

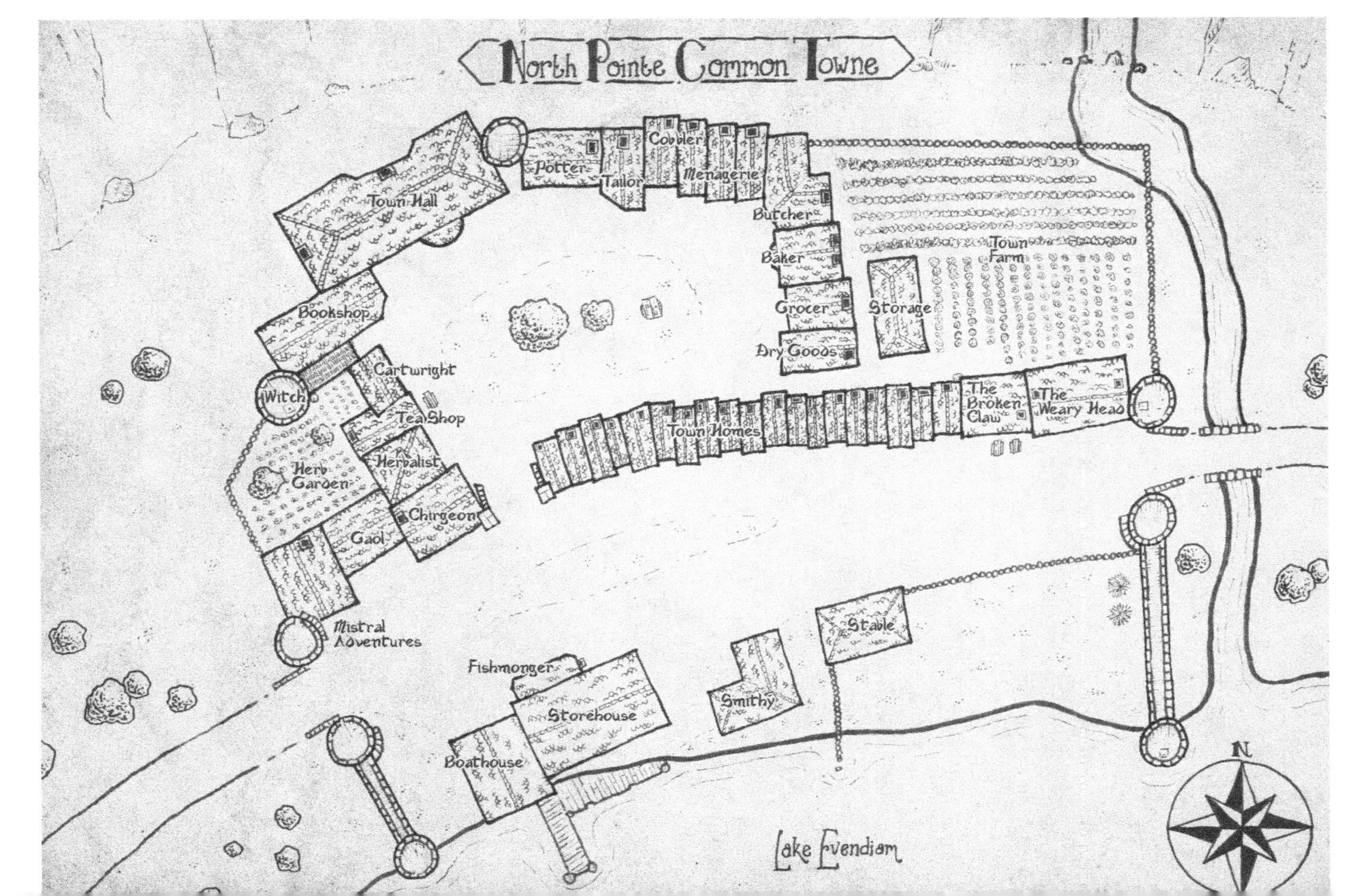

North Pointe Common Towne
Town Hall
Potter
Cobbler
Tailor
Menagerie
Butcher
Baker
Grocer
Dry Goods
Storage
Town Farm
Bookshop
Cartwright
Witch
Tea Shop
Herbalist
Herb Garden
Chirgeon
Gaol
Mistral Adventures
Town Homes
The Broken Claw
The Weary Head
Fishmonger
Storehouse
Boathouse
Smithy
Stable
Lake Evendiam
N

one

· · ·

SUNRISE CAME SLOWLY to the tea shop, as if the day itself preferred to linger in bed a little longer. The morning light eased through lace curtains, sketching honeycomb patterns over every uneven surface: the battered wooden counters, the stone floor swept spotless but eternally dusted with stray tea leaves, the rows of jars and tins crowding the wall behind the counter, labeled in Galhani's brisk, looping script. The aroma that filled the shop was thick and layered: peppery root, tart fruit, resin, smoke, and the pleasant green note of something freshly snipped.

Galhani herself was already awake and in motion. She moved along a row of earthenware jars, fingers trailing, pausing only when her intuition gave the faintest tug. Most days, her hands knew the needs of the day before her brain finished the calculation: this morning, the instinct called for witchhazel, a small twist of bitter orange, the dried yellow heart of borage flower, and a shaving of firevine bark.

She filled the first infuser of the morning, hands nimble and deliberate, and closed the jar with a solid thunk. Water had just begun to bubble in its copper kettle when the bell above the shop door gave a hesitant, apologetic tinkle. She set her infuser in a waiting cup and turned, dusting off her palms.

The traveler who stepped inside seemed to bring the road with him. His coat was road-dust and sweat, and he left behind him a faint trail of sand on the floor. His eyes were the washed-out blue of a sky that had seen too many suns. He shuffled up to the counter and stood, not quite able to rest on his heels, shifting his weight as if unsure if he would be welcome or not.

"Something for the road, or something for after?" Galhani asked, setting out the cup.

"Something for... now," he said, voice barely more than a croak. "I need to be on my feet again by midday, but I could sleep for a year." He considered. "Maybe something for both?"

She nodded, already measuring a pinch of bright starlace into the infuser, and reached for a jar that had been nearly forgotten in the shadowed top shelf: mothmint, its leaves pale as dust, reserved for the most desperate cases. She added a single leaf. He watched, brow furrowed.

"Old remedy," she explained, pouring the hot water over the leaves. "Sharpens you up, then lets you down easy after."

He gave a small smile. "Thank you, mistress."

Galhani offered a smile of her own, then set the cup before him. "Give it two minutes. Any sugar?"

He shook his head. "If it does what you say, it's fine as is."

She moved down the counter as the traveler inhaled, steam rising to his face, and began to work through her checklist: count the honey jars (two left, more than enough), polish the glass display of house blends, rotate the pastries so the cinnamon knots faced out. She reached up to adjust a trailing length of parlor vine that had stretched itself too eagerly toward the morning light.

From the back of the shop came the clack and clatter of someone restocking the drying racks. That would be Lara, no doubt wrangling a stubborn bundle of lemon balm or arguing with the shop's ancient, temperamental scale. The thought brought a warmth to Galhani's cheeks, and she allowed herself a moment to stand on tiptoe and peek through the half-door to the rear garden.

Sure enough, Lara was there: not more than three feet tall, hair tied up in a wild knot, already deep in negotiation with a hunk of ginger root that seemed to resist the knife's edge. She caught Galhani's eye and waggled the knife in mock-threat, then returned to the cutting board with fierce determination.

A second bell tinkle called Galhani back to the front. The traveler had finished his cup and stood taller, as if a small weight had been set down somewhere inside him. He looked at her with a kind of incredulous gratitude.

"You have no idea," he began, and then stopped, eyes shining. "Thank you." He pressed a few silvered coins into her palm—more than enough for the brew—and ducked out, already striding with something like purpose.

No sooner had he left than a new pair entered: a woman, arm in arm with a sullen-faced merchant whose boots bore fresh bandages around the heels. They made their way to a table in the corner, where Galhani already had set a battered sugar bowl and a pot of her own best blend.

"Something to soothe the nerves?" she suggested to the woman, who nodded, eyes darting around the busy shop.

"And for your companion?"

He lifted one foot and scowled. "Something for blisters, I'd wager."

Galhani nodded, her brain assembling the right combination: for the woman, rosehips and valerian, to untwist whatever knot lay in her chest. For the man, a compress of yarrow and ground willow bark, steeped extra strong and served with a small jar of local honey. She brewed with brisk precision, measuring and pouring, then brought both cups to the table. She watched as their shoulders eased by degrees, the woman's jaw unclenching as the first sip took hold, the merchant's frown fading as the warmth seeped through him.

The morning went on this way, the shop filling with the drift and ebb of travelers, townsfolk, and a few bleary-eyed children in search of honeyed milk. Each brought their own troubles—headaches, queasy bellies, stubborn coughs—and Galhani met each with a recipe tailored in the moment, her hands almost moving on their own. The magic of the shop thrummed soft and steady in her chest, guiding her to the perfect ratio of sage to licorice root, or the precise measure of nettle to counter the aftertaste of feverfew.

At regular intervals, Lara would come through the half-door with fresh bundles—marigold, dandelion, sprigs of something peppery and blue-green—and offer them up with a proud smile. Sometimes Galhani would lean in to inspect the harvest, sometimes she'd ruffle Lara's hair, but every time, their eyes would meet and linger for a second longer than needed, and that was enough.

In the early afternoon, a new trio arrived: a rail-thin man, a child perched on his hip, and a grandmotherly woman trailing behind, eyes scanning every surface. The man looked desperate, the child sniffled miserably, and the grandmother's voice was sharp and worried.

"She's had that cough for days now. Can you do something, mistress?"

Galhani reached over the counter and gently took the child's hand, feeling the slight fever, noting the rawness of the throat by the way the girl swallowed. She smiled at the child—who shrank back, but then met her gaze with watery eyes.

"Easy fix," said Galhani. "Marshmallow root, a touch of licorice, maybe a bit of honey if you're very good."

The girl nodded solemnly.

"And for you?" Galhani asked, glancing up at the man and the grandmother.

The man shook his head, exhaustion etched into the lines of his face. "If she's well, I'll be well."

The grandmother considered. "I'd not say no to something for the nerves," she said, gaze softening.

Galhani made two brews, one sweet and gentle for the child, one subtle and earthy for the grandmother. The child's eyes widened at the first taste, then she smiled shyly, the hint of a dimple appearing. The grandmother sipped and closed her eyes, hands wrapped around the cup as if warming herself by a hearth.

A lull followed, and Galhani used the pause to clear tables, brushing away stray leaves and wiping rings from the wood. She glanced around her domain, satisfied to see every customer with a cup in hand, every table occupied by someone at peace—or at least on their way to it. The steam rising from a dozen cups blurred the sunlight, catching in the air and making the whole place feel a little softer, a little safer.

Lara appeared again, this time with a handful of violets, and slipped behind the counter to set them in a glass jar. She reached for Galhani's hand under the counter, squeezed it, and whispered, "You did good today."

Galhani grinned, heart swelling, and leaned over to kiss Lara's hair. "So did you. Never seen better violets."

The two worked in tandem, restocking shelves and preparing for the afternoon crowd, but for a brief moment, the tea shop was theirs alone, filled with nothing but the gentle clinking of porcelain, the sweet haze of flowers, and the sound of their laughter tangled with the rustle of leaves above.

———

Evening in North Pointe arrived with the long, drowsy sigh of the town itself. The wind had dropped, leaving a hush over the cobbles and grass. Vendors in the market square packed their goods into crates and wheeled carts, exchanging last-minute haggles and a few cheerful insults before heading for home, the inn, or a favored corner in the Broken Claw. By the time Galhani turned the sign on her shop from "OPEN" to "CLOSED" and locked the half-door behind her, the sky was already tucking itself into twilight, clouds tinged with fire and lavender.

Lara tugged at her sleeve. "You promised you'd try the cider tonight."

"I promised I'd try it if we survived today." Galhani reached up to pat Lara's arm. "Which, as it happens, we did. Barely."

The two gnomes set off down the flagstone walk, skirts grazing the tips of the overgrown grass. The town square felt oddly still, the calm after a day's storm of travelers and barter. Here and there, a stubborn merchant packed up the last of their apples or parsnips, while children zigzagged between stalls, daring each other to climb the fountain's rim or tap the weathered statues on their stone noses. Overhead, the lanterns that ringed the square flared into life, casting golden puddles on the gray.

As they passed the cobbler's shop—shuttered and dark—Lara whispered, "Did you notice? Not a single morning forager today. Even the old carrot lady didn't show."

Galhani nodded, though she had noticed far more than that. The usual rhythm of the day—predictable as the seasons—had been skipped and syncopated all afternoon. Half the familiar faces were missing. Most customers were strangers, and many had the look of people who planned to move on rather than linger. Even the few regulars in her own shop had seemed distracted, glancing out the windows with the anxious energy of birds before a storm.

She kept those worries quiet, for now. She didn't want to trouble Lara, whose rare evenings off were already too short.

The Broken Claw came into view, huddled beside the inn and across from stables, facing the trade road like a watchful dog. It was a two-story building, plain as a mud pie like the rest of the town, its only concession to extravagance a faded sign painted with a snapped-off bear's paw. The windows glowed, but the warm light was softened by years of smoke and good-natured brawling.

Inside, the din was as familiar as a favorite song: wood-on-wood, the rise and fall of voices, the sweet yeasty tang of beer and the acrid ghost of a thousand spilled drinks. Along the left wall, the battered kegs stood in silent formation, and behind the bar, Sam was polishing glasses with the intensity of someone pretending not to eavesdrop.

Lara grinned and pointed. "Corner table's free."

But the table was not, in fact, empty. Three were already gathered there: Leota in her trailing black dress, looking frail but somehow the center of gravity; Vamir, long-limbed and folded into himself, reading something upside down; and Lucy, arms crossed, bouncing a foot in time to some internal rhythm.

Galhani and Lara slid onto the bench. Leota's eyes flicked up, dark and almost amused. "If it isn't North Pointe's resident miracle workers," she said. "Don't tell me you had an easy day."

"I wouldn't dream of lying," said Galhani. "But if I had, you'd be the first to catch it."

Lara waved at Sam, who nodded and started two small tankards of cider. "What's the story tonight?" Lara asked.

Lucy leaned in, lowering her voice to the sweet spot just above a whisper. "There's more folk on the road than I've seen since I came here. Where do they all come from?" Her accent smeared the vowels, though it warmed the question rather than sharpening it.

"Where are they all going, is what I'd like to know," added Vamir, not looking up from his book. "And why do half of them wear their shoes down in exactly the same way?"

Leota sipped her drink, then turned to Galhani. "Did you hear about the two new shops?"

Galhani blinked. "What, since yesterday?"

Leota nodded. "Right next to Bartram's. One opened just this morning. Sign said 'Darning for Socks.'"

Lara snorted. "That's not even a clever name."

"I know," Leota said, the corners of her mouth curling. "It gets better. Next door is 'Tuning for Harps.'"

Lucy let out a peal of laughter, but Vamir only looked thoughtful. "Perhaps the town's magic is responding to the increased traffic," he suggested, closing his book. "Manifesting useful shops to serve the needs of the community, and calling for people to open them."

Leota shook her head. "It feels off. Like... when you try to whistle, but your lips are too dry. There's something hollow about it."

Sam appeared, setting down two ciders with a practiced thump. "I'll tell you what's off: the noise at the gate this morning. Four wagons, all at once. One with a horse that bit a man's finger, one that nearly ran me over coming up the road, and then two wagons later, a kid who tried to sell me firewood that was still green."

"Doesn't sound that different from usual," Lara said, sniffing the cider.

Sam shrugged. "It's the frequency. Used to be you'd see one or two dozen travelers a day. Now it's five, six dozen or more. You'd think something was pushing them from the other side."

Lucy's foot bounced faster. "It's not just the shops that are off. The whole place feels... stuck." She paused, chewing the thought. "Like there's no air coming in, just a lot going out."

Leota looked over her shoulder, as if checking for eavesdroppers. "Maybe it's nothing. But I swear, the new shops don't feel like ours. They're just—there. No soul."

"Did you visit?" Galhani asked.

Leota made a face. "I tried. Nobody answered the door at 'Tuning for Harps.' The 'Darning for Socks' woman wouldn't look me in the eye."

Galhani frowned, remembering the odd customers from the morning, the way the tea shop's magic had tugged at her hands with more urgency than usual. She thought of the missing foragers, the strangers who seemed to suck the energy from the room, and the sharp, medicinal taste that clung to her fingers after making the last few brews.

"It's not just you," Galhani said softly. "I've felt it too. Like the town's... flavor is changing."

They sat in silence for a moment, each drifting into their own thoughts. Sam, sensing the dip in mood, slid a plate of potato fritters onto the table and changed the subject.

"Did you see the blacksmith's new project?" she asked. "He's working on a sword with a handle so big, I could use it to stir soup for the whole pub."

Lucy grinned. "That's one way to keep peace in the town."

Vamir sipped from his cup, but his eyes were distant. "Sometimes, when you try to preserve the old, you end up breaking it."

"Or you just make it sharper," said Sam, with a wink at Lara.

The laughter rolled around the table, loosening the knots of tension. They ate and drank, trading stories from the day. Even Leota seemed to lighten, her shoulders relaxing under the soft glow of the lanterns. But beneath the warmth and comfort, Galhani felt something else: a faint, sour note, the way you can sense a storm before you see the clouds.

As the evening wore on and the candles guttered low, the friends parted ways, stepping out into the cool night. Galhani took Lara's hand as they walked home, listening to the soft crunch of gravel underfoot and the distant, lingering laughter from the pub. The town was quieter than it had any right to be, the silence stretching out between them and the sleeping buildings.

"I don't like it," Lara said finally. "I don't like it at all."

Galhani squeezed her hand. "Me neither. But it's our town. We'll figure it out."

They ducked beneath the low archway to their shop, and for a moment, Galhani caught the scent of violets—fresh, wild, and stubborn, pushing up through the cracks in the stone. She smiled, held Lara close, and together they slipped inside, into the warmth and the faint, persistent magic of home.

two

. . .

SUNRISE in the tea shop always felt like a private performance, and today was no exception. The lace curtains blushed with the first light, softening every hard edge and turning each dust mote into a floating fleck of gold. Galhani had long ago discovered that the world was best in these quiet, suspended minutes, when the only company was the sleep-heavy plants and the distant whistle of a milkman's cart rounding the square.

She opened for business as soon as the kettle began its gentle whine, propping the sign in the window and sweeping the threshold with two practiced strokes. The rush of foot traffic wouldn't begin until the first bell, but Galhani liked to have the shop awake and expectant well before then. It felt respectful, the way you'd set the table before a guest arrived.

Today, the first to breach the calm was a man past his prime, but still holding to it by the fingernails. He entered in a stoop, brow shadowing his eyes, knuckles already white as they clung to his walking stick. The bell above the door sounded tinny in the hush.

"Mistress," he greeted, attempting a bow and then thinking better of it midway down. "Name's Giles. I was told you might have something for... aches."

Galhani took in the man's posture, the way his knees bent inwards and his left shoulder sagged under the invisible pull of gravity. She offered a smile—not the polite one reserved for finicky merchants, but the softer, genuine kind. "If you're not particular about the flavor, I have just the thing."

He shrugged, trying for nonchalance but missing by a mile. "Long road from Pinehollow. At this point, I'd drink boiled horse piss if it meant I could walk upright by sundown."

Galhani's smile widened a notch. "Fortunately, our standards are a bit higher." She turned to her wall of jars, eyes flicking over the labels with the same rapid focus as a bird picking seeds from gravel. Restorative Tincture required three core herbs: wild nettle for heat and circulation, ground poppyseed for dulling, and just a touch of bloodroot, which lent a faint metallic aftertaste but worked wonders for inflammation.

She measured with care. The nettle first, a finger's pinch straight into the mesh infuser; then poppyseed, crushed into a fine powder that stuck to her fingertip; finally, bloodroot, shaved thin as parchment and set aside on a slip of paper. She prepared the water—drawn cold from the spring, heated in the copper kettle until the first spiral of steam—and poured with a practiced tilt to avoid splashing the counter. As it steeped, a color deep and alive bled through the liquid, amber edged with a faintly alarming red.

Giles, meanwhile, watched as if expecting the herbs to leap out and accost him. "Used to be, I could walk from the mills to my house in the north edge of town and barely feel it. These days, I get halfway there and my legs start drafting divorce papers."

"There's a brew for that too," Galhani said, straining the liquid into a thick-walled ceramic cup. She slid it across the counter. "But this one's friendlier."

He sniffed at the cup, lips pursed. "Smells like a glove-maker's stall."

"Drink while it's hot," Galhani instructed, and watched as he did, in two long gulps and a single wince.

The effect was nearly immediate. Giles's face reset itself like a clock: eyebrows rising, jaw slackening, eyes round with surprise.

"Merciful gods, that's—" He paused, lips moving as he searched for the right word. "It's like I can't feel my knees at all."

Galhani leaned in, concerned. "Is that a problem?"

"Not... exactly." He tried to stand, and his knees didn't so much bend as surrender. Giles grabbed the counter with both hands. "It's just... I was hoping for less pain, not no feeling at all."

Galhani kept her tone light, but a thin line of worry traced her brow. "It should dull and loosen, not... remove entirely."

"Maybe it's the road?" Giles mused, almost apologetic. "Or maybe I'm just a special case."

"Let me make you something gentler, for the evening," Galhani offered, already reaching for the ingredients.

Before she could begin, another set of footsteps approached—quieter, but with a brisker tempo. A woman, perhaps five or ten years younger than Giles, swept in with the air of someone who'd lived her life either just ahead or just behind him. She fixed Galhani with a knowing stare, as if she'd already deduced every step of the previous conversation.

"He made you do the nettle and bloodroot, didn't he?" she asked, folding her hands atop the counter. "That old remedy should come with a warning label. Last time he took it, he fell off a hay wagon and didn't notice for a full candlemark."

"Fair's fair," Giles muttered, struggling to realign his knees.

Galhani kept her gaze on the woman, reading the lines at the corners of her mouth, the veined clarity of her eyes. "And what brings you in today?"

She considered. "He's got a mean case of pride. I have the ache too, but it's more in the hips than the knees. And I need to be able to feel my feet for the rest of the day."

"Understood," Galhani said. She reached for the willowbark, swapped out the nettle for a milder ginseng, and cut the poppyseed in half. This time, she measured with slow, exaggerated care, letting each grain slide from her spoon as if it were the last. The kettle hummed obligingly, and the new infusion glowed pale yellow in the light.

Giles, now perched on a stool, watched with the patience of a man recently unmoored from his corporeal form. The woman—wife, probably, though they shared little resemblance—accepted the cup and sipped gingerly.

The result was the same. She blinked, then wiggled her toes inside her boots. "That's odd," she said, flexing her ankle. "It's like... everything's gone to sleep, but I know it's still there."

Giles grinned, victorious. "See?"

Galhani's worry solidified. She examined the jars, checked the scoop for residue, then glanced at the kettle as if it might be the culprit. Nothing in her process had changed. Nothing in the water or the herbs would account for the acceleration, the over-corrected effects.

She refused their coin—insisted, even, when Giles attempted to tuck a silver piece beneath the saucer—and watched the pair limp and lurch out onto the square, laughing louder than their bodies seemed to permit.

When the door closed behind them, the silence returned, heavier now. Galhani stood a long moment, her eyes tracing the seam between shadow and sun along the counter. The tea shop's magic was subtle, always present but never overbearing. Today, it felt like a cat sitting on her chest: not dangerous, but impossible to ignore.

She thought back to the talk at the Broken Claw, to the way Leota's words had hung in the air after she said, "It feels off. Like... when you try to whistle, but your lips are too dry." The town's flavor was changing, and so was its magic.

Galhani rinsed the cups, set them to dry, and straightened the rows of tins with slow, deliberate motions. Tomorrow, she decided, she'd cut the ratios in half again, or perhaps experiment with a cold brew. But the real problem—the one burrowing under her skin—was not in the herbs or the water, but in the invisible force that made her hands too sure, the remedies too strong, the shop's gift less a gentle nudge and more a hard shove.

It was going to be a long morning.

———

By the time the first bell tolled from the square, Galhani had refilled the water jug, tidied the counters twice, and started a small pan of honeyed oatcakes on the stove. The ritual of it steadied her; the ache in her stomach, less so.

The second visitors of the day arrived not as a pair but as a single, inseparable unit. They entered in a tangle of elbows and giggles, both of them young and sunburned, their boots still crusted with the ochre mud of the northern tracks. One had a smear of dust across his brow and a tan line where his cap had spent too long on his head. The other, taller by a handspan, wore her hair in a wild, knotted braid and blinked at the shelves as if she expected the jars to blink back.

"We were told you make the best salves for, uh..." the boy began, then trailed off, looking sheepishly at his companion.

"For saddle sores," she finished, unembarrassed. "And for skin that's not supposed to be red."

Galhani gestured them toward the stools, already scanning her internal ledger of clients and their needs. "I see a lot of travelers," she said, her tone gentle. "You're in good company."

The girl grinned, dropping onto the nearest stool and swinging her legs with the energy of someone recently freed from a very long ride. "I told you," she said to her companion. "Just like the woman at the bridge said. She said, 'If you need to sit down and not regret it, go to the gnome in the tea shop.'"

The boy winced as he sat, the motion pulling at the skin beneath his thigh. Galhani, despite the weight of her earlier failure, felt a tiny thrill of purpose. She reached for her mortars, the smaller of the two, and laid out a careful row of bottles: plantain leaf, comfrey root, calendula, a hint of golden lanolin, and—this time—only the faintest dusting of poppyseed. She pinched half the usual measure, less even, and showed the quantity to the girl before adding it in.

"I've been experimenting," Galhani said, voice light but purposeful. "Yesterday's batches came out stronger than usual. I'd like you to test it here before you take it on the road."

The boy watched, eyebrows drawn. "You mean, it might do more than numb?"

"Or less," Galhani replied. "I want to be sure before you trust it with your skin." She mashed the ingredients in the mortar, the action soothing, then scraped the thick, green paste into a small crock. "Rub a little on the sorest patch. Wait a few breaths before saying anything."

The girl, unselfconscious, hiked up her trouser leg and dabbed a pea-sized amount onto an angry, inflamed spot above her knee. The boy did the same, with exaggerated care, on his upper calf. For a moment, nothing happened. Then both of them froze, glancing at each other in synchrony.

"I can't feel my leg," the boy said, voice high with awe and a little fear.

The girl giggled, then poked at her own knee. "It's tingly and then —gone."

Galhani's heart dipped. "Describe it to me. Any burning? Pins and needles? Do you still have control?"

The girl considered, then stomped her foot experimentally. "I can move it fine. Just... doesn't hurt. At all."

The boy followed suit, grinning with relief. "It's better than the old stuff. That just smelled like onions."

Galhani allowed herself a small smile, but her insides twisted tighter. "Give it a minute. If the numbness fades too slowly or you notice anything odd, come back. I'll make it right."

They left with the crock and a handful of oatcakes, thanking her profusely and promising to send every other sore traveler her way. As soon as the door swung shut, Galhani turned to her wall of jars and began the inventory anew.

She unsealed each container, sniffing and tasting minute samples, checking for rot, must, or any hint of contamination. The herbs were fresh, the lanolin sweet and golden, the poppyseed perfectly ordinary. Nothing in the raw ingredients explained the acceleration, the amplification. She checked her recipe books, compared ratios, scribbled notes in the margins. The shop was quiet, but her brain was loud: what if word got around? What if a customer got hurt, or worse, lost feeling for good?

A tremor started in her hands as she reorganized the workspace, lining every tin at perfect right angles. Was it better, or worse, that it might not be her fault at all? If the town's magic was changing, her own careful practice might soon count for nothing. That thought frightened her more than the possibility of failure.

By the time the second bell rang, Galhani's notes filled three pages, every possible variable circled and questioned, but the answer remained as blank as the row of empty cups waiting for the day's customers.

————

By the time sun crested the peak of the inn's roof, Galhani had abandoned the front of the shop and retreated to the snug back room she shared with Lara. It was a gnome-sized space, designed by necessity, but crammed with comfort: cushions on the bench, a thickly woven rug on the cold stone, a single table just wide enough for two mugs and a plate. The air was close, scented by bundles of thyme and marjoram that hung from the crossbeams, and bright with the slant of sun that came through the tiny leaded window, casting the dust in living motion.

Lara was already there, feet tucked up, rolling a thin thread of licorice root between her fingers as if it were a worry stone. She looked up, and her face split into that familiar smile—a little crooked, slightly mischievous, and utterly sincere.

"You made it," Lara said, sliding one of the mugs closer. "I was beginning to think you'd melted into the mortar out there."

Galhani sank onto the bench, careful to avoid knocking over the teetering stack of papers and seed packets. "Just busy. Every traveler on the road has a new complaint this sennight. It's like the whole world decided to get a jump on cold moon." She tried for a lightness in her voice, but it landed flat.

Lara considered her quietly, then said, "Is it the shop or the town?"

"I don't know." Galhani found herself tracing a knot in the tabletop with her finger. "I can't seem to get it right. Every batch is off. It's as if the old recipes don't work like they should, or the plants are—" She stopped herself, unwilling to voice the thought aloud.

Lara leaned forward, lowering her voice to the hush reserved for bad omens and small miracles. "If you need a break, take one. Let the shop be a shop for a day. You don't always have to solve everything."

Galhani shook her head, but there was a longing in her chest. "I can't. If I let it rest, it just sits there. Like dough that refuses to rise."

Lara's hand covered hers, warm and light. "Then let's fix it together, after supper. We'll take cuttings from the best beds, check the drying racks, maybe start some new blends. I'll even label the jars with my own terrible handwriting, if it helps."

Galhani managed a thin smile. "That's tempting."

Lara stood and smoothed her skirt, then stooped to collect a woven basket from the floor. "I'm going to the garden. The thyme's gone leggy again, and the sage is competing with the cats for territory."

Galhani nodded, watched her slip through the low half-door and out into the strip of sunlight beyond. She wanted to follow, but the weight of the day held her rooted. Instead, she stared at the patterns the dust made in the sunbeam: always shifting, never settling.

———

The garden behind the shop was narrow but densely planted. Every bit of earth was accounted for, from the neat beds of chamomile and mint to the less tidy rows where feverfew, violets, and foxglove grew in willful abandon. At the far end stood a pair of crooked apple trees, their branches heavy with knobbly fruit, and just beyond that, the weathered stone wall that separated the domestic world from the wild grasses beyond.

Lara moved through the rows with easy purpose, kneeling whenever she found a weed encroaching or a cluster of leaves too dense for new growth. She hummed, low and tuneless, as she worked, sometimes letting the sound vibrate in her chest as she tugged a stubborn root free.

She paused over the feverfew. It had taken over its corner of the bed, crowding out the softer herbs, but today it looked different: the stems seemed stiffer, the leaves a shade brighter, the tiny white flowers reaching for the sky with more insistence than usual. Lara reached out, pinched a leaf, and felt a faint, electric buzz pass through her fingers. She frowned, sniffed the leaf, then tasted it. The bitterness was sharp, but not unpleasant; what struck her was the aftertaste, which lingered at the back of her throat and made her eyes water.

"That's odd," she murmured.

She moved to the sage next, breaking off a sprig and rubbing it between her palms. The fragrance was intense, medicinal, and a little wild, as if the plant had doubled its efforts overnight. Lara checked the mint, then the chamomile. Each was as she expected—healthy, aromatic, perhaps a touch more vigorous than in previous moons, but nothing alarming.

She looked back at the feverfew, then at the row of foxglove further down. Lara knew enough botany to respect the power in those leaves, the way they could heal or harm in equal measure. She moved carefully, inspecting the stalks, and saw that the purple bells were thick and glossy, almost waxy in their perfection. She brushed a finger along one, and again, felt that soft prickle of static.

"Galhani?" she called, voice carrying over the low fence. "Come here a moment."

Inside, she heard the clatter of a mug and the familiar shuffle of slippers on stone. Galhani appeared at the doorway, eyes squinting in the light.

Lara lifted a feverfew stem. "Taste this. Tell me what you think."

Galhani obliged, nibbling the edge and rolling the taste over her tongue. After a moment, she blinked, brow wrinkling. "That's... strong. Like it's been dried in the sun for a whole moon."

"Everything out here's the same," Lara said. "It's all—amped up. The foxglove too. Even the sage."

Galhani considered this, the cogs of her mind already turning. "It's the town. It must be. It's like there's too much of something and nowhere for it to go."

Lara knelt, digging her fingers into the soil. "Maybe it's the people. More travelers, more energy, more... life." She looked up, meeting Galhani's eyes. "You said the recipes don't work the way they used to. What if it's the ingredients that have changed?"

Galhani's gaze flicked over the garden, her own hands opening and closing at her sides. "It makes sense," she admitted. "But I don't like it."

Lara smiled, reassuring. "We'll figure it out. The plants are just keeping pace with the town. We just have to learn how to keep up."

Galhani didn't answer right away. She breathed in the scent of the garden—sharp, wild, alive—and realized that maybe the discomfort wasn't in her own skills after all. Maybe it was in the fact that the world, stubbornly, refused to stay the same.

———

Evening smoothed the day's sharp edges, and the Broken Claw responded in kind. The regulars settled into their preferred shadows, the fire flickered in the long-hewn hearth, and the honeyed light from lanterns overhead made everything seem less dire than it had in the brittle brightness of morning. Galhani and Lara stepped through the low door and paused, letting their eyes adjust. The pub was fuller than usual for a plain evening, with pockets of travelers scattered between the town's ordinary rabble.

Sam was behind the bar, sleeves rolled to her elbows, white hair tied back in a crude knot that exposed the scar on her left cheek in stark relief. She wiped a glass with the measured patience of someone who had spent many candlemarks perfecting the task, her gaze tracking every movement in the room. When she caught sight of Galhani and Lara, she lifted her chin in a silent greeting.

"Evening, mistress," Sam said as they found their way to the corner bench. She set the glass aside and bent to draw two tankards from the keg closest to the counter.

"You look as if you've been dealing with your own share of peculiar," Lara said, sliding onto the seat and patting the cushion beside her for Galhani.

"Peculiar's one way to put it," Sam replied. "Another is that half the town's gone off its leash and started chasing its own tail." She poured a thick, amber cider for Lara and a cloudy wheat beer for Galhani, then leaned her elbows on the bar. "I'm running a tally of new faces, and the sum's coming up larger every day."

"Road's busier than I've ever seen," Galhani said, sipping the beer and letting the foam settle on her lip.

Sam grunted. "Not just that. It's like the town's breeding businesses. Have you seen the square lately? There's a place that only sells bootlaces now. Another that does nothing but sharpen quills."

Galhani choked slightly on her drink. "Quills?"

"Quills," Sam confirmed. "They're open before dawn and close at dusk. Never seen the shopkeeper outside the threshold, but there's always a line. Travelers, mostly. They go in with chewed stubs and come out looking like proper town scribes."

Lara smirked. "And the bootlaces?"

"Same deal. 'Specialized Bootlace Repair,'" Sam recited, with a hand gesture that could have been a curse or a benediction.

Lara exchanged a glance with Galhani, her brow furrowed. "Is it just us, or does that sound... off?"

Sam lowered her voice. "You remember the run on mustard seeds last moon? Or when the tanners all got the shakes at the same time?" She tapped a knuckle on the bar. "This is like that, but sideways. Four new shops in one sennight, and every single one is—" she paused, searching for the word, "—obsessive. Like someone's taken a single problem and built a shrine to it."

A silence stretched out, punctuated by the clatter of a dropped spoon from the far table. The tension was familiar but unwelcome, a thread that ran through every conversation these days.

Sam broke it with a shrug, the lines around her eyes deepening as she leaned in. "Town's never been boring, but it's always had a rhythm. This? This is something new." Her hand drifted to the hilt at her hip—Nailbiter, always within reach. "If it keeps up, I'll have to start serving drinks through a slot in the door."

Galhani tried to smile, but the unease wouldn't let go. "We're seeing it too, in the garden and the shop. The herbs are stronger, the brews are unpredictable." She hesitated, then added, "It's not just the remedies. The whole place feels like it's under a magnifying lens."

Sam snorted. "That's one way to put it. Maybe we'll all shrink if we stand in the sunlight too long."

Lara sipped her cider, thoughtful. "Jen ever seen a town go through something like this before?"

Sam ran a finger along the rim of the glass. "'Not in all my years,' she said. But if I had to guess—" she met Galhani's gaze, the look unwavering, "I'd say something's coming. Might be bad, might be good, but it's going to hit us whether we're ready or not."

The three sat with that truth for a while, letting the sounds of the pub—laughter, clinking, the distant crackle of the hearth—anchor them to something solid. Outside, the light faded into indigo, the lamps on the square flickering to life in their sconces.

Sam, never one for long silences, eventually grinned and banged her fist on the bar. "Well, I'll be damned if we let a bunch of bootlace peddlers and quill sharpeners ruin a perfectly good night. First round's on me."

Lara smiled, the tension easing from her shoulders. "Make it two, and we'll tell you about the wild sage growing behind the shop. Might be strong enough to strip the paint off your tables."

Sam barked a laugh. "If it is, bring me some. I'll use it to polish the bar."

Galhani watched the exchange, a new sense of resolve warming her from the inside. Whatever was changing the town, they'd meet it head-on, together. She raised her glass, and the three women clinked tankards, their laughter carrying into the growing dark like a promise.

three

. . .

THE NEXT MORNING, Galhani found the normally peace-inducing atmosphere of her shop... unbearable. She had slept poorly, drifting in and out while the moon painted watery stripes on the ceiling, haunted by odd dreams in which jars multiplied on the shelves, each one full of a different flavor of static. The air this morning felt charged, brittle. Every time she moved, she risked knocking something over or breaking a seal she'd checked twice already. The first customer arrived half a candlemark before the sign officially flipped, a woman with the hungry look of the night shift.

"I need something for anxiety," the woman said, voice clipped, fingers tapping a fugue on the counter. "I've tried everything, and I can't get warm."

Galhani nodded as if this were perfectly normal, but her hands shook as she reached for the chamomile tin. She selected a soothing blend: lemon balm, chamomile, a sliver of rosehip, then hesitated and cut the valerian root in half, just in case. The water hissed as she poured it.

The woman's eyes darted to the window, then to Galhani's hands. "It's louder out there, isn't it?"

Galhani blinked, not sure what the woman meant, but unwilling to say as much. "If you drink this, you might feel a little drowsy, but it's gentle. Should help with the nerves."

The woman wrapped both hands around the cup the second it landed on the counter. She inhaled the steam, eyelids fluttering. "Thank you," she whispered, and a tremor ran through her that reminded Galhani of the way spiders abandoned their webs before a storm.

After she left, Galhani cleaned the counter twice and stepped outside for air. The square vibrated with a low-grade hum: carts rolling, children shouting, even the pigeons seemed to be bickering more than usual. A man sat near the well, reading a handbill and tearing it into strips as he read, each fragment drifting away on the breeze. Three doors down, someone hammered a sign above a new shop, the letters damp and bleeding: FINE SCRIVENING, in blocky black. No children ran in the grassy square, nobody was lined up at the bakery.

She slipped back inside and tried to lose herself in the inventory, reciting aloud just to anchor her thoughts: "Six tins of hawthorn, five of burdock, four marshmallow, two nearly-empty licorice root." Her words rang hollow in the space, and the sound of her own voice made her want to shout, or maybe run. Instead, she set to grinding a batch of mint for the afternoon blends, losing herself in the rhythm: scoop, crush, pour, repeat.

By mid-morning, she'd had enough. "I'm going to the Claw," she called to Lara, who had been rummaging quietly in the back storeroom all morning.

"Mmm," she replied.

And so Galhani found herself once again in the corner of the pub, unpacking her traveling tea kit. It was an old ritual, one she'd learned from her grandmother—a sacred act, almost, meant to bring calm and clarity to even the most raucous of gatherings.

It wasn't working today.

Her fingers shook as she lined up the infusers, each one polished to a dull patina by decades of use. The wooden box she'd carried since childhood opened with a shudder, revealing the neat squares of parchment, tiny labeled vials, and a miniature pestle that had belonged to her grandfather. She always worked with precision; it was how she controlled the unpredictable, how she made order out of the world's blunted edges. But her hands rebelled against her today, stuttering over each movement, and every accidental tap of glass against wood was louder than it ought to be.

Her client—the traveler from last night, Giles, who had returned in high spirits and with an even higher need for nerve-settling—waited at the small table by the window. He looked more like a man about to receive bad news from a physician than one about to enjoy the promised "Calming Brew." He tapped at the table with two fingers, eyes never quite meeting Galhani's, and when she finally brought the kettle, he started as if she'd poured boiling water on his lap.

"Good day," she greeted, infuser in hand.

He managed a tight smile.

Galhani set down the mug, added a measured spoonful of dried valerian and oatstraw, and then—after a moment's hesitation—barely a whisper of poppyseed. She didn't trust the poppy; it was too strong, too eager, and she didn't need another incident. She made a show of measuring, letting Giles see exactly how little of each ingredient she used.

"Give it two minutes," she said, and turned the sandglass beside the cup.

He watched the sand fall with an intensity that made her uncomfortable. "Funny thing," he said, after a while, "I don't remember yesterday very well. You said it might dull the pain, but I can't recall if I even made it back to my room."

Galhani's mouth went dry. "It's been a strong season. The plants are... potent." It was a lie by omission. The plants were practically feral, half-wild, almost humming with an excess of life and power. It was the town, she was certain—there was a pressure in the air, something that magnified everything, good and bad.

When the sand ran out, she poured. The water frothed, catching an iridescent sheen as it hit the herbs. She stirred, careful not to agitate the leaves too much, and set the cup before him with both hands. "Let it settle," she said. "It's best if you don't rush."

But Giles was not a man of patience. He lifted the mug and drank, and within seconds the change was visible: his posture softened, his eyes drooped, and the tension in his jaw disappeared so completely it seemed to erase years from his face. He set the cup down and stared at it as if it were a puzzle he'd never seen before.

"Well," he said. "That's—" But the word trailed off, his voice lost in the thickening air.

He slumped sideways, catching himself on the table's edge, and then folded forward like a marionette whose strings had been cut. The mug slipped from his grasp and rolled, spilling a thin, glistening trail across the grain. He was out cold.

The nearest two tables turned as one to gawk. One of the regulars, a burly woman with a hairnet, barked a laugh. "Bit strong for breakfast, eh?" she called.

Galhani's face burned. She hurried to Giles' side, heart pounding in her chest, and tried to lift him upright. He was dead weight, his head lolled to one side, and he snored softly—a thin whistle, at odds with the tension choking Galhani's own breath.

Sam was there in a moment, wiping her hands on a bar towel. "What's the diagnosis?" she murmured, kneeling beside the unconscious man. "Did you put him under on purpose?"

Galhani shook her head, fighting panic. "I diluted it. I cut everything in half. He shouldn't even be—" She broke off, unable to finish.

Sam looked at the empty mug, then at Galhani. "Maybe he just needed the sleep. Travelers like him don't stop moving unless someone knocks them over."

"Not like this," Galhani whispered, but she reached for Giles' wrist and checked his pulse, just to be sure.

It was steady, slow but not alarming. She exhaled, some small portion of her terror receding. Sam rose and set the bar towel behind Giles' head, making a makeshift pillow.

"Let him nap," Sam said, voice pitched low. "We'll get him a pie when he wakes. You want a drink?"

Galhani managed a nod, though the thought of ale at this time of day nearly turned her stomach.

Sam poured her a half-glass of cider and handed it over. "I had a fellow pass out from my stout last sennight," she said, almost conspiratorial. "Two sips in. And this was the mild keg, not the reserve. Town's got a case of overachievement lately. Every barrel ferments twice as fast as it should." She sipped her own drink. "You're not the only one."

They both glanced at Giles, whose snoring had grown louder. The room's attention began to drift away, replaced by the quieter background noise of clinking glasses and the low mutter of morning conversation.

Sam leaned in, elbows on the table. "You heard about the inn?"

Galhani shook her head, grateful for the distraction.

"The Weary Head's been giving people dreams so vivid they won't go back for a second night. Two merchants ran out at dawn, said they'd rather sleep in a ditch than in those beds again." Sam lowered her voice. "It's like the walls are whispering. Minnie can't keep up with the laundry—half her sheets end up torn to rags from all the thrashing."

Galhani forced a thin smile. "That's not encouraging."

Sam shrugged. "It's the way of things. Jen says the town's always had its fits. This one's just... bigger." She cocked her head, as if listening to a tune only she could hear. "We'll ride it out."

Giles stirred, grunted, and then groaned as his eyelids fluttered. He looked around, confused, and then at Galhani, as if searching for the line between dream and waking.

"I—" he began, then blinked hard. "How long was I out?"

"Not long," Sam said, offering a steadying hand. "You needed it, by the looks of you."

He rubbed at his temples, then squinted at the half-empty mug. "Tastes like the north woods in autumn. Like sap and cold fog."

Galhani bowed her head, mortified. "I'm so sorry. It shouldn't have—"

He shook his head, slow and deliberate. "I've had worse," he said, but didn't elaborate. He staggered to his feet, waved a clumsy thanks, and lurched toward the exit. As he stepped into the light, he steadied and drew himself upright, the effect of the brew already fading to a dull background hum.

Galhani slumped back into her chair, cradling the cider in both hands. Her palms were slick with sweat. She tried to take a sip, but her mouth had forgotten how to swallow.

Sam watched her, eyes narrow with concern. "You all right?"

"I don't know," Galhani admitted. "I think... I think something's changing. In the town. In the people. It's like everything I do goes too far. Or not far enough."

Sam nodded. "You seen the square lately? Four new shops in three days, and every one more useless than the last." She laughed, but the sound was hollow. "Just this morning, I saw two men almost come to blows over who could fix bootlaces better. Bootlaces, of all things."

"Why is it happening?" Galhani asked, not really expecting an answer.

Sam considered. "Don't know. Town's nervous about something, maybe. Maybe the same thing that's overpowering your herbs is attracting people." She glanced toward the window, where a knot of travelers crowded the stoop, jockeying for space at the bar. "Or maybe it's just that there's more of everything than there used to be. More people, more want, more noise."

As if on cue, the front door banged open, and a trio of newcomers barged in. Their boots clattered on the floorboards, and their voices filled the room before the air had a chance to adjust.

"Did you see the sign?" one of them shouted, his accent sharp and nasal. "Sock darning! That's all they do! You bring 'em socks, they darn 'em while you wait!"

Another, a wiry woman with a face like a hatchet, snorted. "It's the harps next door that'll put them out of business. Tuning, restringing, nothing else. You can't even buy a harp, just get yours fixed."

The third laughed, high and wild, and pounded the counter. "That's nothing! Next to that, they've got a guy who only sells matches. One at a time! Says he's got the perfect matchstick."

Sam leaned close to Galhani, her voice barely above a whisper. "See what I mean?"

Galhani nodded, and for a moment she wanted to cry. Not from embarrassment, but from a deeper, colder fear that she wouldn't be able to keep up, that the town she'd loved and mastered was already slipping through her fingers.

"Sam," she said quietly. "has Jen spoken to the new shopkeepers?" In her role as constable, Jen was usually the one to show newcomers to an empty shop.

Bu Sam shook her head and grimaced. "No. Most of them haven't even been in here for a drink. I can't even get a read on them. It's like they just wander in off the road, see an empty space, and settle in." She shrugged. "Some don't stay. Yesterday—you probably didn't notice—someone opened a shop, first thing in the morning, they probably arrived in the middle of the night, selling hard bread sticks."

"Bread sticks?"

"Thin, crunchy ones. Makota was mightily irritated, I promise you. But here's the thing: by sunset, they were gone, and the shop was empty again." She shrugged again. "Can't tell what the town's up to."

Galhani swallowed heavily and began to pack away her kit, each movement slow and deliberate. The infusers went back into their padded slots. The vials she wiped clean with a corner of her apron, then nested in the velvet-lined rows. When she closed the lid, the tiny latch clicked with a finality that echoed in her chest.

Sam watched her finish, then reached out and rested a rough, steady hand on her wrist. "Hey," she said. "You're not alone in this. If it gets worse, we'll figure something out."

Galhani tried to find words, but they twisted in her throat. She nodded instead, holding onto the warmth of Sam's grip for a heartbeat longer than was strictly polite.

Outside, the sun was climbing into the sky, and the trade road was clogged with travelers. From the pub's front porch, Galhani could see a parade of new faces, all hungry, all moving with a kind of desperate purpose. Every few minutes, someone would pause in front of the pub, or the smithy, or the fish stall, peer inside, then move on. It was a new rhythm, unfamiliar and unkind.

Inside, the newcomers were already arguing over who would get the first tankard of Sam's morning stout. The loudest one knocked over a chair and barely noticed, shouting instead about opening a "letter writing service" that would beat the quill-sharpeners at their own game.

Galhani let herself listen, for a moment, to the chaotic song of the bar. She tried to imagine how she would capture this moment, if she ever had the courage to write it down. Maybe she would begin with the feeling of too many voices at once, of space collapsing, of breath growing short. Or maybe she would start with the memory of the garden, of wild sage and feverfew, and the hope that things might return to normal someday.

But she felt, even then, that the town might never be the same.

She slowly made her way back to the tea shop, dodging travelers on horseback, in wagons, and on foot, lugging her travel kit along. She slipped into the shop, stowed the kit, and then paused with one hand on the "open" sign. She looked past the counter, where Lara was still rummaging around, humming a low, distracted tone, caught up in her own methodical distraction.

She dropped her hand, leaving the "closed" side of the sign facing out, pushed the door open, and stepped back into the square. The bell above the door tinkled slightly as it closed behind her.

———

Galhani found Leota and Vamir in the shadowed back corner of the Broken Claw, hunched over a table so small their elbows touched in the middle. It was the only table in the pub that faced neither door nor window—a trait Leota had once described as "excellent for secrets, terrible for sunlight." They greeted her with a nod and a chair, and the remains of a shared platter: cheese, bread, and a few stubborn olives that resisted capture.

Leota wore her black as always, but today it seemed even darker than usual, her hair slicked back tight against her skull. She looked pale, almost translucent, in the gloom, but her eyes burned with a focused, predatory energy. Vamir was the opposite—loose-limbed, relaxed, with a halo of silver hair that seemed to draw in all the available light. He was whittling absently at a block of wood, sending small curls spiraling onto the table.

"Good," said Leota, not waiting for Galhani to sit. "I was hoping you'd come back. Did Sam tell you?"

Galhani slid onto the bench, brushing a few stray wood shavings aside. "She told me about the inn, the sock-darning, and that I'm not the only one losing control of my craft." She tried to make it sound casual, but the words landed with a brittle edge.

Leota smiled, lips thin. "That's the spirit. Admit to the disease, and you're halfway to the cure."

Vamir stopped whittling, set his knife down. "We've been thinking it through. There's precedent for magical disturbance in towns like ours, but usually it's a surge—everything ramps up, everyone feels wonderful, then the crash comes." He tapped his temple, as if referencing a private archive. "This isn't that. It's more like a thinning."

"Or a graying," Leota interjected. "Everything works, but without flavor. The color is draining, and in its place, something... shallow."

Galhani frowned. "It doesn't feel shallow to me. It feels like a storm in my shop. Even the easy blends come out wrong. Too strong, or nothing at all."

Leota's gaze sharpened. "Because you're closer to the source. Herbalists always are—plants don't lie, and neither do the hands that tend them. What's wrong with your blends, specifically?"

Galhani explained, as precisely as she could, the progression of her failures. "At first, the mixtures were just a little off. Willowbark would numb, but also dull the mind. The sage in the garden started growing wild—one taste and it burned like fire. I halved the recipes, and they still over-performed. Now it's as if every plant has doubled its will, but the effect is... anesthetic." She hesitated. "My last customer passed out cold. He thanked me, but I think he was just grateful to wake up at all."

Leota nodded, as if she'd expected nothing less. "There's an old term for that. Winter-sap, I think. It's what happens when a plant tries to grow during the dark moons: it pulls too much, but the sun isn't there, so all the power has nowhere to go. That's what I'm feeling in the wards, too—the house keeps wanting to cast new spells, but it's getting lost on the way."

Vamir reached for an olive and missed; Poly, the little blue-and-white bird that accompanied him everywhere, had already snatched it from the dish. He didn't react, just adjusted. "In the bookshop, it's even stranger. Every time someone asks for a topic, the shelves produce six or seven tomes at once, some of them almost alive with urgency. I have to lock the history section at night to keep the volumes from crawling out onto the floor."

Galhani looked at him, unsure whether it was a joke. Vamir's smile was serene, as if the idea of carnivorous books amused more than alarmed him.

Leota folded her hands, fingers steepled. "It's not just us. The shops, the tavern, the inn—everyone's reporting overactivity. Even the newcomers. Have you noticed how they talk? The merchants, the ones opening the ridiculous niche stores—they speak as if they've always belonged here, but you can see it in their faces: they're being drawn in. Sucked dry."

Galhani shivered. "It's like the town is hungry."

"Yes," Leota said, pleased. "Exactly that. It's not draining us, per se, but it's consuming something else and leaving us with the residue."

Vamir took up his knife again, working a new groove into the wood. "You said there's precedent for this," he said to Leota. "But I don't remember it from the old stories."

Leota considered. "The only time I've felt anything close was when Aran cut off our gifts entirely. This isn't like that. That was absence. This is dilution. Like a wine cut with water until you forget it was ever wine to begin with." She frowned. "But not even like that. It's like... cutting the wine makes it stronger, too. All at once." The frown deepened. "I can't explain it, and I don't like that."

Galhani let the image sit in her mind, and it made sense in a way that was both comforting and horrifying. "So, what do we do?"

Vamir shrugged, but his eyes were serious. "First, we find the source. If it's the town, maybe it's in the records. If it's the people, it'll be in the patterns."

Leota turned to him, her voice gentle. "Could you check the old volumes? Not just in your shop—go down to your library, the deep stacks. If there's a story, a pattern, it'll be in the banned or forgotten books. The ones the shelves keep hidden from the casual eye."

Vamir's smile was pure mischief. "That's where Poly does its best work."

Leota allowed herself a real smile, then turned her attention back to Galhani. "For now, dilute your mixtures even further. If you can't control the strength, trick it. Use decoys—herbs with similar appearance, but without the power. Give the town what it wants, but don't feed it the real thing."

Galhani nodded, filing away the instructions, though she doubted her ability to lie to the garden. "And you?"

Leota pressed her palms together, as if in prayer. "I'll keep the wards thin. I want to see if the pressure increases, or if it collapses altogether. If anything strange happens, send word."

They lapsed into a silence that was only awkward because of how familiar it felt. Vamir continued his whittling; Leota stared at the wall behind Galhani's head, deep in thought. The hum of the pub around them seemed to fade, as if the three of them were sitting in a bubble, insulated from the rest of the world.

When Galhani finally spoke, her voice was softer. "Is it possible for a town to just... stop being itself?"

Leota smiled, a flash of teeth. "Towns are like people. They change. Sometimes they die, sometimes they shed their skin and come back brighter. But the ones with real magic never vanish. They just learn new tricks."

Vamir added, "And if they can't? The stories say they get stuck. Like a song with no ending."

Leota rose, her movement abrupt, and pulled her cloak tight around her shoulders. "Well then," she said, "let's make sure ours keeps singing." She nodded to both of them, then swept from the table, black dress billowing behind her.

Vamir lingered, watching her go. He turned to Galhani, his eyes gentle. "You're not alone, you know. Everyone's feeling it. Even Poly, though it'd never admit it." He smiled, then stood, brushing the wood shavings from his lap. "I'll let you know what I find."

Galhani stayed at the table, staring at the gouges and scratches in the wood, and felt something loosen inside her. Not hope, exactly, but the sense that she was no longer the only one adrift. She ran a finger over the whorls in the tabletop, wondering what pattern would emerge by evening.

————

Upstairs, the bedroom above the tea shop was cramped, low-beamed, and—until recently—Galhani's favorite place in the world. It was late, the kind of late when the only noises in the square below were drunken songs, dog barks, and the occasional cart rolling by. Normally, the room would have felt like a safe harbor after the day's rough waters, but tonight the walls pressed inward, closer than usual.

Lara was sitting cross-legged at the foot of the bed, a ledger open across her lap and three candles guttering on the side table. She was counting jars and bundles on her fingers, muttering numbers as she tallied the day's yield. She had always been the practical one, able to turn worry into action by sheer will, but even she was starting to fray around the edges.

Galhani tried to settle beside her, but the energy in the room was off: she couldn't sit, couldn't stand, couldn't stop fidgeting with her own sleeves. She found herself pacing from the door to the dresser and back again, hands clasped behind her as if she was a schoolchild about to confess a crime.

Lara paused in her counting. "You're wearing a track into the floorboards," she said, not looking up from the page.

Galhani stopped, unsure whether to laugh or apologize. "Can't help it. The whole shop's off-balance. It feels like nothing I do matters anymore."

Lara's pencil froze. She looked up, her eyes soft, the way they got when she wanted to comfort but didn't know how. "It does matter. It always has."

Galhani shook her head. "No, it really doesn't. Not if the town is just going to eat it up and spit it out." She gestured toward the window, where the lamps from the square flickered through the curtain. "You didn't see what happened at the pub. One sip and he was gone. I might as well be serving poison."

Lara closed the ledger, setting it aside with exaggerated care. "You're not serving poison. You're just adjusting. Every year the weather changes, the water changes, the pests change. We figure it out. This isn't different."

"It is," Galhani said, voice rising despite herself. "We've never had the garden fight back before. We've never had the sage try to choke out the strawberries or the feverfew sprout overnight. I can't keep up, Lara. I don't think I want to."

Lara sighed, rubbing her eyes with the heel of her hand. "You're taking it too personally. Maybe it's not about us. Maybe it's just the world, getting louder."

Galhani's hands went still. She looked at Lara, at the face she'd trusted for years, and tried to find the comfort she usually felt. But there was only a hollow ache, the kind that came from saying something too late, or not saying it at all.

Lara rose and went to the dresser, where she began to organize the jars for morning. She moved with the deliberate care of someone who needed to move, whose body required work to avoid unraveling. After a while, she picked up a small bundle, turned it over in her hands, and held it out for Galhani to see.

"Look at this," Lara said. "The lavender from the south wall." She brought the sprig closer. In the candlelight, the edges of each flower glimmered, but the heart of the stem was oddly transparent, like it was made of glass and not wood at all.

Galhani took it, turning the stem between her fingers. The air around it felt colder, as if the plant was exhaling frost. "That's not possible," she murmured.

Lara shrugged. "It's not just us, or the shops, or the travelers. It's everything. You want to fix it, fine. But start with this." She tapped the stem, her touch lingering. "Figure out why it looks like it's half-here and half—somewhere else. Even though there's more of it than ever."

Galhani nodded, holding the lavender up to the candle. The flame guttered, and the stem seemed to shudder in the shifting light. "Leota thinks the town is diluting itself. Thinning. Like a wine watered down until it forgets what it was supposed to be." She hesitated, wondering whether Lara would laugh or scoff. But Lara only listened, her face unreadable.

"And Vamir thinks the books are starting to breed in his shop," Galhani added, trying to lighten the mood. "He's got to keep them locked up at night."

That got a smile from Lara, small but real. "He always did worry more about the books than the customers." She put a hand on Galhani's shoulder, squeezing lightly. "We'll be fine. We always are."

For a moment, Galhani let herself believe it. She put the lavender on the dresser, where it sat upright in a small glass, the ghostly stem catching and scattering the candle's reflection. She stared at it, searching for a pattern, a meaning, some clue that would let her understand the world again.

They got ready for bed in silence. Lara blew out the candles one by one, the room darkening with each extinguished wick. The moon outside was full and unnaturally bright, but the light that came through the window was fractured, split into strange shapes by the old wavy glass.

They slipped under the quilt, but the usual warmth was missing. Lara curled on one side, Galhani on the other, the gap between them more a wound than a space. Galhani lay awake, staring at the ceiling and listening to the pulse of the town below: laughter, shouts, the clang of a late cart. It felt as if the walls themselves were vibrating, transmitting every sound into her bones.

After a long while, Lara's breathing settled into the slow, steady rhythm of sleep. Galhani envied her the escape, but she couldn't close her eyes—not with the strangeness pressing in from all sides.

She turned toward the window. The lavender glowed faintly in the moonlight, casting an elongated, wavering shadow across the wall. The shadow trembled, splitting at the edges, like it was trying to be in two places at once.

Galhani reached for Lara's hand under the covers, found it, and squeezed. Lara squeezed back, barely awake. "It's just the moon," she mumbled.

Galhani let her eyes close, but the image of the doubled shadow stayed with her, sharp and unyielding. She wondered if this was how it would be from now on: never quite whole, always reaching for something lost in the dark.

In the morning, maybe things would make sense again. But tonight, with the town thinning around her and the world half-gone to ghosts, Galhani counted the heartbeats and waited for dawn.

four

. . .

GALHANI STOOD BEHIND HER COUNTER, a clean, empty space in a shop that now felt like a tomb. She had swept up the last of the fallen herbs, wiped the table where her final customer had grown cold, and locked the door with a final, decisive click. She felt hollowed out, a pot with nothing left to hold. The air, thick with the ghosts of failed brews, was colder than the morning mist outside. She wanted to scream, or maybe just lie down on the floor and let the silence swallow her whole.

A frantic knock at the door startled her. It was Lucy, her face a mask of grief. She clutched a cloth-wrapped bundle in one hand, her knuckles white. "Let me in, Galhani," she said, her voice thin. "I need to talk."

Galhani, surprised, unlocked the door. Lucy stumbled inside, and in the space of a few heartbeats, the shop filled with others. Cole arrived, his basket of produce still clutched in his hand, his clothes splattered with the ruined pulp of a tomato. Warren and Susan walked in, holding hands. Warren's arm was bandaged, and his wife's face was etched with worry. Even Dexter, the town's physician, had left his chirurgery for the morning.

"What's wrong?" Galhani asked, her voice a reedy whisper.

Cole pointed at his basket. "This crop—the one I was so proud of—it's worthless. The carrots snap in my hands, and the tomatoes... they just burst into water." He stared at the floor, his eyes glassy with defeat. "I don't know what I did wrong."

Lucy placed her bundle on the counter and unwrapped it. Inside was a pottery mug, its glaze patchy and dull. With a trembling hand, she gave it a gentle tap with her fingernail. The sound was flat, a dead thud. She looked at Galhani, her chin quivering. "I tried a new glaze, a new firing process. Nothing takes. I worked for days, and the cup turned to dust in the box on the way here."

Warren stepped forward, his huge hands shaking. "It's not just you. I tried to forge a blade for a customer. The metal—it's gone brittle. It snapped in my hands. The shock broke the handle, and I was careless." He held up his bandaged arm, shame and frustration warring on his face.

Galhani looked at her friends, at the small circle of defeated crafters who had gathered in her shop. She no longer felt alone. She felt a profound and painful sense of kinship. Her own failures were not personal sins, but symptoms of a shared malady. She took in the sight of Warren's injury, Lucy's shattered cup, Cole's ruined crop, and understood the true scope of the problem. This was not a storm brewing; it was a plague. She felt a new kind of fear, sharper and colder than any self-doubt she had ever known.

———

By noon, the morning hush had shifted into something close to apathy. The sky outside had faded from blue to a washed, almost translucent white, and the cobblestones radiated a slow, indifferent heat. Galhani kept to the front of the shop, arranging jars and polishing cups to a needless shine, her movements repetitive and tight. She found herself glancing at the clock every few minutes, as if she could hurry the day along by force of will alone.

The bell over the door sounded, hesitant. The man who entered wore the look of someone who had lost several consecutive arguments with the world. His cloak hung limp and patched, his eyes were red-rimmed, and every third breath caught in a rasping cough that seemed to start in his heels. He eyed the counter with suspicion, or maybe desperation.

"I heard you have something for the throat," he said, voice sand-papered.

She nodded, already reaching for her supplies. The man sat at the far end of the counter, as if not wanting to bother the rest of the shop's silence. His cough grew louder with the effort, and Galhani hurried the boiling of water, fumbling only once with the lid of her best honey.

She selected a blend she'd perfected for just this ailment: marsh-mallow, licorice, two curls of lemon peel, and a single bright blue borage flower for the finish. Normally she'd have thrown in a pinch of her best starlace, but after the last few days she no longer trusted it. Instead, she added the smallest dash of sage and set the infuser in the cup.

The traveler watched her hands, and she could feel the unasked question in his stare. When the tea was ready, she placed it before him, and he cupped it with trembling, dirt-stained fingers.

"Will it work?" he asked.

"It's the gentlest blend I have," she replied, and realized only then how little faith she had in the words.

He drank, lips barely parting, letting the steam rise into his nose and eyes. The color returned to his face by degrees, and his cough faded to a dry tickle. For a moment, Galhani allowed herself to hope.

Then he shuddered, once, violently. He set the cup down with a clatter, both hands shaking.

"I feel—" he started, but never finished. His face went ashen, and he wrapped his arms around himself as if seized by a chill. "It's like the sun just set inside me. I'm cold."

Galhani's heart collapsed into a fist. She stared at the cup, then at the man, searching for any sign of what she had done wrong. The recipe had been flawless; the water just off the boil, the measurements exact. Still, something had gone sideways.

"I'm so sorry," she whispered, her throat constricting.

He coughed again, now with a ragged desperation, and wiped his mouth on the back of his hand. "I'll—leave you to it, then," he managed. He fumbled in his coat for a coin, but she waved it away.

"No charge. Please. I—" but the words failed her. She could not meet his eyes as he gathered himself and left, leaving the tea untouched and the air in the shop a degree colder than before.

Galhani stared at the counter for a long time, then at her hands. The skin on her fingers was pale, almost transparent, the nails bitten down to nothing. She tried to recall the last time she had made a mistake in a blend, and could not. Her memory stopped at the edge of last sennight, as if the rest had been pruned away.

With shaking hands, she flipped the sign in the window to "Closed." She locked the door, then leaned back against it, pressing her spine into the wood until her vision blurred. Tears threatened, but she forced them back down, biting her lip until she tasted iron.

From the back of the shop came a sudden, forceful banging. The half-door burst open, and Lara entered with two baskets—one balanced in each arm. Her hair was slick with sweat, her cheeks smudged with dirt, and she had the wild look of someone who had not slept in a sennight.

"Gal!" she shouted, not seeing the distress in the front of the shop. "You have to see this. The rosemary's taken over the whole bed. And the mayseed? There's enough for three years." She dumped one basket onto the workbench: fat bundles of rosemary and mayseed, all shockingly green, some trailing root and clumps of earth.

Lara's second basket was less triumphant. In it lay a few limp sprigs of nightshade and three shriveled flowers of moonflower, their petals collapsed inwards like closed fists.

"The exotics are done," Lara said, voice low now. "I dug all morning. The nightshade's half gone and the rest is dust. Even the foxglove looks sickly."

Galhani wiped at her eyes, turning away so Lara would not see. She forced her voice into a neutral register. "We'll dry what we can," she said. "Maybe I can stretch the reserves."

Lara set down the baskets, her hands on her hips. "Are you crying?"

Galhani shook her head, but the gesture was unconvincing. "Just tired. I had a customer—he was sick, and I think I made it worse. I think I might be getting whatever he had."

Lara's expression softened. "You're not getting sick," she said, gentle. "You're just burnt out. We both are. This time last year, we'd have been drinking our own stock by now."

Galhani tried to smile, but could not manage it. She stared at the mess of herbs on the counter, and found that her vision blurred not with tears, but with something like fear.

"Let's close up early," she said, voice barely audible. "I want to try again tomorrow. Maybe the plants will change their minds."

Lara agreed without argument. She swept up the debris, set the baskets in their places, and gave Galhani's shoulder a squeeze before heading out back.

Galhani remained at the counter, watching as the light crept slowly across the empty shop. She listened to the silence, and to the echo of the traveler's cough in the walls. Her hands were steady now, but they felt as if they belonged to someone else.

She looked at the locked door, at the "Closed" sign, and wondered if she would ever be able to turn it back the other way.

————

Late afternoon pressed itself into the corners of the bedroom, the sun's final angle flooding the space with a golden, sticky light that turned every dust mote into a slow-motion firefly. Galhani sat cross-legged on the wide sill of the upstairs window, her back pressed to the cool stone wall, forehead resting against the glass. From here, she could see the entire square, and—if she craned a little—the sharp line where the last row of houses met the wild edge of the road.

She watched the square as she might have watched a wound she knew would never close: fascinated, horrified, unable to look away. The rhythm of the day was gone, replaced by a current of ceaseless motion. People streamed through the square in knots and clusters, the usual handful of neighbors now multiplied tenfold by an influx of travelers. There were new wagons, new faces, new everything. Even the livestock seemed foreign—sheep with curled horns, a red dog with a tail like a banner, a cart-horse so pale it looked sculpted from old moonlight.

But it was the town itself that seemed most changed. Where, last sennight, several houses had stood empty and shuttered, today two were transformed. One, whose windows had been papered over for years, now shone with fresh glass and wore a bright red sign: "BRIDLE & BITS." There was no recollection of anyone renovating, no word of a merchant buying the place, yet now it stood as if it had always belonged. The other former vacancy, at the edge of the square, now boasted a series of round, porthole-like windows and a painted placard: "Buttonaria— All Buttons, All Times." Behind the glass, strings of buttons in every shape and color trailed from the ceiling, some as large as saucers.

She looked down to the street and saw Dardrad and Makota standing together, both staring at the new shops with the same blank, resigned expression. Dardrad rubbed his beard, muttering under his breath, while Makota held a cinnamon bun in one paw and gestured at the shops with the other. The two exchanged a few words, then Dardrad shrugged, turned, and stomped back toward his own shop. Makota lingered a moment longer, as if waiting for the town itself to explain. Then she too retreated, her tail switching.

Galhani traced circles on the windowpane, her fingers leaving foggy whorls that faded almost instantly. She watched as the newcomers passed below, some peering up at her window, most moving too quickly to care. Every few minutes, someone would stop in front of a shop, consult a list, then move on, as if following a private set of instructions. It was an efficiency that felt almost inhuman.

Her own reflection ghosted on the window, faint and stretched by the glass. She barely recognized herself: the dark hollows beneath her eyes, the thinning hair, the drawn lines around her mouth. She tried to smile, but it only deepened the grooves. For a moment, she pressed her palm flat against the glass, wishing she could push herself through to the other side.

The square was filling up now, the air charged with the energy of market closing. Families corralled their children and herded them toward home. A pair of adolescents in identical brown coats darted behind the well, wrestling for a moment before one sprinted away, howling with laughter. Two old women she'd never seen before, arm in arm, picked their way along the grass, pausing every few steps to survey the growing parade of strangers. Behind them, a trio of merchants in matching waistcoats set up a folding table and began to display what looked like glass beads—tiny pebbles catching the sun as they set them out in neat, obsessive rows.

Galhani closed her eyes, but even then she saw the image of the square, burned into her eyelids. She wondered what it would look like tomorrow—what new shops would appear, what old ones would vanish, which faces would become fixtures, which would fade. She wondered how long it would take before nobody remembered what the square had once looked like, or who had built the houses in the first place.

She glanced again at her reflection, and this time, in the shifting light, she could see Lara's silhouette behind her—moving, always moving, in the bedroom's dim background. Lara was at the dressing table, sorting through a handful of dried flowers, arranging them in tight little bundles that she then set into a box. She hummed, low and tuneless, never looking up. Galhani wanted to say something, to ask if she remembered when the houses had been empty, but the words snagged in her throat. Instead, she watched the way Lara's hands moved—nimble, sure, completely at home in their work.

Galhani let her gaze return to the window. From this height, she could see beyond the square and out through the town gate to the trade road. What should have been a lazy brown ribbon was now a river, choked with wagons, carts, and the distant shimmer of people walking two and three abreast. Even the inn, visible as a slouch of yellow light just beyond the wall, looked overwhelmed: horses lined up at the hitching posts, and lanterns burning in every window.

Everyone was moving with purpose, but none of it made sense. Why would a town need so many bridle bits, or buttons, or hand-baked bread sticks? Who needed a hat for their chicken, or a shop that only sold matches, one at a time? The excess felt obscene, but it was also... deliberate, as if the town was growing toward something. Or preparing for something.

She looked up, and her own reflection met her gaze once more. The face in the glass looked older than ever, and Galhani realized, with a pang, that she could not remember how old she actually was. Not in years, not in seasons. She was as old as the town, and the town was changing.

A soft thump behind her: Lara, closing the box of dried flowers and setting it on the dresser. She crossed the room and sat on the edge of the bed, hands folded in her lap. For a long moment, neither spoke. The sounds from outside—the laughter, the shouts, the hoofbeats—seeped up through the floorboards and circled the room.

"It's not going to stop," Lara said quietly.

Galhani blinked. "The shops?"

"All of it. The new people, the new houses, the way everything gets filled up overnight. You can feel it, can't you?"

Galhani nodded, watching the square. "It's like someone is winding up a clock."

Lara smiled, but there was no humor in it. "I think it's already wound. We're just waiting for it to ring."

They fell into silence again, and Galhani returned her attention to the window. She traced one more pattern on the glass, a spiral that started at the center and worked its way outward, never quite reaching the edge. The motion soothed her, but only a little.

The sun dipped lower, the colors of the square flattening into a single shade of gray. She watched until the last of the children was pulled inside, until the lamps along the road guttered into reluctant flame, until the only movement left was the slow, determined march of travelers arriving from the north.

She stared at the road until her vision blurred, until she could no longer tell if the faces moving toward the town were strangers or ghosts or simply her own memories, doubling back along the path they'd taken every day of her life.

When the first bell sounded from the inn, Galhani uncurled herself from the window and stood, legs numb, spine aching. Lara offered her a hand, and together they left the bedroom and descended the stairs, each step echoing as if it belonged to a much larger house.

She left the window open behind her, the spiral still faintly visible on the glass. By the time they reached the bottom of the stairs, the wind had already erased it.

———

Evening brought a flood of bodies and noise to the Broken Claw. The regulars held fast to their habitual perches—the corner table for Leota, the wide bench for Dardrad, the single high stool by the window for Makota—while the influx of newcomers jostled and hovered near the entryway, clustered in polite but unmistakable exclusion zones. The place buzzed, but not with the easy camaraderie of old times. Instead, the air was charged with the tension of too many stories trying to share a single space.

Sam worked the bar with her usual, cheerful brutality. She filled tankards with cider and ale, wiped the counter with brisk, circular strokes, and kept her one good eye trained on the room. The other, forever marked by the scar that bisected her face, seemed to track the movements of people even after they left her field of vision. Tonight, she wore her hair in a single plait, white as frost, and her shirt sleeves rolled to the elbow to reveal the dense, corded muscle of her forearms. Every time she drew a pint, the veins bulged under the skin, as if even her blood found the night a challenge.

Galhani sat at a round table near the hearth, feeling as though the warmth from the fire barely made it to her skin. To her left sat Warren, slumped forward, massive arms folded on the table like logs of green wood. His hair was wild, his eyes rimmed in red, and his voice—usually a deep, steady rumble—wavered with the uncertainty of a child. He held a dagger in one hand, spinning it by the hilt, the blade catching firelight in brief, unremarkable flashes.

To her right, Leota perched on the edge of her chair, every inch of her shrouded in black. Her hair, black to the roots, fell in two severe braids over each shoulder, and her eyes tracked the room with the wariness of a fox. She had a cup of something dark and bitter in front of her, which she sipped with the slow, deliberate care of a poison-taster.

Across from Galhani, Jen stood rather than sat, her posture ramrod straight, gaze darting between the regulars and the unfamiliar faces at the door. On her wrist, the iron bracelet—the one that turned into her sword at a moment's notice—caught the firelight and reflected it in steady, hypnotic beats.

The conversation, if it could be called that, orbited a single, growing anxiety.

"My forge-dreams are all fog," Warren said, his voice barely above a whisper. "I dream I'm making swords, axes, all for travelers. But when I wake, it's like the metal has turned to mud." He drove the dagger into the table, not enough to stick but enough to leave a small dent. "Look at this. It's for a woman who'll need to protect herself. But it's just—" He let go, disgusted, and the blade clattered harmlessly to the wood. "Ordinary steel."

Leota watched the knife for a moment, then spoke, her voice quiet but precise. "There's a dullness, spreading from the center out. Not just the crafts. The wards on my house are all but gone. The sigils are still there, but the power inside..." She shook her head, as if chasing off a bad dream.

Jen exhaled hard, her hand touching the bracelet in a nervous, habitual gesture. "Town's not integrating. It's absorbing, yes. But the edges don't smooth. There's friction everywhere." She cast a quick glance at the newcomers, who hovered near the door, laughing a little too loudly, their eyes flicking up every time a regular passed close. "It's probably just the chaos of too many bodies in too little space. But it feels wrong. Feels like we're the ones out of place now."

Galhani nursed her cup, which held only water tonight. She found her voice, though it came out a whisper. "Everything's double. The garden. The traffic. The pace of time." She didn't mention the Aegis Brew, or the man she'd chilled to the bone. "I can't predict anything anymore. The blends act as if they've never met each other before."

Warren slumped lower. "I made the same sword three times this sennight. Each time, I dreamed the same face, the same battle, the same ending. But the steel is... less, every time. First it's black and sharp. Second time, it won't take an edge. Third, it bends in my hands. Never seen anything like it, and I've seen a lot."

Leota set her cup down, fingers lingering on the rim. "It's a draining. Quality, not quantity. You said it yourself: twice the metal, half the edge. That's how all the old towns die. Too much of the world wants to get in, and none of it wants to stay." She turned her eyes on Galhani, searching. "What do you think?"

Galhani couldn't answer. Instead, she watched her own hands—thin, pale, trembling slightly as she rotated the cup. She tried to recall the taste of her own tea, but even that memory felt blurred at the edges. She looked to Jen, searching for something sturdy, something permanent.

But Jen was already scanning the door. "See the new ones?" she murmured, almost to herself. "They stick together. Always do, at first. Then they drift, find a regular to latch onto. Sometimes it works. Sometimes..." She trailed off, shrugged.

Sam appeared at their table with a tray of battered potato fritters. She slid the plate into the middle, then poured a splash of cider into Warren's empty mug. "Eat," she commanded. "You'll need it."

Leota raised an eyebrow. "Is there something coming?"

Sam shot a look at the clock above the bar. "There always is," she said, but wouldn't elaborate. Instead, she wiped her hands on a towel and retreated, keeping her eye on the newcomers.

One of them—a tall, sharp-jawed man with clever eyes and a set of jeweler's tools at his belt—broke from the cluster and strode to the bar. He surveyed the room with professional curiosity, lips pursed, eyes noting every detail. When he reached the bar, he addressed Sam by name, as if they were old acquaintances. "Finnian," he said, introducing himself with a practiced bow. "Clockmaker and fixer of oddities."

Sam set a mug down. "Didn't know we needed a clockmaker."

Finnihan grinned, showing an impressive row of teeth. "Every town does, sooner or later." He raised his mug, then turned to scan the regulars, his gaze settling on Lucy, who stood by the hearth, hands still stained with clay.

Lucy caught the look and, with a smile, crossed the room to greet him. "A fellow craftsperson?"

Finnihan nodded, pleased. "I am. And you?"

Lucy's face brightened. "Potter"." She held up her hands and wiggled her fingers.

The two fell into conversation, their voices low but animated. Galhani watched them from her seat, noting the way Lucy's shoulders relaxed, the way her laugh returned—full and genuine, for the first time in days. She tried to feel happy for Lucy, but all she could muster was a small, sour knot of envy.

Across the room, Makota waved at the two, her whiskers twitching. "If you get a minute," she called to Finnihan, "my bakery's oven has a mind of its own. Maybe you can tune it, too?"

Finnihan flashed a thumbs-up. "I'll stop by first thing in the morning." He turned back to Lucy, who was showing him a small, blue-glazed mug she'd pulled from her apron. Finnihan held it up to the light, rotated it in his fingers, then made a series of precise, clockwork gestures as he explained how the handle could be improved. Lucy laughed again, and the two bent their heads close, lost in the mechanics of pottery and time.

Back at the regulars' table, Warren grunted, "He's all right, that one. Odd, but not the dangerous kind."

Jen shrugged. "We'll see."

Leota sipped her drink, her gaze flicking from the newcomers to the old faces. "He fits, because he doesn't try. That's how you survive a thinning. You become what the place needs, not what you want."

Galhani felt the words settle inside her, dense and immovable. She wondered what the town needed her to be, and whether she could even manage it.

Time passed, the candles burning down to nubs, the air thickening with the scents of yeast and oil and the smoke of Sam's pipe. The conversation ebbed and flowed, old stories resurfacing, the regulars inching closer to the newcomers with each refill. By midnight, the two sides had blurred, if not merged: the regulars guarded, the newcomers eager, but all of them—eventually—drawn into the gravity of the Claw.

Near closing, Galhani found herself standing beside Lucy, who was still in close conversation with Finnian. The clockmaker's hands were quick, graceful, almost hypnotic as he described some trick of gears and springs. Lucy's eyes glowed with the thrill of learning. Galhani felt a twinge of relief—maybe this was how it worked, maybe this was the beginning of repair instead of unraveling.

Sam leaned over the bar, her scar catching the lamplight, and winked at Galhani. "Not so bad, is it?"

Galhani nodded, but said nothing.

Behind her, the door opened, and a cold gust swept in, scattering the candleflames. The last of the travelers entered—a woman with sharp features and a cloak that sparkled with frost. She moved through the room as if she owned it, eyes taking in every detail, every secret. She paused at the bar, exchanged a few words with Sam, then settled into a chair by herself, watching the room as if she were a judge at a contest.

Finnian noticed her, and for a second, his smile faltered. Then he turned back to Lucy, as if nothing had happened.

Galhani watched the woman, unease returning. The crowd around her was louder, warmer, but she felt the cold at her back, as if the night itself had followed her inside.

She pressed her hand to her heart, feeling the rhythm—a little fast, a little off-kilter, but still hers. She watched as the new woman pulled a scrap of paper from her sleeve and began to write, her pen moving in neat, mechanical lines.

All around her, the town continued to change, filling itself up with new people, new stories, new dangers. But for a moment, inside the Claw, the world felt steady, held together by the threads of routine and memory and the stubborn refusal of the regulars to give up their place.

Galhani took a last look at the hearth, at Warren's bent head, at Jen's unblinking gaze, at Leota's patient sip. She looked at Lucy, radiant with the thrill of learning, and at Finnihan, who had already found a way to belong.

For a moment, she let herself believe that everything would be all right.

Then the clock above the bar struck midnight, and the world moved forward, one inevitable tick at a time.

five

. . .

THE SUN BROKE over North Pointe in a line of molten gold, burning off the ragged mist and pooling in the tea shop's wide front window. Galhani had opened the place before most of the town even knew it was morning, though her own night's sleep had been punctuated by candlemark-long stretches of just staring at the ceiling, listening to Lara's breathing and to her own thoughts. There was no pretense of breakfast—she'd swallowed a mouthful of cold water and wiped her face with a towel, then gone downstairs to begin the necessary work of being a person.

She set out her cups, three at first, then six, then stopped. Why not more? She counted out twelve, arranging them on the counter in two neat ranks, as if she expected a battalion of customers. The action was automatic and pointless; she knew the morning would bring fewer and fewer regulars. But some habits died harder than hope.

By the time the first knock came at the door, she had already ground and mixed three dozen sachets. She almost resented the interruption, but habit had trained her lips to shape a smile even when she did not feel it. She wiped her hands and went to the door.

The man waiting outside looked more like a memory of a traveler than the real thing. His boots were caked with salt and dust, and his coat was cut for a slimmer, younger man, now hanging off him like a borrowed skin. When she opened the door, he shuffled in without the usual smile or greeting, eyes fixed on the row of jars behind the counter as if willing the right one to appear.

Galhani forced brightness into her voice. "How can I help you, this morning?"

He winced as if the question pained him. "Stomach," he said. "Haven't eaten in a sennight that didn't come back up or through. Lady at the inn said you might have a tea for that." He shrugged, and she saw the cost of the gesture ripple through his frame. "I've got coin. But if it's no use, I'd sooner keep my silver."

It was the sort of problem she'd solved a hundred times. She could see the blend in her mind: ginger for the cramping, licorice root for the ulceration, mallow to calm the lining, mint to lift the bitterness. She said as much, and the traveler nodded, settling onto a stool as if lowering himself onto a bed of nails.

Her hands shook as she measured the powders, but she steadied them against the lip of the tin. The scale didn't lie; she watched the needle settle, then doubled-checked, then checked again. The scale was true. The ingredients were perfect. She dampened the mesh infuser, spooned in the blend, and poured the water in a long, slow spiral. The perfume rose instantly: sharp, sweet, astringent, under-pinned by a hint of woodsmoke. She felt the old thrill of creation— how a handful of leaves could become comfort, how a cup could reset a life. But even as the aroma filled the shop, a new anxiety gnawed at the back of her tongue. Would it be enough?

She set the cup before the traveler. "Give it two minutes," she said, voice barely above a whisper.

He waited in silence, looking miserable, until she nodded for him to drink. He sipped, coughed once at the heat, and swallowed with visible relief. Then he frowned, rolled the flavor around his mouth. "That's—" he started, then stopped. He took a second, longer sip, eyes narrowing. "I don't taste much," he said, his confusion rising to the surface. "Is it supposed to be so... light?"

Galhani felt her stomach turn to ice. "It should have bite," she said. "Let me see." She dipped a spoon into the brew and tasted it. There was nothing. Not even the memory of ginger, or the faint sharpness of mint. It was the taste of boiled air.

Her composure, so brittle these days, gave way all at once. Her hands dropped to her sides, and her chest constricted. She could not breathe. The traveler stared at her, unsure, and she could only look back at him, helpless, before the tears welled over and spilled down her cheeks.

She hated this, hated crying in front of anyone, but it was as if her insides had finally reached their limit and were shedding pressure in the only way left. She turned away, pressing the back of her hand to her mouth, but it only muffled the ragged sound. The man on the stool made an embarrassed gesture, then reached into his pocket for a coin. "If it's not working, you don't have to—" he began, but she cut him off.

"No," she managed, wiping at her eyes. "No charge. Please. I—" She wanted to explain, to say that this was not her fault, that the world itself was conspiring against her teas, that the plants had grown insipid and the air was full of too many ghosts, but her tongue couldn't find the words. She busied herself packing several sachets of her best green tea into a paper envelope, hands working on their own while her mind screamed at her to do something, anything to fix this.

"Try these," she said, voice thick. "It's just plain green, but maybe if you brew it strong..." She trailed off, already knowing it was futile. "I'm sorry. I'm so sorry."

The traveler gave her a look that was half sympathy, half unease. "It's all right," he said. "Maybe it's just the water." He took the envelope, tucked it inside his coat, and left a single copper coin on the counter before turning and shuffling out, head bowed.

She stared at the coin as if it might leap up and accuse her of fraud. The world was quieter now, the sun climbing higher and sharpening every shadow into a blade. Galhani moved to the door, locked it, and then went to the back of the shop and leaned against the wall, staring at her hands. They were red and raw, the skin around her nails chewed to shreds.

The next thing she knew, she was in the storeroom, sweeping the jars off their shelves, dumping the dried herbs into a sack. She upended the baskets of stems, checked the roots for mold, and found nothing amiss. No magic, no bitterness, just bland, compliant plant matter, eager to be forgotten.

She was still cleaning when the front door rattled. Lara appeared in the threshold, her hair streaked with dirt and sweat, hands caked with earth and something darker, almost black. "Garden's done for," Lara said, voice flat. "Every stalk that's not a weed is dead. The exotics are just dust, and I don't know why."

Galhani turned, and Lara's eyes took in the mess, the rows of empty jars, the sack of discarded leaves. She blinked, then blinked again, her usual composure slipping for a moment. "Are you all right?" she asked, and then, after a pause, "Gal, what happened?"

Galhani couldn't answer. Her throat closed up, and her breath came in ragged gasps. For a second, she thought she might faint. Lara dropped the basket she was holding and crossed the room in two steps, putting a hand on her shoulder. She shook her gently, then hugged her hard, getting dirt and sweat all over Galhani's tunic, but neither of them cared.

"It's all right," Lara said, voice gentler now. "It's just a bad season. We'll figure it out."

But Galhani shook her head, and for once, there was no comfort in the familiar words. She let herself sag against Lara, her whole body gone slack with defeat. The garden was dead, the teas were dead, and for all she knew, the town itself was dying by degrees. She felt small and useless and hollowed out.

Lara held her until the shaking stopped, then wiped Galhani's cheeks with the corner of her own apron. For a while, they just stood there, side by side, looking out the back window at the overgrown garden, the weeds already clawing at the edges of the path.

"You want to close the shop for the day?" Lara asked.

Galhani nodded, unable to trust her voice.

Lara took her hand and squeezed it, then together they went to the front and turned the sign to "Closed." The shop, empty and clean and full of ghosts, felt like a museum. Galhani looked at the cups she'd laid out that morning—twelve, perfectly aligned, waiting for a crowd that would never come.

She wanted to sweep them all into the trash, but instead, she reached out and touched the rim of the first cup, tracing it in a slow, careful circle. Lara watched, silent, understanding at last that there were no more words for this kind of sorrow.

Outside, the sun had climbed even higher, making everything bright and unkind. Inside, Galhani stood in the middle of her beautiful, useless shop, and tried to remember what it felt like to be whole.

———

Upstairs, the air was stale with the smell of old linen and potpourri left too long in the sun. Galhani sat on the edge of the bed, shoulders hunched, hands curled into her lap like twin spiders. The window was cracked, letting in a slant of light that seemed almost reluctant to cross the room.

Lara knelt before her, hands gentle but rough, still streaked with black earth from the morning's disaster. She took Galhani's hands in her own, thumb tracing the bruised half-moons under her fingernails. They stayed that way for a long moment, the only sound the whimper of the mattress as Galhani shifted her weight from foot to foot.

"You know," Lara said, voice low and hoarse, "you're worth more than a million dried-up herbs." She squeezed, not enough to hurt, but enough to get Galhani's eyes to rise and meet hers. "You could serve boiled water, and people would still come to see you. It's not the leaves, love. It's your kindness."

Galhani blinked. She wanted to believe it, but the words caught in her throat and dissolved before they could form. She looked at Lara's face, studied the deep lines at the corners of her eyes, the bruised purple beneath each one, the stubborn smear of dirt along her jaw. Lara looked like she hadn't slept in a sennight, and maybe she hadn't. The garden had been a war zone lately, and every time Galhani looked out at it, she found Lara in the thick of it, bent double and tearing at weeds with both hands, as if she could wring a cure from the earth by sheer force of will.

"Did you try watering them with the ash solution?" Galhani asked, just to say something.

"Three times," Lara replied. "Didn't work. The exotics are gone, and the parsley's started growing upside-down." She managed a crooked grin. "If you ever need a tea that tastes like the bottom of a boot, I have you covered."

Galhani tried to smile, and it almost worked. She squeezed Lara's hands in return, then let her head drop forward until her hair hung between them like a curtain. The tears weren't gone, but they were manageable now, leaking out in slow, silent drips. Lara let her cry, stroking her hair in slow, rhythmic passes, the same way she had the first time they'd ever spent a night together, long before they'd learned to live with each other's bad days.

The air in the room thickened. Galhani felt the chill of it settling into her bones. She could have stayed like this forever—just the two of them, hiding from the world—but the world never let them hide for long.

From below, a creak of wood, the scrape of a stool, then voices. Three, at least—one high and bright, one mellow, one almost too soft to hear. Finnian, Lucy, and Leota, if Galhani's instincts were right. She caught the cadence of Finnian's laugh, the way Lucy's words tumbled one over the other, the measured hush of Leota's responses. It was the familiar melody of friendship, and it should have been a comfort, but all it did was tighten the ache in her chest.

She pulled her hands free and wiped her eyes on her sleeve, careful not to let Lara see. "We have company," she said, the words feeling too large for her mouth.

"Let them wait," Lara said, but she was already standing, smoothing her skirt and brushing the dirt off her knees. Her face was set, but not unkind. "Or don't. Maybe you need them. Maybe we both do."

Galhani let herself breathe. She blinked until her vision cleared, then stood, feeling the tremor in her legs but ignoring it. The urge to crawl back under the blanket and never come out was strong, but something else—shame, maybe, or the ghost of curiosity—dragged her forward.

She looked at Lara. "Do I look like I've been crying?"

Lara smiled, soft and sad. "Only to someone who knows you."

"Good." Galhani tried for a laugh, and this time it sounded almost real. "Let's go see what they want."

They crossed the small room together, and for a moment, the world beyond the door seemed possible again.

———

The voices grew louder as Galhani reached the bottom of the stairs, and for a second she froze, hand pressed to the wall just below the landing. She told herself she was bracing, but really, she was buying a few more seconds to become the kind of person who could face other people again. She drew a careful breath, pushed through the last of her tears, and stepped into the light.

Finnian, Lucy, and Leota had claimed the central table. Finnian's back was to her, but even so, he was hard to miss—he wore a vest splashed with every color of the autumn market, and his hair flopped over his brow in a style only a certain type of man could carry without embarrassment. His hands were already at work, arranging three spoons and a salt cellar into an elaborate scaffolding, explaining, she guessed, some mechanical principle to Lucy, who watched with the gentle patience of a big sister letting a child show off a prized stone.

Leota, as ever, looked as though she'd been dragged into the gathering at sword-point. She sat stiffly, arms folded, her black dress creating a gravity well that sucked in every stray shadow. She watched Finnian's display with a kind of cold curiosity, as if trying to decide if the man was an idiot or a genius. Or, possibly, both.

Galhani crossed to the counter and put the kettle on, then set about assembling a tray: four cups, plain and white, nothing fancy, and a single jar of her least offensive green. She knew none of them would want to ask for more, so she filled the cups generously. As she carried the tray over, the conversation wound down.

Finnian looked up and grinned. "You're a sight for sore eyes, mistress. Was just explaining the principle of the escapement to our fine friends here." He tapped the little model he'd made; it collapsed instantly, the salt cellar tumbling and rolling off the table and nearly into Leota's lap.

"Marvelous," Galhani said, and set the tray down. She poured without speaking, the motion hypnotic, a ritual she could still do with her eyes closed. Leota took her cup first, inspecting the color with a wince so small only another perfectionist would notice. Lucy followed, her hands as steady as her eyes. Finnian waited, eager, then lifted his mug to the light and nodded approval at its clarity.

Galhani didn't sit. She leaned against the wall near the window, arms crossed. She wasn't sure if she could trust her voice.

Finnian slurped, then declared, "Excellent. You can tell it's a gnome's brew—the leaves are cut finer than a watchmaker's file." He turned the cup, admiring the spiral left in the dregs. "Nothing in the world compares. Well, except maybe my grandmother's, but she was only half as good and twice as drunk."

Lucy smiled, but it was a careful, wary thing. "What brings you in, Finnian?"

He beamed, more than happy to have an audience. "Can't sleep. Not with the whole town caught up in some grand experiment. There's energy in the air, don't you feel it? It's like standing next to a forge, or right before a thunderstorm." He glanced at Leota, inviting her opinion.

Leota shrugged, took a small sip, and set her cup down. "Feels more like someone's winding up the world and waiting to see if it breaks."

Finnian clapped his hands, delighted. "Precisely! That's the problem with complicated systems: a single misaligned cog, and everything goes sideways. People think it's the fault of the gears, but it's always the smallest thing that throws the whole mechanism off." He picked up two spoons and crossed them, balancing one on his finger. "Like this. If you nudge it, just a little—" he tapped the top spoon, and both fell to the table with a sharp metallic snap. "—the effect is immediate. Chaos from a single touch."

Leota gave him a look sharp enough to shave with. "Are you saying our town is a broken clock?"

"I'm saying," Finnian said, "that you're in the middle of a realignment, no? The old shops, the old faces—lovely, but they're set in their ways. The new shops pop up to fill a gap, but half the time, the gap wasn't even there." He turned to Galhani. "Like your teas, mistress. You adjust your recipe because the world demands it, but the world has already shifted twice before you even realize it."

Galhani stared at her shoes. She wanted to say he was wrong, that she could track every shift, every minute change in the soil or water or humidity. But she knew what he meant. The last sennight had been a blur of recalibration and failure.

Lucy sipped her tea, face thoughtful. "Is there a fix for it?"

Finnian grinned, then sobered a little. "You wait for the mechanism to find a new balance. You can't force it. But you can keep the gears clean, keep the pivots oiled. Sometimes, you need to add a new gear. Or take one out."

The words hung in the air. Galhani felt the heaviness in her chest loosen, just a little. The idea that this was something to wait through, not something she was uniquely failing, gave her a crumb of comfort.

Leota drummed her fingers on the tabletop. "The town's at twenty shops, now. That makes the full icosagon. At least, shops I'll recognize as such. And yet, the center feels hollow."

Finnian shrugged. "Maybe the last piece isn't a shop at all."

Silence. Even Lucy didn't try to fill it.

After a minute, Finnian sat up straighter. "I was actually hoping to ask—do you think the town would accept a clockmaker's shop? Not that I'd compete with anyone. But it feels like the next logical step."

Galhani felt the shift immediately. A warmth ran through her, from the soles of her feet to the roots of her hair—a sensation she hadn't felt since she was a child and the shop's magic had first chosen her. Next to her, Lucy straightened, her eyes wide and shining. Leota blinked, the edge in her stare momentarily blunted by something like wonder.

They all felt it. The town's magic, subtle and ancient, accepting Finnian's idea as if it had been waiting for the offer.

Leota stood, slow and graceful. "You should see if there's a space ready for you. Sometimes, the town gets ahead of its own planning."

Lucy nodded. "I'll show you. The space next to Bartram's would do nicely."

Finnian, flush with excitement, downed the rest of his tea and wiped his mouth on his sleeve. "If it's meant to be, the door will open."

They all left together, Galhani closing the shop door behind them and Lucy already telling Finnian about the best suppliers for springs and the weird old lady who came through once a moon and collected wind-up birds. Leota fell back a few steps, watching them, then turned to Galhani.

"You all right?" she asked, voice more gentle than usual.

"I think so," Galhani said, surprised to find that it was mostly true.

Leota's lips quirked in a half-smile. "The world turns, even when we don't want it to. But sometimes, it lands right side up."

They followed the others. The square was bright and loud now, the energy Finnian had described hanging thick as pollen in the air. They crossed to the space next to the cobbler's shop, where the windows had been dark for so long that even the dust had stopped trying to escape.

Lucy pulled at the door, which opened on the first try. Inside, the air was crisp and clear, as if the place had been waiting with held breath. Sunlight lit up a counter already swept clean, a series of empty shelves, a wide table at the back ready for tools. Finnian stepped in and turned a slow circle, grinning like a man who'd just found the last puzzle piece under the couch.

"It's perfect," he said, then repeated it, softer. "It's absolutely perfect."

Outside, Leota glanced down the street at the line of new shops—Buttonaria, Fine Scrivening, the paper place, and the harps. They were all in place, all running, all exactly as the town had "intended," but they felt different. Temporary, somehow. As if they were holding a place for something better, or just waiting to be replaced.

Finnian's shop, on the other hand, felt as if it had always existed. It fit.

Galhani watched Finnian unpack his traveling kit, already lost in a world of gears and springs. She glanced at Lucy, who smiled in shared satisfaction. Even Leota, for all her practiced cynicism, seemed lighter, as if the balance was starting to return.

"I wonder," Leota said, not to anyone in particular, "what the town is preparing for."

Galhani didn't have an answer. But for the first time in days, she felt less like a failing experiment and more like a part of something living, shifting, and maybe, just maybe, healing.

———

Lucy lingered in Finnian's new shop, the two of them already up to their elbows in gears and fine wire, but Galhani and Leota left them to it and turned back toward the square. The sunlight was harsh now, slanting off the bakery's windows and catching the dust in the street like a blizzard of glass. Galhani didn't speak, but Leota's presence beside her was bracing—a cool, sharp reality after the giddy, uncertain times of the morning.

They reached the tea shop in silence. Galhani unlocked the door, stepped inside, and was struck by the emptiness of the space. For the first time since she'd opened that morning, she noticed how the silence pressed in: the echo of her own footsteps, the tiny hiss of sunlight spilling across the counter. She reset the chairs, wiped the table where the group had sat, then stood with her back to the window, bracing for whatever Leota had come to say.

Leota did not wait. "You're not serving any of your special blends," she said, the words dropping like stones. "Why?"

Galhani looked at the wall behind the counter, at the neat rows of tins, each one labeled in her own careful hand. The answer was everywhere in the room, but she couldn't bring herself to say it out loud. "Nothing's working," she managed. "It's like the magic's been drained out of everything. Even the basics are unpredictable. I can't keep up."

Leota studied her with a predator's patience. "And you think it's your fault."

Galhani shook her head, though a part of her believed it anyway. "I think it's the town. I think it's broken. And I can't fix it."

Leota opened her mouth, but the sound of the bell above the door interrupted her. Vamir entered, his hair in wild disarray, his cloak dusted with what looked like flour and maybe sawdust. In his arms he cradled an ancient, monstrous tome, so large it looked like it could anchor a ship. He nearly dropped it on the threshold, but recovered with a yelp and lurched to the nearest table, where he let the book thud onto the wood.

He stood back, breathing hard, and grinned at the two women. "You would not believe how heavy this thing is," he said, patting the book with a sense of triumph.

Leota raised an eyebrow. "Found what you were looking for?"

Vamir nodded, unslinging his satchel and drawing out a cloth-wrapped bundle, which turned out to be an even older, smaller book, bound in cracked leather. "This is for cross-referencing. But the big one —" he thumped the tome again, "—has what we need." He flipped it open to a chapter halfway through, sending up a cloud of ancient dust.

Galhani watched as he traced the lines with one finger, lips moving as he read. The language was a dense, unfamiliar script, but he translated as he went. "It's called a creative dissonance. Like a parasite, but not evil—just a force of nature, attracted to places with too much magic or creativity and forced to drain it, balance it, until equilibrium is restored." He glanced up, eyes bright. "It's not personal. It just is."

Leota's eyes narrowed. "How do we get rid of it?"

Vamir shrugged, as if the question itself missed the point. "You don't. You outlast it. Or, more rarely, you adapt. Towns that survive usually get stronger, not weaker. But there's a price: the old way has to die off. Otherwise, the thing lingers. Keeps feeding."

Leota absorbed this, her mind already ten steps ahead. "What does it want from us?"

Vamir grinned, delighted. "To be novel. To find a new balance. Or to let go of the parts that won't adapt."

Galhani closed her eyes. The pattern was suddenly clear: the teas, the garden, the shops multiplying and fading, the air thick with unnameable pressure. It was all the same sickness, just different organs failing at their own pace.

Leota bent over the tome, scanning the lines as if she could brute-force a solution from sheer intellect. "If that's true, the town is already changing. But not all at once. Some parts are fighting it."

Vamir nodded. "Exactly. The creative dissonance is not malicious—

it's mechanical. If we can pivot, accept the new shape, it will leave. If we cling to the old, it stays. Simple as that."

Leota straightened, her gaze landing on Galhani. "So we change."

Galhani opened her eyes. "Or we go extinct," she said, but her voice was calm now, the words settling into her like a new root system.

Vamir set the book aside and smiled. "I vote for change. If you need a new blend, I have a hundred ideas. Most of them are terrible, but a few—" he winked, "—might even surprise you."

Leota laughed, a short, incredulous bark. "Surprises are the only thing keeping us alive these days." She turned to Galhani, her expression softening just a fraction. "You were never the problem. But you can be the solution, if you want."

Galhani looked at her hands, which were finally still. She thought of the morning's failures, of Lara's dirt-stained fingers, of Finnian and Lucy and the odd new shops that came and went like dreams. She felt the heaviness in her chest, but it was softer now, almost like an anchor instead of a stone.

She reached for the nearest tin, opened it, and inhaled. The aroma was faint, barely there, but she could smell the ghost of possibility. She measured a pinch, then another, improvising as she went. She set the kettle to boil, eyes fixed on the rising curl of steam, and found herself breathing in time with its gentle rhythm.

She poured the water, let it steep, and waited. When she finally tasted it, the flavor was subtle—a whisper of what it used to be—but she found she didn't mind. It was new, and it was hers, and it would have to do.

She poured a second cup and handed it to Leota, who sipped and nodded approval, then to Vamir, who tasted and made a delighted face.

"It's good," he said. "Different, but good."

Galhani smiled, for real this time, and looked out the window. The light was softer now, the afternoon sun painting gentle patterns across the street. In the distance, she saw Finnian and Lucy laughing, arms loaded with boxes, and she thought of all the things that had to break before they could heal.

"But," Vamir continued softly, "it's not *special*, is it?"

Galhani's throat tightened and she shook her head.

"It doesn't need to be," Leota said firmly. "Special can come later. For now, tasty is more than enough."

Galhani gave the witch a hesitant smile. She went to the door, flipped the sign to "Open," and let the air carry the new scent out into the world. She had no idea what would happen next. But for the first time in ages, she was curious to find out.

six

. . .

THE CLAMOR of the bell above the tea shop door brought Galhani out of her late afternoon lull, halfway through prepping a new blend of mild chamomile and desperate optimism. The bell was insistent, as if rung by someone trying to summon the entire neighborhood at once, and for a moment Galhani braced herself for an unhappy customer. Instead, Makota arrived in a blur of brown fur and striped skirt, tail lashing so violently it nearly knocked over the display of honey jars beside the entrance.

"Change of plans, mistress!" Makota announced, not even waiting for Galhani's greeting. "There's a party tonight. I've decided.""

Galhani blinked. "A party?"

"A town-wide celebration. On the square." She planted both hands on the counter and leaned in, whiskers forward, eyes bright. "Everyone brings something—food, drink, music, chairs, an instrument if you own one. And nobody gets to say no."

From the back, Lara's voice floated in: "Did I hear we're having a party?"

Makota pivoted, tail flicking, and beamed. "The whole square, Lara! And I'll have you know, I bullied Sam into pouring three kegs for the occasion. Dardrad and Dalossalda are on sausages. Vamir's bringing entertainment. Bartram's promised to lead us in a dance."

Lara poked her head through the half-door, eyebrow arched. "Is this to welcome the new people? Or to flush out whatever's haunting the old ones?"

"Both!" Makota shouted, then turned to Galhani again. "You're on cordials and crowd control. No arguments."

Galhani opened her mouth to protest, but Makota had already begun rummaging through the jars behind the counter, her paws a blur. "Not that one, too bitter. Yes, that one, perfect for mixing. Do you have any of the sweet syrup left, the one with the blue cap?"

She did, and she handed it over before she really thought about it. Makota grinned, unscrewed the top, and took a long, unselfconscious swig straight from the bottle.

"I'm inviting everyone. Even the new shops, even the ones with the weird signs and stranger smells. It's time we all met, and if the town wants to double up on itself, it can do it in public."

And with that, Makota was gone, off to spread her gospel of forced festivity to the rest of the square. Galhani stared at the aftermath—the syrup bottle still wobbling, three tins of her best tea upended, and a new sense of urgency in the air. She glanced at Lara, who was already sorting through the shelves for their best glassware.

"Is it possible to have a town-wide party and not break anything?" Galhani wondered aloud.

Lara shrugged, sweeping her hair back and tying it with a twist of old blue ribbon. "We'll find out. At least if something does break, it'll be our own fault."

"True," said Galhani. She started lining up bottles, already thinking about which blends would be safest for a crowd.

The next candlemark was a flurry of preparation. Word of Makota's plan had spread even faster than her cinnamon rolls: Galhani could hear the shouted arguments and speculative laughter drifting in from the square, punctuated by the occasional curse as someone tripped over a cord or dropped a stack of folding chairs. A group of children wrestled chairs and benches onto the grass, while Jen borrowed a handcart from Cole to help haul kegs out from the tavern's storage.

When Galhani stepped outside to check the lay of the land, she found the square already halfway transformed. Someone had strung a line of lanterns between the big tree and the bakery's front porch, and paper streamers drooped in the gentle wind. Lucy, dressed in her best working tunic and with splatters of clay up both forearms, had laid out dozens of her simple bowls on a trestle table near the center. Dardrad and Dalossalda, both in full butcher's regalia, were constructing a brick firepit with the grim determination of engineers building a fortress.

Makota presided over the chaos, darting from station to station with a ledger in one paw and a pastry in the other. She barked orders at anyone who stood still long enough to hear them, and when someone objected, she simply shouted louder until the protestor relented.

"Potluck, potluck!" she was yelling now. "Everyone brings something, or they eat last!"

A chorus of "aye!" and "yep!" and "I'll bring a salad!" followed, as people returned to their homes to raid pantries and root cellars. Galhani caught the sound of music—someone tuning a fiddle, another plucking at a thumb piano, and Finnian, humming as he set up a clockwork contraption by the food tables.

Back in the shop, Galhani and Lara worked side by side to blend the night's cordials. Lara took the lead, zesting lemons and slicing rounds of cucumber while Galhani lined up the glassware and checked her notes for the best calming (but not sedating) herbs. The resulting mix was a pale green and almost alarmingly clear; Galhani sniffed it, frowned, then tried a sip.

"It's... nice," she said, surprised by her own hesitance. "Not as sharp as I'd hoped, but better than nothing."

Lara nodded. "It'll do."

They boxed up the cordials in two heavy baskets, wrapped the glassware in tea towels, and made their way to the lawn.

The scene that greeted them was part carnival, part disaster. The lawn was awash with color—picnic cloths, banners, borrowed rugs thrown down as makeshift seating. Children darted between clusters of adults, some in costume, some in their best hand-me-downs, all sticky-fingered from sampling the sweets. Near the tree, Makota had set up a table of savory pastries: hand pies, spiral buns, and crescent-shaped tarts lined up in military precision. The sign above it read, in her careful script, "FREE FOR ALL—ONE PER HAND."

Dardrad was already grilling, his beard singed at the edges, as he tended a row of sausages so fat they bowed the metal grates. The smell was intoxicating, but even from a distance, Galhani could tell something was off: the usual sizzle was missing, the smoke less fragrant than it should have been.

She poured a glass of cordial for herself and watched as the first wave of townsfolk claimed their seats. Dalossalda set up a carving station and began slicing thick slabs of sausage onto plates. Lucy arranged her bowls in an artful pattern, offering them to anyone who needed something in which to ladle food, and Makota patrolled the periphery, ensuring every guest had a pastry.

As the sun slipped behind the western roofs, the lanterns' flames flickered wildly, turning the lawn gold and orange. Music started: a thin, reedy flute joined by the steady thump of a frame drum, then the unmistakable pulse of Finnian's mechanical bird as it chirped in perfect rhythm with the human musicians.

Galhani sipped again and felt the flavor dissolve, bland and watery. She frowned, tried a sausage, and found it savory but unremarkable. Even the pastries, which Makota had undoubtedly made with her own hands that morning, tasted flat. Not bad, just... lacking.

Around her, the townsfolk hardly seemed to notice. They ate and laughed and compared stories, and if anyone found the flavors off, they kept it to themselves. Galhani watched the clusters of people—old-timers and new arrivals, children and elders, the peculiar and the plain. Every so often, she caught a stranger's face: the new shopkeepers, awkward at the edges of conversation, their expressions wary but hopeful.

Lara nudged her and pointed to the far end of the lawn, where

Vamir was holding court. He'd set up a tiny stage (probably borrowed from the schoolhouse), and was in the process of reading from a massive, leather-bound tome to a rapt audience of children. Poly, the bird, flitted from shoulder to shoulder, occasionally interrupting the reading with a high-pitched whistle that sent the kids into fits of laughter.

Galhani watched, half-amused, half-melancholy. The town had never looked more alive, but the sense of muted flavor in the air unsettled her. She wandered among the tables, refilling cups and exchanging pleasantries, always aware that the sharp edge of the world had dulled somehow.

She found Leota near the lantern line, watching the crowd with her usual intensity. The witch's black dress absorbed the sunset, her hair a stark slash against the fire-lit faces around her. She sipped from a chipped mug, lips pursed, eyes scanning the square as if trying to see through to some other world.

"Enjoying yourself?" Galhani asked, settling beside her.

Leota snorted. "I'm enjoying Makota's show. She's a born tyrant, that one. If she'd been in charge of my coven, we'd have conquered the continent by now."

Galhani smiled. "It's not so bad. Everyone seems... almost happy."

"Almost," Leota echoed. "It's a nice illusion. But the new faces don't blend, do they? They hover. Like they're waiting for the moment to slip away again." She finished her drink and set the mug down. "And the food's gone flat. That's a bad sign."

Galhani nodded, heart heavy. "I noticed."

Leota's expression softened. "It'll pass. Things always do, for better or worse. For tonight, you should pretend it's all perfect."

They stood together, watching the party spiral outward as the night grew deeper. The music swelled, the voices grew louder, and the paper lanterns flickered in the wind, their light casting wavering patterns across the grass.

As Galhani raised her glass to her lips, she caught a glimpse of Finnian in the crowd, surrounded by children and several adults, his arms flailing as he acted out the climax of a story. For just a moment, she heard genuine laughter, clear and strong, and she let herself believe that, even with the world's edges sanded off, the heart of the town still beat true.

———

The evening stretched and thinned as twilight painted the grass in blue shadows and gold. At the center of it all, the party ebbed and surged, the music growing wilder, the conversations fragmenting into dozens of laughing, hungry knots. Galhani floated from table to blanket, cordial in hand, offering greetings and tasting each moment for what it was: pleasant, communal, and just a shade insubstantial, like bread made with too little yeast.

After a time, she remembered the second half of Makota's decree—that the new shopkeepers should be welcomed, drawn in, made part of the whole before the town grew another layer of strangers. So she set out, weaving between the old-timers, who called out her name and invited her to sit, and made for the clusters of unfamiliar faces at the party's periphery.

It was harder than she expected. Some of the newcomers had gathered in small, defensive groups, speaking in quiet voices and nursing their drinks. The few who mingled did so with the nervous energy of guests at a wedding where they barely knew the bride or groom.

The first stranger she introduced herself to was a tall, thin man with pinched features and hands that trembled slightly as he poured himself a cup of water. He wore a black vest and a necktie patterned in silver clefs, which she recognized instantly as the universal sign of a musician who wanted people to ask about his instrument.

"Galhani," she said, extending a hand. "Herbalist and tea-monger."

The man gripped her hand delicately, as if her bones were made of spun sugar. "Pleasure," he said. "I'm the harp repairman. New in town."

"From the shop near the corner? I've admired your sign," she replied. She tried to conjure his name from the haze of her memory, but it hovered just out of reach.

"Yes," he said, blinking owlishly. "That's me."

They exchanged a few pleasantries about the party, the weather, the music, and the way the food tasted slightly off tonight. He told her a story about a harp that broke every time the wind shifted, and she laughed at the appropriate place. When she tried to introduce him to someone else, though, the name was gone. By the time she circled back, he was chatting with a different group, and she doubted he'd remember her either.

The sock-darning woman was next. She wore a cardigan the color of creamed butter, and a headscarf with tiny chickens printed along the edge. Her smile was fixed, her eyes soft and indirect. Galhani asked if business was good, and the woman replied that it was "adequate, for the time being," but she hoped for better if winter arrived early.

They talked about darning versus knitting, and the different breeds of wool, and the oddness of living in a town with so many specialty shops. "It's like the place wants to be a market square and a village at once," the woman said, and Galhani agreed, but again, the exchange slipped from her mind as soon as she moved on. She turned, intending to find the woman again and ask her about the chicken hats Makota had mentioned earlier, but she was already gone, blending into the party as if she'd never been there.

It was like trying to remember a dream: vivid in the moment, but gone the instant you reached for it.

Of the new shops, only about half had sent anyone at all. The others remained dark and shuttered, despite Makota's invitations. The newcomers that did attend seemed mostly content to linger at the margins, observing more than participating, their laughter always a second slower than the rest.

She found herself drifting back toward the center, drawn by the gravitational pull of familiarity. Dardrad was telling war stories at a table packed with fishermen and bakers, their faces bright and open in the lamplight. Makota held forth at the pastry table, regaling a group of children with stories of "the time I caught a thief with only my claws and a rolling pin." Sam had abandoned her post at the kegs and was now wrestling in mock combat with two of the regulars, both of them twice her size but half her stubbornness.

Galhani watched these scenes with a warmth that was real, but also with a creeping sense of loss. The town was still itself, but the edges were fraying. She tried to picture the party a year from now, or ten, and could not decide if the new faces would blend or simply replace the old.

Then, from the far side of the lawn, she heard a burst of laughter so true it startled her. She followed it and found Finnian, cross-legged on a picnic blanket, surrounded by a loose ring of children and adults. In his lap, the mechanical bird chirped and spun, and as Finnian gestured and performed, he made the bird's movements seem part of his story.

"—and then the watchmaker told the king, 'This bird only sings at midnight, and only if you're not looking at it directly!'" Finnian's hands shaped the story in the air: now a bird, now a king's crown, now the tick of a clock. "So, of course, every night the king waited, staring and staring, and every night he heard nothing. But the rest of the palace was kept up by this wild, midnight music. Until one day, the queen gets clever—she covers every mirror in the castle, and the bird can't see itself, so it sings all night long, and the king is forced to admit that he has never heard anything so beautiful in his life." He bowed, the bird chirped on cue, and the children howled with laughter.

It was as if a patch of the world's color had condensed around Finnian, resisting the slow drain that had leached so much from the evening. Galhani felt herself smiling without effort. Even the adults looked brighter in his presence, the stories binding them together in an easy, temporary family.

She stood there, just outside the ring of light, and watched Finnian tell another story. He didn't seem to notice the divide between old and new; he welcomed anyone who wandered close, folded them into the story, gave them a line or a sound to perform, and sent them back into the world a little lighter than before.

The mechanical bird hopped from his hand to a child's, then to another, and each time it moved, a ripple of delight followed. It was a small, ridiculous miracle, but in that moment, Galhani decided that maybe Makota was right: sometimes the only answer was to throw a party, and let the world fix itself around the edges.

She was still standing there, half-lost in the patterns of Finnian's hands and the bird's unflagging song, when Leota appeared at her side. The witch was quieter than usual, her black-on-black dress catching the last light in odd, iridescent shimmers.

"Notice how he fits?" Leota murmured, barely moving her lips. She nodded at Finnian, now orchestrating a game where the bird assigned a silly animal call to each child and then tried, with ever-increasing speed, to make them all chime in sequence.

"He's the only one who does," Galhani said, not bothering to hide her admiration. "I tried talking to some of the others. It's like… the conversation never lands anywhere."

Leota's eyes followed the arc of the story circle. "Of all the newcomers, he's the only one who belongs. Not sure if that's a comfort or a warning."

Galhani shrugged, sipping her still-bland cordial. "Maybe both. At least he doesn't make me feel like I'm missing a joke."

"Town's up to twenty-one shops now," Leota said. "At least twenty-one I recognize as such. The icosagon is overfull." She arched an eyebrow at her own word, as if daring Galhani to laugh. "Means someone will be leaving soon. Or something will break to make room."

The phrase set a tremor through Galhani's chest. She didn't like the idea of any of the old shops closing, of any of her friends leaving.

"Maybe we'll get lucky," she said. "Maybe it's just a phase."

Leota scowled, rubbing her temples. "Nothing is ever just a phase in this town. I half-expect to wake up tomorrow and find the carving in my house changed from a twenty-sided star to a fifty-sided monstrosity. The town is impossible to understand right now."

Galhani laughed, but the sound came out thin and uncertain. "At least the party's working. People are together, even if it's only for tonight."

Leota's eyes narrowed, but not in anger. "That's the whole trick, isn't it? If you hold the center long enough, maybe the rest comes back."

For a while, they stood together, silent, as the music faded into soft talk and the children started to yawn and collapse into laps and blankets. Someone began to gather up the leftover plates; another started stacking the folding chairs. Even the clockwork bird seemed to sense the mood, slowing its flapping wings and chirping only when prompted by a child's gentle poke.

Galhani felt a strange, deep gratitude, not just for the event itself but for the simple fact that her friends were still there. Leota, with her barbed wisdom. Lara, who had found her way back to Galhani's side, basket in one arm and a sleepy child from the neighbors cradled in the other. Sam, hoisting a keg over her shoulder like it weighed nothing. Even Dardrad and Makota, exchanging good-natured insults as they swept up crumbs and cleared tables.

It almost felt normal.

But the flatness lingered, even as she helped gather the bowls and pass around the last cups of cordial. It was as if the world had been made of canvas all along, and only now could she see the thin places where the color had faded.

The children lined up, each one taking a turn to pet the mechanical bird or thank Finnian for his stories. He took their bows with the grace of a real performer, doffing his imaginary hat and flourishing a low, theatrical bow that sent the smallest ones into fits of giggles.

Leota smiled, just a crack. "If we're doomed to be replaced, at least the next generation's got some taste."

Galhani watched Finnian, saw how he paused, just for a second, to look back at the adults. He met her gaze, smiled with that crooked, earnest energy, and for a heartbeat she believed in the future again.

She glanced up at the lanterns, at the stars coming out overhead, at the shivering, ordinary beauty of the world as it was. "Do you think it'll ever go back to how it was?" she asked Leota, softly.

Leota shook her head. "No. But sometimes new is enough. You just have to make peace with the shape it takes. You know that. We've seen our share of people come and go."

They finished their tidy-up in companionable quiet. When the last lantern was doused and the children herded home, Galhani stood at the edge of the empty lawn and felt a little less hollow. The town wasn't healed, and maybe it never would be, but for a moment the party had held the center.

She watched Finnian disappear into the dusk, mechanical bird perched on his shoulder and a trail of tired, smiling children following after him. She wondered what shape the town would take next—and whether she'd still recognize it when she woke up in the morning.

seven

. . .

AT DAWN, the square was empty except for the slow sweep of morning mist and the thin, determined shape of the herbalist pressed to the window. Galhani had opened the shop a candlemark before the sun, but the air inside was already warm with her restlessness. She kept her cheek nearly to the glass, staring past the condensation that gathered there, eyes fixed on the space between the main road and the low stone boundary of the gate.

A new wagon had appeared overnight. Not unusual, not this season, but this one was not just a cart; it was a self-contained shop, a squat box painted the color of salt, with a hatch that folded down into a tidy display. The man who owned it—she'd learned his name was Silas by listening to the rhythm of it as he barked orders at his own shadow—stood by the stall with his arms folded and an expression of icy composure. He was a tall human, with thin, gray-streaked hair, pale hands, and a tendency to arrange every object on his table twice: once for symmetry, once for show.

From her vantage, Galhani watched him line up tin after tin of pre-packaged blends, each canister identical but for a neat black-inked label, clearly printed by some kind of machine, not hand. She squinted at the words: Calm. Focus. Remedy. Cleanse. The labels themselves—

glossy, with a faux-wax stamp pressed into the corner—made her scalp itch.

He worked with a speed that felt mechanical, and even as he set each container down, the restock of the row behind was ready to slide forward and fill the gap. No empty space was left for longer than a heartbeat. In a quarter candlemark he had completed the setup, checked and re-checked it, and then stood to face the morning with the stiff, unyielding patience of a cold season.

Galhani tried to turn away, to focus on her own counter and the familiar comfort of wooden shelves, but her gaze kept drifting back to the new stall. She caught a faint reflection of her own face in the glass —creased with fatigue, eyes two dark stones, hair knotted and in need of combing. She didn't recognize the bitterness in her mouth, or the sensation of her own fingers curling hard enough to hurt.

She heard the first customer before she saw her: the scrape of shoes on the flagstones, then the low, apologetic mutter of someone trying not to be seen. It was Cole's youngest, the one with the cowlick and the habit of breathing with his mouth open when nervous. He ducked his head and hurried past Galhani's window, barely glancing in. His trajectory—direct to the wagon, a nervous hop from foot to foot as he waited for Silas to acknowledge him—was so practiced that for a moment Galhani felt as if she were seeing a play acted for her alone.

She watched as the boy handed over a coin, received a paper-wrapped bundle in return, and then, unable to help himself, peeked back over his shoulder. He met Galhani's eyes. The guilt was as obvious as the morning sun. The boy bolted, clutching his package to his chest.

By seven, there were four more in line, none of whom she recognized as travelers. She pressed harder against the window, unable to stop herself. They came singly, always with their eyes averted, and each left with the same white package, tucked away in a pocket or basket as if it were a stolen thing.

She let the curtain fall and sagged back, one hand bracing her against the sill. The familiar scent of her own shop—peppery, sharp, undercut with the sweetness of drying flowers and old wood—felt suddenly too thick, as if the walls were closing in. She rubbed at her arms and paced a slow circle behind the counter. She pulled down a jar at random and re-shelved it. She straightened the row of honey pots, then did it again, then again, the jars clinking softly as she set each one to its precise angle.

By the time the door bell sounded, she had nearly worked herself into a sweat.

The first true customer of the day was not a neighbor, but a woman with the open, hungry stare of a traveler. She wore a clean dress, hands red from washing, and when she stepped inside, she paused at the threshold as if waiting for the shop to recognize her. Galhani smiled, welcoming her with a practiced warmth, but the woman's eyes flicked from jar to jar with a fevered restlessness.

"I saw the sign," the woman said, nodding toward the window, "and I wondered if you had anything for nerves. Something gentle, but quick."

Galhani could have filled the order in her sleep. "We do," she said, voice steady despite the tremor she felt behind her lips. "Would you like it as a tea or as a cordial?"

The woman hesitated. "I'm not sure. The man outside has a powder, but—" she cut herself off, glanced away. "I heard from someone that yours is better."

Galhani ignored the sting, and began to measure out a blend. "You can try both," she offered. "On the house. If you don't like the taste, no obligation." She set water to boiling, then fished a mesh ball from her kit and scooped the right ratio of linden, lemon balm, and a pinch of her own dried lavender. "It should work in three minutes. Sit, if you like."

The woman perched on the nearest stool, hands splayed on the counter. She waited in silence, eyes never settling for long. Galhani poured the brew, set it before her, and watched the first cautious sip. The woman's jaw relaxed. She took a second, deeper drink, then a third, before looking up.

"This is good," she said, almost surprised.

Galhani nodded, but the usual pleasure of a job well done didn't come. "It's an old blend," she said, tucking her hands behind her back. "Works better if you don't rush it."

The woman drank the rest, thanked her, and pressed a coin into Galhani's hand. "I'll tell my friends," she said, and left with a final, grateful nod.

Galhani watched her go. She returned to the window just in time to see the woman pause at Silas's wagon, speak with him, and then, after a brief, almost embarrassed conversation, buy one of the packages anyway.

She wanted to throw something. Instead, she turned from the glass and took a slow inventory of her shelves, running a finger along the edge of each tin, reading the hand-painted labels: Soothing, Fortify, Heartmend, Dreamless. She paused at the end of the row, then went back to the start and did it again.

The bell rang a second time, and she started, nearly dropping a jar. Lara stood in the doorway, arms cradling a basket heavy with fresh-picked lemon verbena and a sheaf of wild mint. Her hair was tangled and her nose red from the cold, but her face brightened when she saw Galhani.

"Back already?" Lara said, lifting the basket high as if in salute. "They're not pretty, but they're ours."

Galhani forced a smile. "They'll work," she replied, and moved behind the counter to greet her. "Thank you."

Lara set the basket down and dusted her hands. "You're pale," she said, peering at Galhani. "Did you forget breakfast again?"

"Not hungry." The lie was familiar and unconvincing.

Lara glanced at the window. "You saw, then."

Galhani felt the heat rise in her cheeks, and hated herself for it. "It's fine," she said, but her voice thinned out at the end. "He's just... efficient. People like that."

Lara came around the counter, close enough that the shop's old wood floor creaked beneath them both. She touched Galhani's shoulder, fingers light but insistent. "You are not a powder in a box."

"No," said Galhani, fighting the urge to laugh or scream or both. "I'm not."

The silence that settled between them was heavy. Lara studied her for a long moment, then pulled her into a tight, brief hug, smelling of cold air and crushed mint. "Come on," she said. "There's still bread left from last night. You need something in you."

Galhani nodded, not trusting herself to speak.

The two moved into the small back room where a pot of porridge had cooled on the iron stove. Lara ladled out two bowls and set them on the table, then poured a mug of hot water and nudged it toward Galhani. "Drink," she said, and there was no arguing with that tone.

They ate in silence, the only sound the quiet scrape of spoons and the hollow thud of a wagon wheel as it hit a rut outside.

After a while, Galhani's hands stopped trembling. The sun had crept higher, painting the inside of the shop with slanted gold, and she felt the knot behind her sternum start to loosen, just a fraction. She set her spoon down, wiped her mouth, and looked at Lara.

"Do you think it's going to be like this every day?" she asked.

Lara tilted her head. "Maybe. Maybe not. The world has a way of favoring novelty, but it doesn't always last. People will remember the difference, if it matters."

Galhani nodded, unsure whether to believe it.

Lara smiled, then stood and stretched. "I'm going to clean up the garden. You should stay out here, watch the world for a bit."

Galhani watched Lara's retreating figure, grateful and more than a little ashamed. When she heard the back door close, she wandered to the window again and watched Silas, who was already restocking his wares, the little white packages a perfect, soulless army on display.

She set her jaw and turned away. She would not be a powder in a box.

She went to the counter and opened the first tin, inhaling the memory of what her craft had always been: precise, personal, impossibly alive. She took down a second, and a third, and lined them up with a meticulousness that bordered on defiance.

When the bell rang again, she was ready.

———

By noon, the square had thawed from its morning stasis, patches of winter grass softening underfoot as if unsure whether to die or grow.

Galhani made her way to the center, basket crooked in the elbow, keeping her head low but her ears wide open. A crow perched on the well's handle, picking at something that wasn't there. The air smelled faintly of iron, as if a storm was hiding just beyond the ridge.

Lucy was already waiting, seated on a low stone bench with her legs splayed in front and a blue-glazed pot cradled in her lap. She rolled it between her palms, turning it over and over, her thumbs worrying the rim.

Warren arrived next, stride a little off, eyes darting from one end of the square to the other as if he half-expected to be ambushed by chores. His green skin was duller than usual, his white hair gone to a frizzy halo from working too close to the furnace. He carried a cloth-wrapped bundle in one fist.

Prudence came last, trailing her infant son in a pram that looked two sizes too large. She parked herself on the opposite bench and spent a long moment folding and refolding her hands, gaze never quite touching the other three.

Dexter joined them with little warning, emerging from the far side of the well with a physician's grace—smooth, silent, already measuring the group for signs of illness. He nodded to each in turn, said nothing, and perched on the well's edge.

Galhani took her seat last, setting her basket down beside her feet. Nobody spoke at first. The silence stretched, twisting between comfort and threat. Eventually, Lucy broke it, holding up the pot as if it were evidence in a trial.

"It's just...clay now," she said, giving the vessel a gentle tap with her fingernail. The sound was a dull thud, not the bright ring it should have been. "Fired it twice, tried every slip and glaze I know. Nothing takes. Not even the blue stays blue."

Warren looked at the pot, then at Lucy, then at his own bundle. He unwrapped it with a tenderness that seemed out of place for someone with hands like shovels. Inside was a dagger, plain as a carrot. The blade was perfectly straight, perfectly sharp, and perfectly dead. No shimmer, no play of light, not even the memory of a gleam.

"It's not the ore," he said, voice hoarse. "It's not the fire, neither. I tried the secret batch from the bottom of the bin. Just comes out...less, every time."

Prudence glanced from the dagger to the pot, then reached into her satchel and pulled out a bolt of fabric. She let it unspool across her lap, fingers running the length of it. The silk—her best, her signature—looked gray in the light, the intricate pattern faded to the point of invisibility.

"It's not holding the spellwork anymore," she said, eyes on the cloth. "Or maybe I've forgotten the touch. Last year, I could have stitched a dress with a sennight's work. Now it takes twice that, and it still ends up dull." She made a show of tucking the fabric away, but her hands lingered, folding and smoothing the same three inches over and over.

Dexter waited for the silence to return, then drew a small jar from his coat. Inside, a salve the color of bone marrow. He unscrewed the lid and held it under Galhani's nose. She sniffed, expecting the astringent punch of yarrow or willow, but found only the bland, waxy scent of fat and chalk.

"I've been brewing this for three days," Dexter said, voice barely above a whisper. "Every time I add something to it, the base just eats it. No scent, no heat, no bite. Even the strongest blends flatten out by morning."

They all looked at Galhani, waiting for her contribution to the litany. She considered telling the truth—the real truth, about Silas and his factory-perfect wares, the way her own hands had started to betray her, the growing suspicion that something essential had gone missing from the world—but instead, she shrugged.

"The garden's still growing," she said. "But the leaves taste like nothing. Even the wild stuff. Lara says it's just a cold snap, but I don't know." She felt the words as she said them, thin as the broth they used to serve at the orphanage when she was small. "Maybe the soil's tired."

Lucy smiled at her, but it was a hollow thing. "Maybe it just needs more time."

Warren grunted. "Time's all I got. Still don't help the swords."

The toddler in Prudence's pram let out a short, sharp squawk, then settled. Prudence rocked the pram with her foot, each movement as precise and measured as her embroidery.

Dexter recapped the jar and set it on the stone beside him. "It's spreading," he said, matter-of-fact. "If it was just one of us, I'd call it a rut. But all together? Something's off."

The group nodded, heads bobbing in slow, defeated unison.

For a moment, Galhani almost laughed. There they were—a seamstress, a smith, a potter, a healer, and a herbalist—each the best at what they did, each losing the thread of their craft. It should have been funny, but the laughter wouldn't rise past her chest.

They sat in silence a while longer, watching the wind move the weeds around the edges of the square. A pair of sparrows landed near Dexter's feet and pecked at the dust, finding nothing.

After a while, Lucy stood and tucked the pot under her arm. "I have a shipment to finish," she said, not meeting anyone's eyes.

Warren gave a half-salute with the blade, then wrapped it again and shambled off toward the forge. Prudence packed away the silk and wheeled her son toward the seamstress's shop, jaw set in a line that promised no comfort for anyone who interrupted her work.

Dexter remained at the well for a long moment, then caught Galhani's eye. "If you ever need a tonic, I'll try to make it," he said. "No promises."

"Same," Galhani replied, her voice thin but honest.

He left without a backward glance.

The square emptied, the only movement the stubborn crow, who'd managed to scavenge a crumb from somewhere.

Galhani stood, stretched her legs, and made for home. The sun was high, the shadows short and sharp, but she still felt cold. She let herself into the shop, hung her basket on its hook, and shut the door behind her with a decisive click.

Inside, the light was different. The shelves looked closer together, the colors of the jars muted. The air held the scent of something gone overripe.

She crossed to the workbench and cleared a space, then pulled down her most precious stash: a tin of night-blooming cereus, dried by hand two summers before; a pouch of white ginseng, a gift from Lucy last new year; the last of her bee-balm, bright as spilled blood.

She measured, mixed, and crushed, working the pestle with deliberate care, breathing slow and even. She heated the water to the precise degree, steeped the blend for exactly five minutes, and poured it into her favorite cup.

She let it cool, watching the surface for a ripple or a sign. Nothing.

She raised the cup to her lips, sipped, and waited.

It tasted like nothing at all.

She stared at the cup for a long time, then, with a sudden, sharp motion, poured it into the sink. The liquid drained away, leaving a faint brown ring around the porcelain.

She washed the cup, dried it, and set it on the shelf. Then she leaned against the counter, arms crossed, and let her eyes close.

She stayed that way until the light changed and the square outside grew quiet.

———

The afternoon drifted in like a slow hemorrhage—nothing dramatic, just a steady leak of color and warmth from the world. Galhani found herself walking the short way to Dexter's chirurgery, a parcel of basic healing herbs bundled in wax paper and tucked under her arm. She told herself it was a delivery she'd meant to make all sennight. In truth, she just needed to see if he was still there, or if the last few days had hollowed him out, too.

The front door of the clinic was open. Inside, the air was cool and almost hospital-clean, but not the way it used to be. The usual sharpness of disinfectants and dried sage had flattened into something sour and faintly metallic, like a bandage left too long on the skin.

Dexter was at the main table, hunched over a pile of ledgers. His movements were precise, but lacked their former edge—he didn't look up until Galhani's shadow stretched across the floorboards.

"On time as always," he said, but there was no bite to it. "Set it on the counter."

She did. He reached for the bundle, sliced it open, and prodded through the leaves, his fingers thin and quick. "Looks fine," he muttered. "You washed these?"

"Three times," she said, and waited for a reprimand about wasting water. None came.

He pinched a stem between his thumb and forefinger, held it up to the light, then set it down. "You know," he said, voice low, "half of what's in the books doesn't work anymore." He gestured to the ledgers, flipping through a few pages. "I tried to patch a cut with willow poultice yesterday. Did nothing but stain the bandage."

Galhani nodded. "Same here. Even the blends I've made for years are..." She shrugged. "Empty."

Dexter raised an eyebrow. "It's happening to you too, isn't it?"

She hesitated, then nodded again.

He closed the ledger and pushed it aside. "I figured as much. Town's been running hot for sennights, but now it's gone dry. Like a fever breaks, and there's nothing left to sweat out."

Galhani ran a finger along the edge of the counter, trailing a line in the dust. "Lara thinks it's a cycle. Things will swing back. But I've never felt anything like this before. It's as if..." She struggled for the words.

Dexter finished the thought for her. "As if something is bleeding the creativity out of the place." He turned to a wall of neatly arranged jars. "Look at this." He unscrewed the lid from a squat, cobalt jar and scooped out a dab of pale salve. He smeared it on the back of his hand, waited, then wiped it away with a cloth. "I made that batch a moon ago. Used to numb a man's whole arm. Now it's just ointment."

She leaned in to sniff. There was a whiff of camphor, but the rest was nothing—no bite, no burn, not even the cool tingle that always signaled a good batch.

Dexter replaced the lid. "I've tried different ratios, different suppliers. Even borrowed some of Warren's forge water—he swears it's enchanted. It's not."

They stood in silence for a moment, watching the light creep across the floor. It felt like being in a room with a patient you knew you couldn't help, just waiting for the end.

A shout broke the quiet—a thin, angry sound from outside. Dexter moved to the window, lifting the bottom edge of the curtain with two fingers. "Another one," he said, voice sharp for the first time all day. "You see?"

Galhani came to look over his shoulder. A second merchant wagon had pulled up near the corner of the square, this one painted green and gold, with the word "CLAYWORKS" stenciled across the side in block letters. On the makeshift shelves lining its open hatch, dozens of mugs, vases, and plates—each identical to the one beside it—were stacked in rows, flawless and featureless as eggs.

Lucy stood a few yards away, fists clenched at her sides, her face a mask of betrayed fury.

The potter from the wagon—a squat, balding man with a dusting of red hair—stepped down and, with theatrical flourish, handed a mug to the first passerby. The mug was too large, too smooth, its blue glaze a mockery of Lucy's best work. The customer smiled, held the mug up to the light, and walked off without paying.

Lucy's lips moved, but from this distance, the words were lost. She glared at the merchant, then wheeled around and strode away—past the bakery, past the smithy, straight for The Broken Claw.

Dexter let the curtain drop. "Guess she'll be drinking tonight."

Galhani pressed her hand to the glass, watching the wagon. Already, two children and an old man were comparing plates at the display, oohing and aahing over the uniformity. "Is it going to be like this for everyone?" she asked, not expecting an answer.

Dexter returned to his table, began to arrange the herbs into neat piles. "Might be," he said. "Or maybe just until the town gets bored of the new stuff and wants the old back." He didn't sound convinced.

She stayed a moment longer, then turned to go. "Let me know if you want me to try anything different."

He nodded, but didn't look up. "Take care, Galhani."

The road outside was quiet for a change, the only sound the low, greedy clatter as the merchant restocked his display. Galhani forced herself to walk past without looking, but she felt the weight of the newness in the air, the gravitational pull of what everyone else seemed to want.

She reached The Broken Claw and slipped inside. The pub was less than half-full, and the usual glow of the place had dimmed to a weak, watery orange. Even the hearth seemed to burn at half-strength.

Lucy sat hunched at the end of the bar, her new pot—one of her last—upended in front of her like a threat. Sam stood behind the counter, arms folded, face unreadable as she poured a double measure of something dark into Lucy's mug.

Galhani slid onto the stool beside her friend.

"Don't say it," Lucy muttered, gripping her drink with both hands. "I know it's stupid to care, but it's mine. It's all I ever had."

Sam said nothing, just wiped the counter in front of Lucy with slow, circular strokes. Her usual jokes or threats of ejection were nowhere to be found.

Galhani reached out and set her hand over Lucy's, feeling the tremor in the potter's fingers. "You're allowed to be angry," she said.

Lucy barked a laugh. "I'm not angry. I'm... erased." She took a long pull from the mug, winced, and set it down. "First my pots lose their spark, now this. People buying cups that look like they belong in a counting house." She pushed the mug away. "Even the ale tastes like nothing."

Sam offered a sympathetic grunt, then poured a shot for herself. "You should have seen the last travelers," she said, voice rough. "Asked for cider, then asked if I had it in a different flavor. Said something about a place called 'fusion bar' out west." She made a face. "I almost threw them out."

Lucy managed a smile. "Did you?"

Sam shrugged. "No. We need the coin."

They sat in silence for a while, the three of them anchored to the bar, each lost in their own shrinking world. Around them, the pub moved with a kind of lethargy: a pair of men in the corner played a hand of cards with all the enthusiasm of a funeral, and a woman near the hearth nursed a pint for so long the condensation ran down onto the floor.

The door banged open and closed. A cold wind swept in, but nobody paid it much notice.

Lucy finished her drink, wiped her mouth with the back of her sleeve, and stared at the empty pot. "What's going to happen to us?" she asked, her voice so small it was almost a child's.

Sam leaned across the bar and laid a heavy hand on Lucy's shoulder. "You'll figure something out," she said. "You're stubborn enough."

Lucy nodded, but didn't look convinced.

Galhani studied the two of them—the way Sam's hand lingered, the set of Lucy's jaw. Even in defeat, there was something vital about them, something that hadn't yet been ground out by the new order. Maybe that's what would save them in the end, or maybe it would be the thing that got them pushed aside. She had no way of knowing which it would be.

Sam poured another round, this time without being asked.

They drank, the three of them, together in the quiet, while outside the square bristled with strangers and everything that had once made sense slipped just a little further away.

eight

. . .

THE NEXT MORNING arrived with the promise of summer, but Galhani found little of it in her bones. She took her time dressing, giving the tea shop a desultory once-over tidying, and then wandered out into the square. She lingered outside the bakery, where Makota and her kits were setting out trays of bread and arguing over whether to dust the rolls with caraway or poppyseed. Makota waved her in, but Galhani ducked her head and drifted on, drawn to the patch of grass at the square's heart, where the real business of the day was underway.

Cole, the grocer, stood ankle-deep in the dewy grass, basket in the crook of his arm and a look of mounting dread on his face. Leota had already claimed a spot on the curved stone bench that bordered the square, her black skirts spread like a shadow behind her, fingers drumming a jittery rhythm on the stone.

"Morning," Galhani said, as she slid onto the bench beside Leota. The witch gave her a sidelong look, then nodded at the basket in Cole's arms.

"Show her," Leota said, voice pitched low.

Cole grunted and tipped the basket forward. "Just picked these from the north field. You see it?"

Galhani leaned in. The carrots on top were straight and unblemished, but the orange was pale, as if someone had soaked the color out with lye. She picked one up, snapped it in half, and watched the two pieces shatter into splinters. There was no snap or moisture, just a papery crunch. The core was a tunnel, hollow all the way through.

She rolled the carrot in her palm, then handed it back. "Happened overnight?" she asked.

Cole's mouth twisted. "Started two days ago. First the greens wilted, then the roots went soft. Half my onions turned to mush, and the strawberries—I won't even bring those out. They look like someone stepped on them in the dark." He dug deeper in the basket and pulled out a tomato, round as a moon and glossy as ever. "Looks fine, right?"

Galhani nodded. "Perfect."

Cole squeezed the tomato gently. It gave beneath his fingers, then burst, splitting its skin and oozing a stream of watery red onto his palm. There was no scent, just the faint chemical sweetness of overripe flesh.

Leota stared at the puddle forming between Cole's fingers, her lips pinched white. "When's the last time we had a crop like this?" she asked.

Cole wiped his hand on the grass, eyes fixed on the horizon. "Two summers ago, when we lost the gifts. Before that... never." He let the ruined tomato drop and set the basket down at his feet.

Galhani reached for another carrot, examining the fracture at its core. She sniffed, expecting at least a ghost of earth or bitter green, but it was empty. "The new shops are doing fine," she said, almost to herself. "Makota's bread rose twice as high as usual, and Warren's been getting triple yield from the winter rye. But your produce—"

"It's not just mine," Cole interrupted. "I saw Dardrad yesterday, said his beans tasted like sawdust. Even the kids won't eat them, and they'll eat anything." He lowered his voice. "Is it the parasite? The one Vamir talks about from his books?"

Leota's eyes narrowed. "Perhaps."

Galhani braced her elbows on her knees and stared at the grass. "If it is something like that, it's clever. It's not killing the town, just draining the flavor out of everything. Maybe it wants to see if we'll starve on sameness before we starve for real."

Leota was quiet for a long moment. "Could be," she said finally. "But if it's a parasite, it's only going after things that matter. Your blends, Lucy's glazes, Cole's crops. The other shops—the new ones—they're immune, or close to it."

Galhani thought of the tidy rows of tins at the outsider's cart, the way the contents never lost their color or bite, even after days in the sun. "Maybe it's only targeting gifts," she said.

Cole shifted his weight, looming over the two women. "Could it be spreading from the new shops?" he asked.

"Could be," Leota said. "Or it could be the old gifts are thinning out on their own. There's only so much magic to go around, and the more shops we get, the less there is for the rest of us." She made a small, frustrated gesture with her hand, as if trying to swat away a fly.

"Your magic feels different, too?" Galhani asked, keeping her voice neutral.

Leota scowled, her fingers curling into the stone of the bench. "It's vague," she admitted. "Fuzzy around the edges. The wards on my place are still there, but they take twice as much effort to hold, and I can't get the focus I used to."

"Can you show us?" Cole asked, voice low and eager.

Leota hesitated, then reached into the pocket of her dress and pulled out a withered sprig of thyme. She cupped it in her palm and whispered a single word, one that should have been enough to coax color and life back into the stem. Nothing happened. She frowned, then closed her eyes and tried again, this time using the careful, old-fashioned pronunciation she'd learned in her youth.

A faint shimmer ran along the length of the sprig, a pale green halo that lasted only a moment before guttering out. The thyme lay in her palm, unchanged.

She shrugged, tossed the herb aside. "See?" she said, her voice edged with bitterness. "It's like trying to light a fire with wet wood. You get a little spark, then nothing."

Cole's shoulders slumped. "So there's nothing to do?"

Leota looked at Galhani. "Unless you've got a miracle up your sleeve."

Galhani shook her head. She ran a hand through her hair, leaving bits of dried lavender tangled in the curls. "I thought about making a blend to boost the old gifts. I have a few ingredients left that are still strong enough, but if the soil's tainted, it won't last."

They sat in silence for a while, watching the morning fill with people—most of them regulars, a few of them strangers, some even less familiar than that. The new shopkeepers opened up with a kind of forced cheer, laughing a little too loudly at the empty air between them and the rest of the town. The bakery's window caught the light, sending a white glare across the square. It made the world look hollowed out, washed in bleach.

Finally, Cole stooped to gather the spilled carrots and tomatoes, returning them to the basket. "If you come up with anything," he said, "let me know. I'll try it, even if it tastes like last winter's boots."

Leota grunted agreement. "If you want company, I'll be at the Claw by noon. Sam's got a shipment coming in—maybe it'll be the old stuff, not the new."

Galhani stood, brushing grass from her skirt. "I'll be by," she promised.

Cole tucked his basket under his arm and strode off toward the grocery. Leota lingered on the bench, her gaze tracking the cracks in the flagstones.

"Do you really think it's a parasite?" she asked, after Cole was out of earshot.

Galhani hesitated. "I think it's something we made," she said. "Or let happen. Maybe it's both."

Leota's mouth twisted into a wry smile. "That's the problem with cleverness. You can never tell if it's the solution, or just another part of the curse."

They parted ways, Galhani to her shop and Leota to her dim, cold house on the far side of the square. The grass under their feet was damp and resilient, but Galhani wondered how long it would last before it, too, went hollow.

———

The Broken Claw was more crowded than usual, the humid air sloshing with sweat, ale, and too many voices raised just below the threshold of a fight. Galhani paused in the entryway and let her eyes adjust to the gloom, picking out the familiar shapes among the bodies: Leota's black silhouette folded into a corner booth, Warren's hunched form bracketing the end of the bar, Lucy's head a painted orb among the lesser lights.

Sam worked the bar, arms and jaw in perpetual motion as she poured and wiped and refilled, her single good eye sweeping the room for trouble the way a lighthouse swept for rocks. The other eye—surrounded by scar as it was—gave her face an asymmetrical threat that matched her demeanor. She nodded once at Galhani, then went back to polishing a glass so fiercely the rag squeaked.

Two men at the bar, travelers, were bent in a quiet conversation. Galhani stood next to them for a few moments, listening to them.

"I'm telling you," the first said in a low, gravely voice, "it's not just the little goblins tribes you have to worry about, anymore. We'd come close enough to dealing with them. A double stockade, watchers on the moonless nights."

"The Goblin King," his companions said, nodding.

"They don't act like *goblins* anymore," the first continued, frustration evident in his tone. "Used to be like wild dogs, come at you all in a wave, but not organized. Now they're... *organized*. One weak spot in your defenses and they'll spot it at once, and they all aim for it."

"He's united them," the second man said.

Galhani stepped away as they continued their discussion. The idea of a united goblin nation was terrifying—the Gnomelands abutted goblin territory to the south—but everyone knew goblins, with their cold blood, would never venture this far north. *She* was likely safe, but she suddenly understood the travelers' concerns and urgency far better. If there was an air of desperation in the pub, she could understand it. That was part of the place's purpose and balance, in times like these.

But it was the newcomers who threw the pub off that balance. They gathered in a knot at the far end of the room, closest to the door, their faces red with drink or nerves or both. They wore clothes a little too fine for travel and talked in a dialect that leaned heavily on hard consonants and laughter that never reached the eyes. Even at a glance, Galhani could tell they were watching the regulars, waiting for a misstep.

She moved past the first table, nodding at Dardrad, who was already half a pint down and in the process of explaining to a pair of farmers why barley beer was better than wheat. The farmers were not convinced. She heard one of them mutter, "Try growing barley with no rain," and Dardrad only grunted, raising his glass as if to toast the futility of the whole world.

Warren caught her attention with a shout: "Gnome! Over here!" He pounded the bar with one fist, sending his mug rattling and drawing a reproving glance from Sam. Galhani slid onto the empty stool next to him, careful to keep her feet out of range of his boots.

He leaned in, the smell of steel and char heavy on his breath. "You seen the forge today?" he demanded. "Dead as dirt. I tried to run the morning's batch, and the fire wouldn't even take the edge off the ore. Never seen metal so stubborn." He slammed the mug again, less to emphasize his point than to bleed off the frustration. "I need you to fix it," he said, as if that were a reasonable thing to ask.

Galhani managed a smile. "If I could fix fire, I'd charge double. Maybe your metal's just tired."

Warren grunted. "It's not just tired. It's giving up. Look." He reached into a satchel at his feet and pulled out a length of what should have been sword blank. Instead, it was a gray, pitted strip, warped at the edges and dulled by some invisible rot. He slapped it on the bar. "Would you want to fight a goblin with that?"

Sam eyed the sword, then eyed Warren. "I wouldn't want to fight a goblin, period. I've done it already."

Warren bared his teeth in what might have been a laugh, then slid the metal back into the bag. "World's getting soft," he said. "And it's not just me. Lucy's glazes are running, Leota's wards don't hold, and I heard the best honey in town has gone bitter."

Galhani looked for Lucy, who sat at a table near the hearth, a row of blue-glazed cups lined in front of her like a jury. She cradled one in both hands, running her thumbs over the surface as if trying to will a design into it. When she saw Galhani's gaze, she shook her head and mouthed, "No good."

At the next table, a trio of travelers huddled over their drinks, voices low and urgent. One of them kept glancing at the door, as if expecting someone—or something—to burst through at any moment.

A sharp, cold draft swept the room. Galhani looked up to see the inn's bell-ringer pushing inside, face red from the cold. He stomped over to Sam, exchanged a few words, and then departed, leaving the door swinging on its hinges and the gossip behind him rippling like a dropped stone.

The volume in the room built, first slowly, then in waves, until Galhani could barely follow the threads of conversation. She heard her name twice, once as a compliment and once as a curse. She ordered water, which Sam poured without comment, and tried to catch Leota's attention. The witch only raised her mug in silent salute, then returned to her slow survey of the newcomers.

The next event began as a minor commotion—someone at the travelers' table laughed too loud, and a local snapped back with a pointed comment about manners. Another traveler retorted. Within seconds, the whole room was a single, rolling argument.

"It's your lot that's the problem," said Dardrad, brandishing his mug at the newcomers. "Who needs a shop full of buttons?"

A woman in a green dress shot back, "Maybe if the town had something worth buying, we'd have more custom."

"Try the bread, then talk to me," Makota called from the kitchen doorway, voice sweet and lethal.

The woman snorted. "Your bread tastes like old air."

Makota started toward the woman, but Sam blocked her path with one arm, the other hand still polishing her glass. "Let the customers argue," Sam said, "unless you're planning to bake them into a pie."

Galhani felt the pressure rising in the room, a kind of static that buzzed at the edges of her teeth. She closed her eyes for a second, trying to remember the last time the Claw had been this tense, this close to a breaking point. She couldn't.

The voices overlapped, a rolling, guttural tide.

"It's the newcomers ruining things—"

"—maybe if you didn't treat us like dirt—"

"—old shops are the only reason this place exists—"

"—well, maybe you should adapt—"

Leota rose to her feet, the movement so abrupt her chair toppled. She didn't bother to right it. "Enough," she said, and somehow, the word carried. The noise guttered, then stilled, as all eyes turned to the witch.

She stood in the space between the clusters, her hands folded behind her back, her posture loose but somehow dangerous. "We're not dying," she said. "We're changing. There's a difference." Her gaze swept the crowd, stopping on the new faces. "The town's always been magic. It will keep being magic, even if none of us know what kind."

A voice from the back—one of the travelers, his accent thick—said, "Easy for you to say. You have a home here."

Leota smiled, a flash of teeth. "I earned it the hard way. And if you want to stay, you'd better do the same."

There was a long silence, broken only by the sound of Sam setting a fresh glass on the bar, as if to underline the point.

Galhani's heart thumped against her ribs. She thought of her theory—the one Vamir had suggested and she'd refined, late at night, staring at the ceiling: that the old shops drew their strength from a deep, creative magic, but the new arrivals, with their efficient, dead flavors, didn't need magic at all. They only needed to be repeatable, identical, marketable.

Maybe it was the new magic draining the old.

She found herself standing, the words escaping before she could stop them. "What if it's not about who was here first," she said, voice rising above the hush, "but about what kind of magic we're using? The old shops—ours—needed magic because they were about invention, about making something unique. But the new ones, they're about repeating a recipe, not making one."

Heads turned. Some faces were angry, others thoughtful.

"Maybe that's why everything tastes less," she went on. "Maybe the new shops are eating the magic instead of making it."

A murmur ran through the crowd, and then Dardrad shouted, "So what? You want to run them out?"

Galhani shook her head, cheeks hot. "No. I want to find a way for us to survive."

The words set off an explosion. The room broke into a dozen arguments at once. The travelers shouted that they had as much right to the town as anyone, the old shopkeepers bristled at the idea of change, the handful of laborers and passers-through just looked for the nearest exit. Mugs slammed down, voices doubled in volume.

Galhani felt herself shrinking, the Claw's walls suddenly too tight, too close. She ducked Warren's arm, skirted Leota, and made for the door, half-expecting a mug or worse to follow her out.

She stepped into the night, the cold air hitting her like a slap. For a long moment, she stood there, breathing in the hush, her ears still ringing with the aftershocks of the fight.

The door banged open behind her. She tensed, but it was only Sam, stepping out for a smoke.

Sam didn't look at her. "You didn't have to say all that," she said.

Galhani hugged her arms to her chest. "Somebody did."

They stood together in silence, the only sound the whistle of wind through the eaves and the dull, distant roar from inside.

After a while, Sam spoke again. "You're right, you know. But being right doesn't help much when the world's already made up its mind."

Galhani looked at the orange glow in the windows, the silhouettes shifting inside. "I wish I could fix it."

Sam shrugged. "Sometimes you just have to wait it out. Or outlast it." She turned and went back inside.

Galhani stayed on the stoop, letting the cold soak into her skin, her hands clamped together so tight her knuckles ached. The Claw buzzed and howled behind her, but the town beyond was quiet, every window dark, every door shut tight against the future.

She wondered what kind of world they'd find when the doors finally opened again.

———

The tea shop was dark, save for the thread of lamplight in the back room. Galhani hunched over the work table, surrounded by the ruined debris of another day. The surface was a ruin of stems, seeds, and spilled powders, every inch dusted in the ghosts of failed brews. Her hands moved with a nervous energy, snatching jars from the shelf and measuring pinches onto the scale, dumping and re-dumping, weighing and reweighing until the needle's slow sway became a metronome for her desperation.

She'd started with the old blends, hoping that routine would bring her back to center. But the first attempt tasted like boiled linen, and the second left a film on her tongue that reminded her of well water after a long drought. The third—her favorite, the one she'd poured years into perfecting—was so bland she spat it out and watched the pale brown stain run down the drain.

Lara moved through the room with the soundless caution of a night nurse, hands folding and refolding the dish towel as she swept up the worst of the mess. She gathered the dried leaves that had escaped Galhani's grasp, pressed them into small, neat piles, then wiped the table in careful circles. Every few minutes, she reached out to rest a hand on Galhani's shoulder, and every time, Galhani shook her off, too wrapped up in her own failure to accept the comfort.

The only smell was crushed herb and burnt-out hope.

Galhani tried again: a blend of chamomile, wild fennel, and a twist of dried orange peel. The scent was promising, but when she poured the water, the leaves just floated, refusing to bloom. She tapped the side of the glass, willing the color to deepen, but it remained stubbornly clear. She let it steep longer than she should have, then lifted the cup to her lips and drank.

Nothing. Not a trace of flavor, not a hint of the sweet tang she'd built her reputation on.

She set the cup down with a force that threatened to crack the porcelain.

Lara approached with the quiet determination that had always made her infuriating, and perhaps irreplaceable. She set a clean cup in front of Galhani and filled it with fresh water from the kettle. "Try again," she said, her voice gentle but flat.

Galhani grabbed a fresh jar—lemongrass, this time, her best crop from two seasons ago—and pinched off a handful. The blades crumbled between her fingers, but they smelled of dust and little else. She weighed it, measured it, crushed it in the mortar with a fist that ached from use. She steeped it, timed it, strained it.

She sipped. A faint, bitter nothingness.

She exhaled through her nose, wiped her eyes with the back of her hand, and reached for the next jar. She told herself that it was the dryness in the air, the heat of the lamp, the strain of the past sennights. But in her heart, she knew: the magic was gone.

She went faster, hands shaking, muttering the old ratios under her breath. Every blend was a memory, and every memory failed her. She tried the sweet root, the mossy lichen, even the single dried berry she'd saved from the last festival. All useless. The water in her cup was always just water.

Lara came back, this time carrying a damp cloth. She dabbed at the rim of Galhani's eye, then brushed the hair from her face. "You've been at this for candlemarks," she said. "You need to sleep."

Galhani didn't look at her. "If I stop, I might not start again."

Lara knelt so that their eyes were level. "You're not alone," she said, the words as steady as the sunrise. "It's not your fault."

Galhani ignored her, grinding the next handful of leaves into a fine green powder. She measured, steeped, strained, tasted, and spat it out. The bitterness made her tongue curl.

Lara reached for her hand, but Galhani pulled away, clutching the mortar as if it could anchor her in place.

The lamp flickered. The worktable was a wreck, the air thick with the scent of failed alchemy. On the far wall, the clock ticked off the minutes, each second a pinprick in Galhani's skull.

She tried one last time, a reckless blend of everything left in the drawer. She pressed it into the bottom of the cup, poured the water, and watched as the mixture curdled and frothed. She took a deep breath and drank it down, not caring that it burned the roof of her mouth.

She gagged. The cup slipped from her hand and rolled across the table, splashing brown liquid onto her notes. The glass cracked, a thin line zigzagging from rim to base.

She stared at the crack, numb.

Lara came forward, wrapping both arms around Galhani's shoulders and pulling her close. For a moment, Galhani resisted, but then her body went limp, and she let herself fold into the embrace.

They stood like that, surrounded by the debris of lost craft and the ache of a vanished world.

"I'd rather have you than your tea," Lara whispered, lips brushing the top of Galhani's head.

The words hung between them, heavier than grief, sharper than any failure.

Galhani closed her eyes and listened to Lara's heart, steady and strong, and wondered if she had the courage to accept it.

nine

. . .

THE SUN ROSE over the tea shop, but it didn't so much illuminate the place as call attention to how many corners the light no longer reached. Galhani woke to the sound of her own pulse, pounding at the base of her skull, and the sick sense of déjà vu that she would spend this day the way she'd spent the last: faking the motions of hope, waiting for the truth to catch up. She rolled out of bed, nearly pulling the blanket with her, and stood for a long moment in the muted light of the bedroom, watching the soft rise and fall of Lara's shoulders. If there was any justice, Lara would keep sleeping—maybe she'd dream of a better world, or at least a world that didn't taste like failure. But Lara was already awake, eyes open and patient, and she didn't say a word as Galhani dressed in silence and slipped out the door.

Downstairs, the shop felt colder than usual. Galhani set a hand to the glass window. Condensation had left it slick, but even after wiping it with the sleeve of her shirt, the outside world looked the same: more wagons on the trade road, and a new sign advertising "Buttonaria" in an indecent shade of pink. She drew a finger down the pane, then let it fall.

The day's ritual was so ingrained it should have been a comfort: set up the cups, open the jars, boil water, count the coins in the box. But today, each action snagged, caught on itself, then started over. She lined up a row of twelve cups, then stared at them until her vision blurred, then took away two, as if it would hurt less to be disappointed by ten empty chairs instead of twelve. She set out the tea—just the plain black, nothing fancy, because what was the point of blending when none of the old flavors worked anyway.

The bell above the shop door announced Leota with a flat, metallic clang. Galhani didn't look up at first, just listened to the scrape of boots and the low rustle of Leota's black dress against the doorframe.

"You're early," Galhani said, voice gravelly with sleep.

Leota shrugged, dropped a battered satchel onto the nearest table, and made her way to the counter. "I needed air," she said. "Too many nights staring at parchment. Not enough results." She reached for a cup and inspected it, turning it in her hands. "You look terrible," she added, not unkindly.

"So do you," said Galhani, and surprised herself by meaning it as a compliment.

The door chimed again. This time it was Vamir, carrying a stack of books cradled against his chest and blinking at the world with the air of a man who'd just been delivered from a cave. He nodded at Leota, then at Galhani, and set the stack down with a thud.

"Morning," he said. "Or whatever we're calling it these days."

Leota eyed the books. "You find anything?"

Vamir thumbed through the top volume, pages yellowed and thin. "A few references to psychic parasites. Some historical cases in the Western Reaches, and a nasty one in Minnevar about forty years ago. Nothing exactly like this." He rapped the cover, then looked up at Galhani. "You brewing, or is it just water today?"

Galhani forced a smile, though it didn't touch her eyes. "There's tea," she said. "It just won't taste like much."

She moved behind the counter, her movements deliberate, almost ceremonial. She measured out the leaves, even though she knew the balance by heart. She let the kettle boil longer than needed, just for the sound. She poured the water in a slow spiral and watched as the color bled into the cup, pale and uncertain. She carried the tray to the table, set it down, and then retreated to the window.

Leota took a sip first, then grimaced. "You're not wrong."

Vamir tried his, made a face, then shrugged. "Could be worse."

Leota reached into her satchel and produced a folded scrap of parchment, covered in her own dense handwriting. "Let's get this over with," she said, flattening the note on the table. "Symptoms?"

Vamir answered before Galhani could speak. "Loss of flavor, loss of color, general decline in magical effect. Crafters losing their knack, wards going thin, even the physical stuff—dye, glaze, steel, and so on —turning brittle or lifeless." He paused. "And more shops every morning."

Leota ticked off each item with the tip of a stubby pencil. "Any new reports?"

Vamir shrugged. "Dexter says his salves are going flat. Jen's sword bracelet jammed last night, almost took her wrist off." He looked at Leota. "Anything from your end?"

Leota's mouth twisted. "The wards on my door are so weak I could break them with a sneeze. And every time I try to recharge them, the energy just slips away. It's like pouring water through a sieve."

Vamir leaned forward, lowering his voice. "So. We agree it's a parasite, yes? Or something very like it."

Leota nodded. "But not a natural one. It's too targeted."

Galhani, still at the window, spoke without turning around. "So what do we do?" She pressed her forehead to the cold glass, hoping for clarity.

Leota hesitated, then said, "You kill a parasite by starving it. Or you outlast it. Or you feed it so much it bursts."

Vamir shook his head. "Not this kind. The cases I found—they don't respond to brute magic. In fact, the more power you throw at them, the more they feed. It's not about energy; it's about creativity. Novelty. They crave it."

Leota frowned, then tried a small gesture with her fingers, the beginning of a ward. A spark leapt from her palm, then guttered out, leaving only a faint singe on her sleeve. "So we can't brute-force it," she said. "Fine. But what's left?"

Vamir tapped his book. "In the case in Minnevar, they broke the cycle by organizing a mass event. A festival. Everyone in the town made something—anything—at the same moment. The parasite couldn't keep up with the surge, and it just... let go." He set the book down, then looked at Galhani. "It's not about magic. It's about reminding the town what it's for."

Leota mulled this over. "So we throw a party for the parasite?"

Vamir smiled, just a little. "If you want to think of it that way."

Galhani finally turned from the window, her shoulders hunched, her eyes rimmed with red. "You really think people will go for that?" Her voice was so flat it could have been a piece of slate.

Vamir shrugged. "It's worth trying."

Leota took a deep breath. "I'll talk to Jen and Sam. Maybe Dardrad and Makota. If anyone can organize a town-wide event, it's those two." She shot a glance at Galhani. "Will you help?"

Galhani didn't answer right away. She looked at the row of cups, the hollow brown tea inside, the way the steam rose in perfect, scentless lines. She wiped a circle on the counter with her sleeve, then let her hand drop.

"What's the point?" she asked, her tone so mild it sounded like politeness. "Everything I make turns out wrong anyway."

Leota's face darkened. She started to say something sharp, but thought better of it. Instead, she closed her notebook, finished her tea in a single, shuddering gulp, and stood.

"Then try something new," Leota said, and the words hung in the air like the last note of a song.

Galhani watched as Leota and Vamir gathered their things and left, the bell above the door a brief, bright punctuation in the gray morning. She returned to the window, watching as the two walked together down the square, already lost in urgent conversation.

The shop was quieter than ever, and when Galhani finally sat down, she realized she had no idea how long she'd be sitting there.

———

The Broken Claw always looked smaller in the afternoon. With the sun hanging westward, its light ducked under the eaves and spilled across the floor in mean little stripes, igniting the dust but leaving the rest in a kind of perpetual twilight. Galhani hesitated outside the threshold, rehearsing the first words she might say, then gave up and just stepped in, letting the door close behind her with a reluctant groan.

Sam was at the bar, as always, her long white braid a whiplash against the dark oak of the shelf. She didn't bother with a greeting—just lifted her chin in a way that said "sit, or don't, it's all the same." Jen was already installed on a stool, her hair tied in a severe queue, posture as rigid as an accusation. The two of them were bent close, voices low and grim, each nursing a mug that had been drained and refilled more times than anyone wanted to count.

Galhani slid into a seat at the far end of the bar, keeping a safe three-stool distance. Sam poured her a cider—no words, just the sound of the tap and the brief, bitter hiss as the glass filled. Galhani raised it, then left it untouched.

Jen was the first to break the silence. "You seen the road today?" she asked, not looking at Galhani.

Galhani nodded. "Buttonaria. And there's a man selling pressed herbs out of a wagon near the gate."

Sam "And another selling little knives. Had the gall to set up just outside the smithy. But Warren says they're all pressed out of metal, not forged. Cheap. Worthless."

Jen grunted. "They'll keep coming. I tried to run them off this morning. Thought I'd at least make a show of force."

Sam snorted, then jabbed a finger at Jen. "Tell her what happened."

Jen's jaw clenched. "I said I'd fine them for unlicensed trade. Told them to pack up and move on before I came back with the real paperwork." She took a slow pull from her mug. "Didn't get to finish the sentence. The town—" She let out a breath, the sound as sharp as a blade being drawn. "Town's compulsion hit me right behind the eyes. *Serve all who come in peace, stay in peace, and leave in peace.* That's the rule. I know it, but it's never tripped me up before."

Sam nodded, her eyes glinting. "That's the magic at work. Long as we have a constable, nobody's allowed to bring violence through the square." She looked over at Galhani, voice softer. "But it works both ways. You can't run them out unless they break the rules first."

Galhani felt the skin at the base of her neck go cold. "So we can't even stop it? Why are they all coming here?"

Jen looked at her, finally, and there was real fear behind the exhaustion. "Because we're still safe," she said. "Rest of the trade road's gone to hell. Half the towns between here and the river have lost their protection, or just vanished. If you're a seller, or a drifter, or someone looking for a new start, you come to the one place where the gift's still in force."

"There's more," Sam said slowly. The other two women looked at her. "Look, I haven't been here long enough to forget why I came here. How I came here."

"You'd cashiered out of your merc company," Jen said.

"True, but why come north? Something... drew me. I mean, I let my horse have his head, but... something turned it here."

"Nate was sick," Galhani said.

"And the town knew I'd be needed," Sam agreed. "It's *drawing* these newcomers. These wagon-merchants."

"We assumed it was the increase in traffic," Jen said slowly. "You're suggesting it's something else."

"Maybe it *does* want change," the bartender shrugged.

"What, we should all leave?" Galhani snapped.

"No. We've earned a place here," Sam said quietly. "But maybe we *have* fallen into a rut."

"Leota says," Galhani ventured, her voice now soft, "that if it's a parasite, sapping our creativity, we could try to overwhelm it."

"Feel pretty overwhelmed myself, right now," Jen muttered. "Too many newcomers all at once."

Sam set her glass down with enough force to threaten the rim. "And the more that come, the weaker it gets. We all feel it. Used to be, a fight would barely make it onto the street before Jen here had it cooled off. Now? It's a struggle to keep the peace in the taproom."

Jen's hand flexed on the bar. "I thought I could handle it. But it's like the whole town is straining at the leash. If we don't get ahead of it —" She didn't finish the sentence, just let the words hang.

They sat in silence for a long minute, each working through their own calculations of doom.

It was Galhani who spoke first. "Leota is talking about organizing a festival—some kind of group effort to flood the system, give it more than it can handle. It worked in another town, once, Vamir said."

Sam made a face. "A festival? That's certainly Makota's answer to everything."

Jen managed a thin smile. "Maybe it's worth a shot. The alternative is letting the place rot."

"We had the party," Sam pointed out.

"Must need to be more," the constable shot back.

Galhani picked up her glass and stared at the bubbles crawling up the side. "Do you think people will do it?"

Sam shrugged. "If you tell them it's a party, maybe. If you tell them it's life or death..." She grinned. "In this town? If everyone knows the stakes, they'll show up. It's what we do here."

A pair of strangers entered, shaking dust off their boots and blinking in the gloom. They slid into a booth near the window and waited, eyes darting from Sam to Jen and back again. Sam poured two ales and set them on a tray, moving down the bar with the easy menace of a woman who'd fought her way through much worse than new faces. She dropped the mugs at the table, made a joke that didn't quite land, then returned to her post with a deliberate slowness.

Jen watched the newcomers, lips compressed. "If it keeps up, there'll be more of them than us."

Galhani found herself nodding, though she didn't want to agree. "So we do nothing, or we do the festival?"

Sam grinned, a wolfish flash of teeth. "If we're doomed, we might as well go down drinking."

Jen looked at her mug, then at Sam, then back at her mug. "Could be worse," she said, and this time the humor stuck.

The three of them huddled there, sharing the brief warmth of an alliance forged in mutual resignation. The air in the Claw thickened, filling with the scent of hops and burnt wood, and the steady pulse of voices, old and new, rising and falling as the afternoon bled into evening.

By the time Galhani left, there were twice as many people in the pub, and every single one of them looked like they were waiting for something to break.

———

By nightfall, the Claw could barely contain itself. The long-time residents packed in elbow to elbow at the long trestle tables, and every stool at the bar was double-booked. Even the standing room near the hearth was claimed by a cluster of newcomers, huddled together like children on the first day of school. The old order of the place—the quiet bench for Leota, the broad seat for Warren, the corner for Vamir and his book—was lost in the crush. Sam worked the room with both hands, topping off pints and serving up her own special brand of intimidation with every refill.

Galhani took the farthest table, as close to the window as she could get, and watched the slow-motion disaster build. The noise was not the cheerful chaos of a festival or the reckless din of a wedding, but a raw, serrated edge. Laughter cut too high, arguments hovered just below a shout, and every now and then a crash of glass or a jostled elbow sent a ripple of tension through the crowd.

She traced the rim of her empty cup, trying to remember what it felt like to want a drink.

Near the fire, Warren rose to his full, impossible height. He planted one ham-sized fist in the center of a table, making the tankards rattle, and held up a blade with the other. "Look at it!" he bellowed, his voice somehow managing to clear a pocket of silence in the din. "No shine, no edge—just metal. You could as well fight a bandit with a spoon!"

A chorus of jeers and groans followed, but not all were mocking. Calder, the fisherman, raised his head from the bar, eyes rimmed red. "You think that's bad?" he said, voice pitched low but deadly clear. "The lake's turned sour. I set three lines today, caught two fish. Both of 'em had white eyes, and the meat fell off the bone."

Warren brandished the blade in Calder's direction. "It's the whole town, then. Not just me."

Alred, the grocer, piped up from somewhere behind a stack of crates. "Mold in the beans. First I thought it was just a bad shipment, but I switched bins twice and it still comes back. Even the dried stuff spoils now."

Tyran, broad as a barn and twice as loud, pounded his table for attention. "Half the gear in my shop's no good. Saddles won't hold a seam, rope unravels if you so much as look at it. And the shelves—" He shook his head, genuinely unsettled. "They used to organize themselves every morning. Now I have to do it by hand."

More voices joined, a flood of complaint that drowned out the smaller conversations:

"Prudence can't get her silks to take a dye."

"Dexter's poultices are just water and wishful thinking."

"My son's toys all fell apart in a day—"

"I can't even keep yeast alive long enough for a loaf—"

Sam moved between tables, shutting down the worst of it with a glare or a word. She kept her sword at her hip, the hilt visible and shining, but everyone knew it was for show: nobody in North Pointe had seen a real fight in years, and if anyone did, Jen would be there to break it up before the first punch landed.

For a moment, Galhani thought a brawl might actually break out. But Sam stepped in, grabbed both by the shoulder, and said, "If you want to fight, take it to the road. I'm serving peace tonight, and you're going to drink it."

The noise dipped, then surged again, even louder than before. Every face was red with drink or anger or both. The walls themselves seemed to pulse with heat and tension.

Galhani sat through it, every word landing like a drop of acid on her nerves. The voices blended until she couldn't tell which complaint belonged to which neighbor, which grievance was a real threat and which was just someone's way of not drowning.

It all became a single, sick chorus.

She stood, not sure what she meant to do until she was already on her feet. The motion drew a few glances, then more as she stepped away from the table and into the open space near the bar.

"This is worse than when we lost our gifts completely," she said, voice steady and clear. "At least then we knew what we were dealing with. This—" She swept her arm around the room, catching every face in turn. "This is like watching everything we love slowly die."

A silence fell, abrupt and total. Even the fire crackled more quietly.

"We used to be a town," Galhani went on, her own voice rising. "We helped each other, we made things nobody else could make. Now all we do is talk about how nothing works, and whose fault it is." She forced herself to look at Warren, at Calder, at Sam and Jen and even the woman in the green scarf. "If this is all we are now, maybe we deserve to be hollowed out."

Nobody spoke. Some looked away; some glared as if she'd insulted them personally. Sam's jaw set, but she didn't say a word. Galhani waited for someone to shout her down, to throw a cup or a punch, to break the moment.

But in the silence, all she could hear was her own heart pounding and the faint, hopeless sigh of the wind against the walls.

She sat back down, hands trembling, and didn't lift her eyes again for the rest of the night.

The arguments resumed, louder than before, and so it took a long time for anyone to notice that Finnian was standing. He'd been perched by the hearth all evening, working at something small and mechanical—nobody cared what, not with the bar at full boil—but when he straightened, he did so with the casual authority of someone who expected to be obeyed.

He raised one hand. The hush came not all at once, but in a slow ripple: a table here, a cluster there, until most of the room had quieted enough to listen.

"I once visited a town called Meridian," he began, his words pitched to carry. "Not far from here, but a little out of the way. Lovely place. Good food, good company, better than average weather." He smiled, as if sharing a private joke with the walls. "Except, after a while, everything became... ordinary."

A few in the crowd scoffed, but Finnian pressed on. "It started with the cheese, I think. Suddenly, it all tasted like the same wheel. Then the beer. Then the tools. Even the clothes—couldn't tell one seam from the next. People didn't notice at first. They just went on as usual, until one morning, they realized the world had gone gray."

He scanned the room, his eyes bright and unhurried. "So they did the only thing they could. They stopped trading, stopped buying, stopped pretending it would fix itself. And they built something, together." He gestured as if drawing a circle in the air. "A machine. Nobody remembers what it did, but that doesn't matter. It was the act —the making of it, the shared sweat and cursing and pride. And when it was done, things started to taste like themselves again. Just a little, at first. Enough to notice. Enough to want more."

A handful of regulars muttered, others looked away. But a deeper quiet took root, a stillness that wasn't just the absence of noise.

Finnian shrugged, sat down, and returned to his work. The story, like a pebble in a pond, sent out its ripples. For a time, nobody argued, and even the newcomers sat with their thoughts.

Sam, who'd heard more tall tales than she could count, was watching Finnian with a strange look—half gratitude, half suspicion, as if trying to decide if she'd just been conned or inspired. She gave him a nod, and he returned it with the smallest, most genuine smile.

Galhani felt something shift, a brief loosening of the rope around her chest. She caught herself standing, saw that she'd drawn stares, and sat back down quickly, burning with embarrassment. The memory of her own outburst returned, heavy and mortifying.

She waited for the arguments to start again. This time, they didn't.

Instead, the pub began to thin out. The regulars drifted home, the newcomers finished their drinks and left in knots of two or three, their conversations low and thoughtful. Sam wiped down the bar, slower than usual. Jen, who had listened to Finnian's story without a word, rose and walked out, her silhouette rigid in the doorway.

Galhani watched it all, numb.

When the room was nearly empty, she stood, smoothed her skirt, and crossed to the door. Finnian caught her eye as she passed. He didn't say anything, just held her gaze for a moment, as if to acknowledge her pain and offer nothing but honesty in return.

The night outside was crisp and sharp. Galhani hugged herself and walked home, her feet scuffing the stones. The square was deserted, the new shop signs dimmed for the night, the old ones sagging under the weight of whatever tomorrow might bring.

Don Jones

She unlocked the door to the tea shop, stepped inside, and relocked it behind her. The darkness was total. She didn't light a lamp, didn't set water to boil, didn't even bother to brush off the day's accumulation of dust from the countertop.

She just sat, alone, the world narrowed to the circle of her own breath and the faint, bitter taste of everything she'd failed to do.

ten

. . .

GALHANI SPENT the entire morning in bed, a tangle of limbs and sweat-soaked sheets, with the curtains drawn so tightly that not even the blue daylight could wedge itself in. At some point, Lara brought her a mug of broth and set it on the crate beside the bed, but the steam went cold before Galhani managed to drink. The cup was greasy, slick with chicken fat and resignation, and when she finally took a sip, it tasted like loss.

From the hallway, she could hear the thud of feet as Lara cleaned, the dry snap of kindling in the stove, the scrape of knives against the chopping board. Once or twice, the front door rattled, and voices rose and fell—a customer, a delivery, maybe even a friend—but none of it reached the bedroom. The world shrank to the width of the blanket pulled over her head.

She wasn't crying, not anymore. She wasn't even sure what she was doing, except running a single phrase over and over through her skull, like a pestle crushing roots to powder: "If you want to starve a parasite, you outlast it." Finnian's story haunted her, and not for the reasons he probably intended. Galhani kept thinking about the town in the story, the one where nothing tasted like itself, where even the cheese lost its bite, and how the only way out was to build something

—anything—together. It made her want to punch him, a little, for being right in a way that left her with nothing but the problem.

Around noon, Lara knocked, waited, and then entered with the patience of a cat approaching a snake. She set another bowl of broth beside the bed, this time with a wedge of bread, and then perched on the edge of the mattress.

"You can't stay in here all day," Lara said. Her voice was gentle, but the words had claws.

"I know," Galhani said, but she stayed anyway. "I just need—"

Lara waited.

"—to think."

Lara smoothed a hand across the blanket, then got up and left. The door closed with a click, and Galhani let herself drift. She picked at the crust of bread, letting it dissolve on her tongue, hoping for a jolt of flavor, but it only tasted like dust and the memory of poppyseed.

She considered the problem the way she'd always approached a stubborn blend: test the ratios, invert the process, start with the solution and work backwards. But every time she tried to imagine the town whole, she only saw the cracks, and the cracks were growing. The new shops nearly outnumbered the old, some of the townsfolk were already patronizing the wagon-merchants, and the more the town changed, the more it felt like nothing would ever change back.

When the sun began to set, a knock on the door startled her awake. She'd slept through most of the day, and in her dreams, the town was already gone—replaced by a grid of identical stalls, each one manned by a pale, hungry face selling the same unremarkable wares. Galhani tried to laugh at the bleakness of it, but the sound stuck in her throat.

Lara's voice filtered in, muffled but insistent: "Vamir says the meeting's in the main room. He'd like you there, if you feel up to it."

Galhani didn't answer. She waited for the footsteps to recede, then swung her legs over the edge of the bed. Her joints popped in protest, but she ignored them. She stripped off her nightshirt and dressed in the plainest tunic she owned, running her fingers through her hair until the knots surrendered. She caught her reflection in the dark window and almost didn't recognize the woman staring back.

The town felt colder than usual when she stepped outside. The sky was the color of watered milk, and a lazy wind pushed at the back of her neck, nudging her toward the square. As she made her way down the narrow walk, Galhani counted the new shops: the button place was still open, its awning freshly scrubbed; two more stalls hawked paper and ink, though nobody in town had written a letter in moons; and the harp repairman was holding court in front of his shop, strumming a minor chord that made the whole square vibrate with unease.

But what caught her eye was the line of wagons parked along the trade road, just beyond the low stone boundary of the gate. There were at least a dozen of them now, each painted a different shade of disappointment: gray, dun, the dull red of dried blood. Their windows glowed with lamplight, casting wobbly shadows across the rutted path. Galhani recognized none of the faces behind the counters, but the wares were all too familiar—perfect, soulless, massed in ranks as if ready for a funeral.

She hesitated in the street, heart racing as she realized she was being watched. Silas, the tea seller, stood by his wagon, arms folded and gaze fixed on the road. He didn't acknowledge her, not even a nod. His eyes were on the travelers—three of them, heads together, comparing the labels of his blends with the grim focus of a jury weighing the value of life.

She moved past without a word, but she felt his attention follow her, a chill crawling up her spine. The rest of the road was in motion: travelers' kids running between the bakery and the grocer, a pair of old men from the inn arguing over the price of lamp oil, and, near the entrance of the Broken Claw, Prudence in her severe black dress, pushing her pram with the deliberate precision of a general inspecting the troops.

Galhani entered the Claw. The warmth inside was a shock to her system, her skin tingling as her eyes adjusted to the glow of lanterns and the dense heat of bodies. The place was packed—every bench, every stool, every inch of the bar crowded with faces both new and old. The air thrummed with conversation, a hundred voices raised just enough to be heard over the din. She spotted Sam behind the bar, her white braid swinging as she poured drinks with mechanical efficiency, her face set in a mask of brittle cheer.

She found a spot at the far end, tucked behind a pillar, and sat with her back to the wall. She didn't order; she'd brought her own mug from the shop, filled with the last of the night-bloom tea, though she doubted it would taste like anything.

At first, she just watched. Vamir was at a table in the center of the room, surrounded by a cluster of regulars—Lucy, Warren, Makota, even Dexter, though he looked as if he'd rather be anywhere else. They leaned in close, speaking in clipped tones, occasionally glancing at the door as if expecting someone to burst in and change everything.

Every so often, a fight would nearly start. The newcomers kept to their side of the room, but the divide was as clear as if someone had drawn a line down the center of the floor. Cole, the grocer, was locked in a silent standoff with a man in a traveling cloak, the two of them staring each other down over mugs of what passed for ale these days. Dardrad was louder than ever, arguing with Makota about whether it was better to bake bread that tasted like air or to not bake at all. Jen sat at the end of the bar, her face unreadable as she scanned the room for trouble.

For a long while, Galhani said nothing. She nursed her mug and let her mind wander. She wondered if the magic in the town had been spread too thin, or if it had simply gone brittle from neglect. She thought about the parasite, and how it didn't care if the hosts died, as long as there was something left to feed on. She thought about Finnian's machine, and whether it had ever really existed, or if it was just a metaphor for hope.

As the sun dipped below the roofs outside, the crowd shifted. The travelers drifted out in ones and twos, replaced by townsfolk coming in from the fields or the shops. The noise in the Claw swelled, then settled into a steady, nervous hum. Galhani finished her tea and let the empty mug sit in her lap, hands cradling it like a memory.

Eventually, she caught Vamir's eye. He nodded, a small, encouraging gesture, and she nodded back. She knew the meeting would happen soon, and that she was expected to have something to say, some insight or spark that would change the tide. But right now, all she could do was sit and watch, letting the moment draw out as long as possible before she had to rejoin the world.

Outside, the wagons glowed like embers in the dusk, and the street was alive with the sound of bargains and the soft, sweet promise of nothing at all.

———

Before long, the Broken Claw was full to bursting—no, past bursting, the air itself swollen with the press of bodies and the pungent reek of sweat and road dust and beer spilled a dozen times before. Every bench and barrel had been pulled from storage and repurposed for sitting or leaning, and even the steps to the door were claimed by travelers with the hollow, hard faces of people too tired to care who they offended.

Galhani and Vamir had managed to snag a narrow table by the window, but only because Vamir had snapped at two travelers to move their elbows before he "snipped them off like ragwort." His voice, always so gentle in his shop, had a cold edge in the Claw. Even after the fishermen left, Galhani could see Vamir's jaw working, as if he were chewing the words he wished he'd said.

The noise in the room ebbed and surged, a wave that built and crashed in unpredictable patterns. There was laughter, but it was sharp and too loud, each joke landing like a thrown cup. Arguments sparked and guttered in the corners. At the bar, Sam moved with a speed and precision that seemed barely controlled; she poured, wiped, slammed mugs with a violence that was more warning than service.

Nobody here was drinking for pleasure.

A new crowd had pushed in after sundown: a clutch of traveling musicians, hands raw from the road, who'd bought one round and then started playing for tips; a family of five, the youngest child still stained blue around the mouth from eating unripe berries off the hedge; a handful of mercenaries who weren't even pretending to be peaceful, only resting their sword arms while they drank. Between them, the locals looked beleaguered, their faces set in the exhausted defiance of survivors.

Galhani sipped her tea, which by now was nothing but water and memory. She had brewed it herself, used the last of the night-bloom, but it tasted no more than warm air. She watched Vamir twist the stem of his cup, over and over, until the fragile pottery seemed ready to snap.

The door opened with a bang. The sound cut through the noise like a sword and left behind a momentary vacuum.

Elspeth Riverpine entered. A kind-looking, grandmotherly figure, she was not tall, nor broad, but she seemed to fill the room all the same, the way a drawn blade commands silence even before it's used. Her cloak was coated in a patina of dust, the hem frayed from rough ground. She gripped her staff with a hand that trembled only slightly, but each step was measured, her gaze sweeping the room with the efficient ruthlessness of someone who had long since run out of patience.

She stopped at the threshold, surveyed the crowd, and then walked directly to Galhani and Vamir's table. Nobody said a word until she sat, her staff thunking to the floor beside her.

She didn't say hello. "It's a circus," she announced, voice low and flat.

Vamir gave a cautious nod. "Haven't seen you in a moment."

"I regret that," sighed Elspeth, brushing dust from her lap. "But there are three dozen questers living in my woods right now, and if I spend another night with them, I'll drown myself in a creek."

Galhani raised an eyebrow. "Questers?"

Elspeth snorted. "Every idiot with a sword and a rented horse. Most want directions, the rest want me to bless them or hand out the magic swords. It's this damn Goblin King in the west. It was bad enough last year, with everyone wanting some magical protection for their village, but now... it's like a frenzy."

"It's been busy here as well," Vamir murmured. "And not to our benefit."

"Tell me about it." Elspeth turned her attention to Galhani. "You look like you haven't slept in a sennight, and this entire place feels like drinking dishwater."

"I haven't," said Galhani, not bothering to lie.

Elspeth reached over, plucked the mug from Galhani's hand, and took a sip. Her mouth twisted. "Speaking of dishwater...?"

"Don't remind me."

The noise in the room had returned, but at a lower pitch. Galhani could feel eyes watching them, a nervous energy that crackled and snapped from table to table.

Elspeth set down the mug and laced her fingers together. "There's a man in the wagon camp selling charm bracelets. He claims they're mine." She glanced at Vamir. "You know anything about that?"

Vamir shrugged. "If they were real, they'd be selling for ten times as much."

Elspeth's lips curled in satisfaction. "That's what I thought." She looked at Galhani. "You're awfully grim, for a gnome."

"Not much to be happy about."

"Goodness," Elspeth said with a long, indrawn breath. "Wouldn't have guessed a few busy fortnights would put *you* lot under the weather." He brow creased with concern. "But things *don't* feel right, here."

"A half-dozen new shops," Vamir sighed softly. "But they're all little things, opportunistic things."

"And these wagons along your road," Elspeth said.

Vamir nodded. "The town... did something. it's drawn them in. But it's drawn something else in, as well. Something hungry."

Elspeth's lips quirked into a frown. "We're linked, this town and I. All of you."

"And?" Galhani asked.

"My questers have been ill-prepared. Shoddy weapons, shoddier tents. Hungry, and not just in their stomachs. Gaunt. They've had a gray haze in their eyes. Desperation."

"I don't think we're being very helpful right now," Galhani mumbled.

"No, I—"

There was a crash, and then a shout: Cole, the grocer, had flung a mug at Warren, who caught it one-handed and crushed it in his fist. "Try forging something that isn't soft as pudding!" the grocer yelled, spraying foam. "Maybe then the tools will last a day in the field."

Warren's face went purple with rage.

Sam appeared between them, slamming down two fresh mugs and

fixing both men with a glare. "Drink, or leave," she growled. "If you want to fight, do it outside."

They drank, and silence fell, but the tension lingered, a stench thicker than the smoke in the air.

Elspeth looked alarmed. "What's this?" she whispered.

"The town's magic has gone flat," said Vamir, "It's making people tense."

Lucy was next, her voice sharp as vinegar, cutting through the din from her table near the fire. "I wouldn't wrap a fish in that fabric," she said, staring at Prudence, who sat stiffly, her hands folded over her infant's pram.

Prudence's reply was as thin as the cloth she sold. "At least I try to make something new, instead of churning out the same blue pots until the world is sick of them."

Lucy bared her teeth, the smile as predatory as it was amused. "Well, if you ever want to borrow a real dye, come by the shop. I'll show you what color looks like."

Sam poured herself a drink, then another, ignoring the spillage as she filled the glass to the brim. Her hands shook, just a little.

"Is it always like this now?" Elspeth asked, but the question wasn't for anyone at the table.

Vamir leaned back, letting his gaze sweep the crowd. "They're scared. All of them. Even the ones who act like they're above it." He hesitated, then added, "Especially them."

Galhani's own fear was more subtle, like the numbness that follows a burn. She wondered if anyone here even remembered how things used to be—the spontaneous laughter, the way the Claw had once felt like a home rather than a bunker.

Elspeth exhaled, her breath clouding in the air. "I've seen it before," she said, her tone softer. "Fear. I lived in one of the rosefruit towns, you know. A long while ago. Small towns, each with their own character. When the fighting came, they split. The brave stayed to fight. The greedy as well. The rest ran for the road. People will go mad for territory."

Vamir's eyes narrowed. "Rumor has it, the goblins aren't just fighting for territory. They're clearing a path. For something bigger."

Elspeth nodded. "The so-called Goblin King. Nobody knows what he wants, but the little settlements fall just the same." She looked at Galhani, and for the first time, there was pity in her eyes. "You're not wrong about there being something hungry. I can feel it. But my magic isn't rooted in creativity. That's not my role. But it's not the parasite that kills you. It's what you become when you try to live with it."

There was a moment of silence, one of those perfect pauses when even the air seems to hold its breath.

Then, from the other side of the room, a glass shattered. Someone screamed. Sam leapt the bar with a speed that belied her years, but by the time she reached the source, the violence had already passed. A traveler—one of the mercenaries, probably—clutched his hand, blood streaming between his fingers. He looked up at Sam, eyes wild, and spat something that was more curse than language.

Sam barked a command. The room responded at once: chairs scraped back, people surged to their feet, but nobody moved to help the injured man. He was an outsider, and it was as if his blood was less real than the beer on the floor.

Galhani watched the scene, her stomach turning. She set down her mug and looked at Elspeth.

"What would you do?" she asked, her voice barely audible.

Elspeth's considered that. "Remember why you're here."

That's what Finnian said, Galhani thought. *Basically.*

"And," Elsepth added, "remind everyone else why they're here."

The words didn't comfort Galhani, but they did settle something in her chest. She understood, now, that the fight was not just against whatever was hollowing the world, but against the desire to give in, to let yourself be nothing.

The mood in the Claw had shifted again. The locals closed ranks, the outsiders nursed their wounds. Sam returned to her post, her hands red from cleaning up blood, but her eyes clear.

Elspeth stood, collected her staff, and nodded to Vamir and Galhani. "That's enough I think," she said. She glanced once more at the room, then pushed her way out, the heavy door swinging shut behind her.

Galhani watched her go, then looked at Vamir, whose fingers were white where he gripped his cup.

"Do you think she's right?" she asked.

Vamir shrugged. "Sometimes, the only answer is to outlast the problem." He glanced at the bar, at Sam, at the cluster of locals who still clung to their tables as if they could anchor the world in place. "But sometimes you have to make something, even if you're the only one left to build it."

They sat in silence, the noise of the room growing once more. The arguments resumed, but the mood was different—desperate, but also hungry, as if everyone understood that things would never be the same, and they had to fight for whatever scraps of themselves remained.

Galhani felt a bitter laugh building in her chest, but she swallowed it. She raised her empty mug to her lips, tasted nothing, and set it down with a finality she hoped was enough.

Outside, the world spun on, relentless as ever. Inside the Claw, the storm had only just begun. Galhani shook her head and moved toward the door.

———

The night air was sharp, and Galhani felt it bite into her lungs as soon as she stepped out of the Claw. For a moment, she just stood on the stoop, letting the cold and the quiet eat away at the memory of the heat and noise behind her.

Elspeth lingered just outside the light thrown by the windows. Her staff made a dull thump on the ground as she tapped it, more to feel the earth than to steady herself. She stared out across the square, where the lamps from the new shops flickered like ghostly eyes, casting long, warped shadows across the dirt.

"I used to come here for the stillness," Elspeth said, voice pitched for Galhani's ears alone. "Now I can't even hear myself think."

Galhani hugged herself, wishing she'd brought a coat. "It's not so bad, out here," she said. "You get used to it."

"That's the problem," said Elspeth. "Everyone gets used to it. Nobody remembers what it was like when the world had quiet."

Footsteps approached—deliberate, careful. Leota emerged from the night, the hem of her black dress trailing dust. She nodded to Galhani, then to Elspeth, her mouth a tight line.

Elspeth gave a half-smile, the lines at the corner of her eyes deepening. "Witch," she said, and it wasn't an insult.

Leota nodded back with a small grin. "Enchantress." For a moment, the air was charged, two kinds of power in the same space, each testing the other for weight.

Elspeth seemed to approve of the challenge. She leaned her staff against the porch railing and turned to Galhani. "You know," she said, "there's more than one kind of magic." Her tone softened, almost conspiratorial. "Some magic is too loud to be heard. It drowns everything around it. But the quietest magic..." She trailed off, as if the wind might steal the secret.

Galhani waited. "What about it?"

Elspeth's eyes glinted. "It's the most powerful, in the end. Because nobody notices until it's gone."

Galhani frowned, feeling the words like a pebble in her shoe. "I don't—"

But then Finnian arrived, his steps silent except for the faint click of metal from the pocket-watch he carried. Leota introduced him with a tilt of her head. "This is Finnian. He's the new clockmaker."

"Never met a clock I couldn't fix," said Finnian, with a crooked, earnest smile. "Or break. That's usually the same thing, in the long run."

Elspeth studied him, then looked at Leota. "He's unenchanted."

Leota shrugged. "Little enough to go around these days."

Elsepth shook her head slowly, then sniffed, as if tasting the air. "There's plenty enough. It's just... hmm."

"Spread too thin," Leota grumbled.

"No. It's just forgotten who it wants to be with. Distracted with all the noise."

Finnian tapped his pocket-watch, the gears inside making a soft, whirring song. "A clock with a hundred perfect parts will still fail if just one tiny spring is misaligned. People forget that. They think it's the big cogs, or the hands on the face. But usually, it's the tiniest thing that sets the whole system off."

Elspeth's gaze softened, as if she saw something in Finnian that reminded her of a better time. "Your trade is safe from the draining, then."

He shrugged, not so much modest as matter-of-fact. "It's still all just gears. Some spin, some freeze. Towns are the same."

For a moment, nobody spoke. The silence pressed in, more honest than any of the conversation inside.

Leota broke it, her voice gentle. "Your magic still works, doesn't it?"

Elspeth nodded. "It does. But it doesn't matter. If the world around you is all broken springs and dead weight, what good is power?" She tilted her head at Galhani. "It's like a blend with all the wrong notes. You can force the flavor, but you can't make it true. As I told them, we're linked, you all and I. I can't make my quests easier just because the questers aren't prepared. So neither of us are filling our roles."

Galhani tried to smile, but it caught on her teeth. "So what's the answer?"

Elspeth's reply was little more than a whisper. "Wait for the quiet. And when it comes, fill it with something new."

She picked up her staff, gave the three of them a curt nod, and melted into the darkness. The sound of her footsteps faded long before her presence did.

For a long moment, the three remained on the porch, each lost in thought. Finnian wound his watch, Leota watched the wind play with a strand of her hair, and Galhani stared at the horizon, searching for a glimpse of the old world, or maybe the next.

Behind them, the Claw roared on, but out here, the quiet magic gathered strength.

Galhani took a deep breath and headed back inside.

Inside, the Claw had shed even the pretense of harmony. The new arrivals from the porch found the atmosphere sharper, the noise cut by the edge of desperation. Galhani could feel it before she stepped fully into the room—voices pitched higher, laughter stuttering on itself, all the small acts of courtesy and care worn away by fatigue and irritation.

Makota was at the bar, her tail lashing the legs of a stool as she argued with Jen. "It's theft," Makota said, ears flat and voice razor-thin. "They're selling hardtack right out of a wagon, not even baked here. It's old, it's dry, it's not even food."

Jen's reply was a stone dropped in a bucket: "Town says anyone can trade, long as they stay in peace. I tried to move them, Makota. The rule held. I could as well order the wind to stop."

Sam kept wiping the same patch of bar, the motion so mechanical it seemed to grind a groove into the wood. She glanced up as the argument escalated, but her eyes were unfocused, her face drawn tight. "If you want my advice," she said, "don't eat the bread. It tastes like old socks. That's all I'll say."

From the back of the room, a traveler in a patched green coat upended his mug. The beer spread across the table, then the floor, and for a heartbeat, everyone stared. Nobody moved to help. The man dabbed at the mess with his sleeve, muttered a curse, and let it stand. Galhani watched, and something inside her turned cold.

Lucy was gone; Warren had fallen into a sullen, silent drinking contest with Dardrad. Prudence sat alone, cradling her infant and staring at the wall. Even the regulars seemed to keep to their own islands, afraid that speaking would only draw more of the storm down on their heads.

Galhani sat, but only just. She felt like a visitor in her own town, the person least equipped to fix what had gone wrong.

Vamir caught her eye from across the room. His expression was grave, and she understood immediately: there was no fixing this. Not tonight. Maybe not ever.

She rose, leaving her empty cup on the table. She didn't say goodbye to anyone—there was nothing left to say. The noise of the Claw closed behind her, muffled only slightly by the door.

Outside, the night had gone colder. A thin mist drifted through the square, softening the lamp-lights but doing nothing to blunt the feeling of loss.

She started home, but halfway there, she stopped and looked back.

The windows of the Claw were brighter than ever, the lantern-glow a sickly yellow against the dark. Inside, the voices clashed and howled, and for a moment, Galhani wondered if the walls themselves would hold.

She realized then that the town had become something new—a thing with a beating heart and a hunger all its own. Maybe Elspeth was right: maybe the only thing left was to wait for the quiet, and to be ready when it finally arrived.

But as Galhani turned away, she knew the storm wasn't over. It hadn't even begun.

eleven

. . .

VAMIR'S SUMMONS arrived before Galhani finished her morning inventory. He didn't send a note, or even a child with a message—he simply appeared at her window, eyes glinting in the early light, and tapped three times with a deliberate, patient rhythm. When she finally noticed, he gave a brief, apologetic bow, then motioned for her to come outside.

She met him at the threshold, the shop's door groaning as if in protest at being opened so early.

"Apologies," Vamir said, his voice as smooth as always. "I know you have your routine. But I thought you might want to see something." He paused, looking past her at the silent jars and the faded sunlight that struggled through the shop's front glass. "You could bring tea. If you wish."

She considered refusing, or at least putting him off for a few candlemarks. But something in his tone—gentle, but urgent, the way you might speak to a child with a fever—made her simply nod, grab the first tin in reach, and follow.

The green outside was mostly empty, the morning not yet awake. The shop fronts all faced inward, forming their little ring of civility, but none had raised shutters or opened up for the day. Even the bakery's windows were dark, though Galhani caught a brief whiff of stale, cooling bread as they passed.

They crossed the square in silence. Vamir's gait was long and efficient, but he slowed every few steps to make sure Galhani could keep up. He wore a neat black coat over his robes, and his pale hands were gloved in lambskin, though she doubted he needed the warmth. At his shoulder, as always, perched Polyocular—a dense, blue-feathered orb of a bird, its three eyes blinking in perfect sync.

Vamir's bookshop stood next to the town hall, set a little back from the green, as if embarrassed by the grandness of its arched door and stained-glass transom. Inside, it was close and dim, the air as thick as honey from the weight of centuries of parchment and ink. The smell was the first thing that struck you—an instant, unfiltered shock of mildew and dust, undercut by the sharper tang of lemon oil and candle smoke.

Vamir held the door for her, then ducked inside, closing it with a decisive click. He did not speak as he led her through the labyrinth of shelves, past the front desk, and down a tight aisle at the back. The shelves was just far enough apart for one—Galhani's shoulder brushed the books' bindings as she passed.

The way opened a tiny clear area, a nook of sorts, featuring a diminutive table that might have been custom-made for a gnome. Vamir gestured for Galhani to sit. Polyocular hopped off his shoulder and landed at the edge of the light, three eyes trained on her with the intensity of a scholar awaiting a lecture.

He waited until she was seated before speaking. "You remember the texts Leota mentioned? The ones about the parasite?"

She nodded, feeling the morning's fog recede as the familiar ritual of research took over.

"I found more," Vamir said, and his voice dropped half an octave. "But not where I expected." He pulled a thin, battered volume from the pile on the table. It was not much bigger than her hand, but the leather was cracked and stained, and the corners had been nibbled by silverfish. He opened it with reverence, as if it might break apart in his hands.

"The Westcroft Collection," he explained. "Most of it is nonsense—

alchemical speculation, rumors about curse outbreaks in the Red Cities. But this—" He turned to a page marked by a sliver of dried grass. "This is different. Read."

Galhani squinted at the ink, which was a faded brown, barely visible against the warped paper. The script was dense, written in a hurried, looping hand:

"When the art of a place begins to unravel, look for the parasite not among the things most cherished, but among those most despised. For the parasite is a thief of contradiction. It thrives on dissonance, finds purchase in that which opposes the heart's purpose. When once it lodges, the true craft is hollowed, and all attempts to restore it must fail until the original discord is resolved."

She let the words settle. "It's not attacking what's strong," she said, "but what's opposite to us."

Vamir nodded. "That's how I read it." He tapped the page with one delicate finger. "It attaches to the anti-gift. The thing you wish didn't exist in your community."

Polyocular trilled, hopping closer. Galhani reached out and smoothed the page, then looked up at Vamir. "Is that why the new shops are thriving? Because they're the inverse of us?"

"It seems so," Vamir said. "And the more they multiply, the more they anchor the parasite."

Galhani stared at the little book, at the curl of Vamir's finger on the margin. She tried to picture the town as it once was—every shop with a purpose, every craft unique, nobody competing for the same coin. Now the square was half filled with forgeries: knockoff pottery, mass-bottled teas, even someone selling charm bracelets stamped from tin.

She felt her breath quicken. "So we're doomed," she said, "unless we can get rid of all the junk merchants."

Vamir frowned, then shook his head. "Not exactly. The next part is stranger." He turned the page, and the script changed, the lines more frantic, slanted as if written during an earthquake.

"The only cure is renewal of purpose," it read. "The parasite cannot abide in a place that remembers its reason for being. But beware—when the new order is not a true order, but a mockery, the parasite only grows stronger. Community must have a center, or it becomes a hundred empty circles. The cure is in the making, not the unmaking."

Galhani let the words trickle through her mind, but they pooled and went nowhere.

"What's that supposed to mean?" she asked. "How do we 'renew purpose'? None of us even agree what the purpose is."

Vamir smiled, but the expression was tight, anxious. "I think that's the problem." He closed the book, and Polyocular squeaked in protest.

"Is there more?" Galhani asked.

"Not in this volume." Vamir gestured to the long table, which held a dozen more books in various states of disrepair. "But the library downstairs—" he hesitated, as if unsure how much to reveal. "It's not like other libraries. It listens. It shows you what you're looking for, if you know how to ask."

He watched her carefully, as if gauging how much she could handle.

She squared her shoulders. "Then we ask," she said, her voice steadier than she felt.

Vamir nodded, then rose, gesturing for her to follow. "This moves itself every so often," he said almost apologetically. "Keeps me on my toes." He reached toward a shelf and tilted one battered old volume forward. With a *click*, a narrow section of bookcase swung open on silent hinges, revealing a narrow stone spiral staircase. "Come."

It was not a normal library, then. But Galhani hadn't expected a normal anything when it came to Vamir. She followed him, clutching the tea tin to her chest, and let the hush of the bookshop settle over her like a second skin. At the threshold of the secret stair, Polyocular hovered for a breathless moment, then dove ahead, three eyes bobbing in the dim.

The spiral was cut crudely into the bedrock, each step worn concave by centuries—or by the same pair of feet, running this route a thousand times in a thousand emergencies. Galhani felt the temperature drop as they descended, the air shifting from the syrupy warmth of old paper to a damp, mineral chill shot through with the tang of potash. After three revolutions, the last threads of natural light vanished, and Vamir drew a slender rod from his sleeve and snapped it, conjuring a thread of blue-white radiance that lit the way but cast no shadow.

At the base, the stair let out into a vast, rectangular chamber that looked nothing like the snug upper floor. The ceiling was lost in darkness, and the walls were masked by bristling towers of books stacked to the rafters, some bound in leather, some in bark, some in stitched-together sheaves of what looked like beetlewing or felted hair. There were aisles, but they wandered, interrupted by precarious ladders, mismatched stepladders, and the occasional pile of stacked crates left as stepping stones. Polyocular immediately began to flit between the shelves, scanning titles with a microscopic twitch of feathers.

Galhani had never seen so many books in her life. There were probably more here than in the entire Gnomeland. It made her head swim. The air was thick with the smell of old knowledge, but also something sharp and astringent—a note of iron, maybe, or ozone.

Vamir led her to a workbench that had been excavated from the stacks, its surface almost clear except for a heavy, open ledger and the detritus of a half-completed repair: scraps of vellum, a bottle of glue, a wooden clamp. He set the battered volume aside and gestured for her to sit on a tall stool.

"I'll try to focus it," he said. "But it helps if you think about what you're looking for. The stronger the need, the better the system works."

She didn't know what to focus on. What did you even call this kind of hunger? The hollowing? The anti-gift? She tried to imagine the town as it had been—a single, humming instrument, every part in tune—and then pictured what it might be, emptied out and filled with forgeries. The ache in her chest sharpened.

Vamir placed two fingers to his temple and closed his eyes. Polyocular, perched atop a nearby shelf, mimicked the gesture with a tiny wing. There was a low, vibrational hum, almost below the threshold of hearing, and the stacks seemed to groan around them.

Galhani stared at the walls, expecting to see nothing change. But the aisles began to shift, the angles of the shelves warping as if flexed by invisible hands.

Vamir, looking intently as the shelves and books seemed to momentarily settle themselves, crossed to a shelf at the far side of the room. Polyocular followed, hopping along a thin table, wings flicking in anticipation. He ran a hand over the spines, murmuring to himself, then selected a volume that looked less like a book and more like a stack of pamphlets stitched together with catgut. He set it before Galhani and motioned for her to open it.

This one was written in Gnomish, the script familiar but archaic. Galhani's eyes widened as she read, the words tumbling out in a rush:

"There are places in the world where the center holds, and places where the center breaks. When the latter occurs, the parasite of dissonance is inevitable. It is not alive, not as the world understands it, but it is hungry, and it will not rest until it eats itself to sleep or is starved by purpose restored. Beware the temptation to eradicate the parasite by force; it will only retreat and return. The solution is to find the pulse, the reason, and let all things return to their core."

She looked up, startled. "It's not just this town," she said. "It's happened before."

Vamir inclined his head. "Often. Usually in places where the community loses itself."

She closed the book, her hands trembling. "So what do we do? Throw a bigger party? Build a statue? Make a new holiday?"

Vamir considered. "Perhaps. But it's not about the act. It's about the belief. Everyone has to want it. Or at least, everyone who matters to the heart of the town."

For a moment, neither spoke. The only sound was Polyocular's faint, high-pitched chirr as it groomed a patch of feathers.

Galhani looked around the library—the way the shelves curved, almost protectively, the way the books on the end seemed to lean toward her, as if offering comfort. She felt the weight of the musty air, the cold at her ankles, the warmth of Vamir's lamplight.

She let the silence lengthen, then finally said, "I don't even know what I want anymore. Or what this place wants."

"That's the hardest part," Vamir said. "But you're the first one to admit it."

He placed a hand over hers, gentle but unyielding. "If you can find your purpose, the rest might follow. Or it might not. But at least you'll know where to look."

Galhani felt her throat tighten, but she didn't look away. She thought of Lara, asleep upstairs, and the smell of the dried herbs in her shop. She thought of Sam's determined rage, and Leota's dry wit, and even the way Warren barked at the morning like it owed him an apology.

She realized, with a tiny flicker of hope, that she wanted all those things to survive. She wanted the town to stay what it was, but also to become something new.

Vamir watched her with those pale, ancient eyes. "You're thinking something," he said.

"I'm thinking it's not the parasite that matters. It's what happens after."

He smiled, and this time, it was real. "You'll be all right, Galhani. The world needs more people who remember what comes next."

She laughed, a short, startled sound. "I hope you're right."

Polyocular shrieked, then darted up onto her shoulder. Its three eyes blinked in sequence, and for a moment, Galhani saw her reflection in them—small, tired, but alive.

Vamir offered her the tiny, battered volume. "Take it," he said. "If you need more, the library will know."

She tucked it into her pocket, then stood, brushing off her skirt. The cool air bit at her, but she barely felt it. For the first time in days, she could taste something on her tongue. It wasn't much—just the ghost of possibility—but it was better than nothing.

"Thank you," she said.

Vamir only nodded, his expression grave but kind.

When she left, the shelves seemed to close behind her, sealing off the secrets until she—or someone like her—was ready to ask again.

———

Galhani retraced her steps through the bookshop's anteroom, her mind running in loops over what she'd just read. The morning sun had brightened, flooding the square and sending angled stripes of gold across the worn flagstones, but inside her head the world was dimmer, focused only on the slow, stubborn pulse in her chest.

She stepped out onto the stoop and paused, letting the air bite at her cheeks. The ground outside was glazed with thin frost that the sun had only just begun to soften. In the hush of the square, she heard the distant crunch of boots and the brittle whistle of wind through eaves. She closed her eyes, and a memory surfaced, vivid and unbidden.

It was the day she and Lara had first arrived in North Pointe Common Towne, five years ago but still raw enough to sting. The wagon had dropped them a mile out, and they'd walked the last stretch by hand, their two bags and one battered box slung between them. She remembered the soil—still dark and rough from a spring plow, flecked with last season's straw and the scent of fresh earth so sharp it made her eyes water. Lara had led the way, boots punching holes in the frost, and Galhani had followed, trying not to slip, trying not to laugh at how utterly ill-suited they looked: two city gnomes, one too tall, the other too loud, both carrying everything they owned in a box that smelled faintly of onion and regret.

Their new home was nothing but a cold shell, a single window cracked at the corner, a floor scattered with dead moths and the black skeletons of last year's flies. But Lara had only grinned, cranked the window open, and let the morning's air in. "Smells like a clean start," she'd said, and Galhani had believed her, if only for a second.

They'd unpacked in silence, each arranging their world the way they liked best—Lara with her neat rows of jars and knives, Galhani with her chaos of pots and crushed herbs. She remembered Lara's hands, the warmth of her grip as they stood together in the raw kitchen, the way she'd pressed her thumb into Galhani's palm like a promise.

"We'll make it ours," Lara had whispered, and for the first time, Galhani had believed that was possible. She'd felt the hope flicker, brief but enough, and it had carried her through the next sennight, the next moon, the whole brutal winter after.

Now, standing in the town square, she felt that same hope, battered but still alive, pulsing just below her ribs. It hurt, but in the way that means you're not dead yet.

Elspeth's words echoed, as clear as if she'd just spoken them:

"Remember why you're here. And remind everyone else why they're here."

Galhani looked at the little book in her hand, the Gnomish script already smudged by the sweat of her thumb. The parasite didn't want to kill the town; it just wanted to break it into pieces, each shop and each person isolated in their own tiny orbit, until the center gave out and nothing was left but dust.

She realized she'd been holding her breath. She exhaled, and the cold air made her cough. She felt a strange, greedy energy surge through her arms, a need to do something—anything—to hold the town together. She pressed the book tighter to her chest, her heart hammering in time with the memory.

A shadow fell across the stoop. Vamir, as if summoned by the change in her breathing, stood at the door. He studied her for a long moment, head tilted, eyes bright and intent.

"You found something," he said, not a question.

She nodded, but didn't speak, not yet.

Vamir gave a small, satisfied smile. "It's good to see the fire return," he said softly. "Polyocular thinks so too." The bird, perched on his shoulder, bobbed its head in agreement, feathers fluffed against the cold.

For a moment, Galhani almost laughed. She looked down at the book, then back at Vamir, and her eyes stung with the beginnings of tears she didn't want him to see.

She forced a smile. "I did. Thank you for the library. And for knowing I needed it, even before I did."

Vamir bowed, then reached out and squeezed her shoulder, careful and brief. "You'll tell them," he said. "When you're ready."

She nodded again, unable to speak for fear of crying. Instead, she let the book anchor her, let the memory of Lara's hand and the bite of cold soil steady her legs. She stood on the stoop a little longer, gathering herself.

———

The upstairs rooms of Vamir's bookshop were, if anything, even more peculiar than the warren below. They weren't simply private—they were insulated from the rest of the world by a deliberate eccentricity, a kind of enforced silence that resisted the usual clamor of town life. The main parlor was crowded but clean, with pale wood floors and a pair of mismatched chairs angled just so around the fire. The hearth was cold, but sunlight found its way through the stained glass above, painting slow-moving color onto the floor and making every motion seem more significant than it was.

Finnian was already there, perched on a three-legged stool beside a battered tea cart. His hands worked methodically at the guts of a pocket watch, extracting pin-sized gears and setting them in careful lines on a dish towel. The table beside him was cluttered with more clockworks in various states of disrepair, plus two plates of sweet biscuits, a wedge of cheese, and a small mountain of napkins folded with impossible neatness.

He didn't look up as Galhani and Vamir entered, but his fingers slowed, then paused, as if to acknowledge their presence without risking a misstep on the delicate cog he was holding.

"Morning," he offered, his tone kind.

Vamir poured himself into the nearest chair, as if relieved to be back in the realm of books and clocks. Polyocular settled on the top of the stained-glass window and began a low, trilling whistle, the sound so close to a mechanical tick that Galhani felt a shudder of kinship between the pet and the clockmaker.

Galhani, restless with the energy of her revelation, reached for the kettle. Her hands shook, but she didn't spill. She brewed a simple tea —just plain black, nothing fancy—because that was what Lara always did when the air in the room felt too thick for words.

Vamir wasted no time in sharing their findings. He laid out the facts with a scholar's restraint, emphasizing the pattern of creative dissonance and the role of the parasite in finding and amplifying contradiction.

Finnian listened, his eyes on his work, mouth tightening as the story took shape. At last, he set down his tweezers, wiped his hands, and looked up. "So the town's become a clock with too many hands, and no idea which time it's meant to strike."

"That's one way to see it," said Vamir.

Finnian's face took on the absent, thoughtful cast of a man weighing gears in his head. He picked up the watch, rotated it, then snapped the case shut. "You know," he said, "sometimes people bring me a watch that's perfectly good, but it doesn't keep time. They'll swear the springs are sound, the jewels intact, but when I open it up —" he gestured with the watch "—there's always one gear out of place. Usually a tiny one, the kind nobody notices because it doesn't even connect to the hands directly. But if it's crooked, the whole thing falls behind, or else it spins out of control and snaps the mainspring."

Galhani watched him, fascinated despite herself. There was something comforting in the simple clarity of a mechanism, even if the comparison stung. "You do keep saying that," she said softly. "One little piece."

Finnian looked at her with the blunt sincerity that made him both easy to trust and easy to misunderstand. "So maybe it's not about fixing every piece. Maybe you just find the first thing that went wrong, and set it straight."

Vamir nodded slowly, as if weighing the idea against a lifetime of study. "The trouble is, the first thing to break isn't always the most obvious."

Finnian shrugged. "Still, worth a look."

Galhani poured the tea into three mugs, set them down, and tried not to notice how her hand trembled as she offered one to Finnian. He took it with both hands, sipping with a grateful, almost reverent air.

The conversation lapsed into quiet. Outside, the day had advanced enough that the sounds of town life filtered up—the clang of Warren's hammer, a snatch of laughter from the bakery, the distant, hollow ring of the bell at the gate. In here, the only sound was Polyocular's even ticking and the faint chime of clock parts as Finnian sorted them into rows.

Galhani sipped her tea, then set it down, suddenly overcome by a wave of exhaustion. She looked at her hands, at the pale lines etched into her knuckles, at the ink stains that never really washed out.

She thought again of the town, and the "first broken gear." The image wormed into her brain and would not leave. She remembered how, moons ago, her own blends had begun to fail—the first in the town, though she hadn't realized it at the time. She'd blamed the weather, the water, her own inattention. But now, seeing herself reflected in Finnian's metaphor, she wondered if she had been the first gear to go crooked.

She closed her eyes, felt the hot pinprick of tears, and tried to swallow them down.

But the silence of the room was too gentle, and the words of Elspeth, the notes from the parasite text, even Finnian's earnest, unknowing wisdom—all of it piled up in her chest until it overflowed.

The first sob escaped with no warning, as much a hiccup as a cry. She clapped her hand over her mouth, but the next one came louder, wracking her whole frame and sending her mug trembling across the table. She tried to stop, but the effort only made it worse.

Finnian froze, unsure what to do. Vamir rose, circled the table, and set a warm, steady hand on her shoulder, just enough pressure to keep her from floating away.

"It's all right," he said, the voice low and soft, but not condescending.

Galhani shook her head, but the tears came faster, blurring the stained glass and the neat rows of clockwork. She pressed her face to the crook of her arm, muffling the sounds, but the grief was too old, too tired to be polite. It poured out in shudders, mixing with the scent of tea and old books, the smell of a life she'd loved and might lose.

Polyocular abandoned its perch and landed gently on the back of her chair. It didn't chirp this time, but leaned forward and brushed its head against her hair, a strange, feathery comfort that nearly made her laugh, even through the sobs.

She wept for a long while. When she was done, Finnian handed her a napkin, carefully unfolded and crisp. She blew her nose, dabbed her eyes, and tried to apologize, but the words stuck.

Finnian looked at Vamir, then at her, and said, "It's always the finest ones that break first."

This almost started her crying again, but instead, she snorted and coughed, the sound ugly but honest.

Vamir knelt, meeting her eye. "If you are the first broken gear, it only means you're also the first to know how to fix it." His hand squeezed her shoulder, gentle but unwavering.

Galhani nodded, not trusting herself to speak.

They sat in silence, together, as the town's day passed below and the world outside their window spun on, indifferent and persistent as a wound that refuses to heal.

————

Leota arrived just after midday, slipping through the front of the bookshop as if she'd been expected all along. She wore her customary black-on-black—today, a fine-woven wool over a simple dress, every thread so dark it seemed to suck the lamplight from the corners of the room. Her hair was still wet from a hurried rinse, combed back and left to dry in inky strands. The only color about her was the bruised blue of her lips, which she pressed into a sharp line as she surveyed the trio.

Galhani was not surprised that Leota found them instantly, nor that she read the emotional wreckage like a trail of spilled ink. She closed the parlor door behind her, ignoring the usual pleasantries, and walked straight to Galhani's chair.

"Looks like you've been raked over the coals," Leota said, voice pitched low for Galhani's ears alone. She placed a cool, dry hand on the gnome's shoulder, the weight somehow both comforting and impossible to ignore.

"I have," Galhani said, voice raw but steady.

Leota offered a ghost of a smile, then turned to the others. "Gentlemen," she said, "I see the scholar and the tinker have solved the world's mysteries, or at least made a noble start of it."

Vamir gave a dignified shrug, Polyocular echoing the motion with a bob of its three-eyed head. Finnian just nodded, wiping a final streak of oil from his fingers onto his apron.

Leota scanned the room, taking in the clock parts, the crowded shelves, the thin slice of sunlight painting the floorboards. Her gaze lingered on the tea tray and the untouched biscuits, then on Galhani's puffy eyes. "Did you learn anything that's not going to make me cry?" she asked.

Galhani managed a weak smile. "That depends. Are you much for metaphor?"

"I make my living on metaphor. I was trained in it by women who could turn a curse into a song and back again." She squeezed Galhani's shoulder, then pulled up a chair with a scrape of wood and bone.

"Here's the short version," said Vamir, and repeated their findings in brisk, academic tones, ending with the phrase: "The only cure is renewal of purpose."

Leota snorted. "If that's all it takes, the world would be a paradise of purpose by now." She fixed her gaze on Galhani. "What's your angle?"

Galhani picked up the battered book from the library, running her finger along the broken spine. "The angle is that the parasite doesn't kill you. It just... starves you. It waits for the host to forget what it was ever hungry for. And then, it eats what's left."

Leota considered, then nodded. "I've seen the same thing in a war-coven. Few of them last more than a decade."

A knock at the shop's glass pane startled them all. Vamir rose, stepped to the window, and peered through the colored glass. "You'll want to see this," he said, and waved them over.

From the upper story, they had a perfect view of the square and the new arrival: a wagon painted a grim, gray-brown, with none of the flourishes or pride of a craftsman's shop. A man in a drab felt cloak unloaded bolts of cheap cloth, piling them in the slush at his feet. Another, younger, unrolled a makeshift sign and nailed it crooked to a slat: "CLOAKS 4 SALE. NO QUESTIONS."

A line had already formed—five townsfolk, two travelers, and, awkwardly, one of the local children, whose mother yanked him back by the collar before he could paw at the goods.

Leota's mouth twisted. "What a disgrace."

"That's not even the best part," Vamir said, gesturing with his chin.

Jen was approaching the wagon, a study in slow, deliberate menace. She wore her constable's coat, sleeves rolled to the elbow, and her long, gray-streaked hair was tied in a tail that swung like a warning behind her. Her right hand hovered near the thick metal bracelet at her wrist, and every step made it clear she was not here to shop.

The two men at the wagon watched her come, one nervously shuffling his feet, the other standing rigid behind his display.

"Place your bets," said Leota, sotto voce. "Does she go for words or wrists?"

Galhani watched, fascinated, as Jen stopped directly in front of the wagon and leaned in close, her body language coiled as a spring. The taller of the two men started to speak, but Jen silenced him with a finger raised to his lips.

She stood like that for a long moment, then spoke in a low, measured tone that carried just enough for Galhani to catch through the window: "Town's peace keeps you alive. The minute you forget that, you'll wish you were dead."

The man flinched, but tried to keep a smile fixed in place. Jen withdrew her finger, then flicked the bracelet on her wrist with a sharp snap. The metal band shimmered, almost imperceptibly, the first motion of Hellsting's hidden blade. Galhani could almost feel the magic from this far away—a coldness in the air, a taste of iron on the tongue.

The constable lingered another second, then turned on her heel and strode away, leaving the wagon men visibly shaken, their hands trembling as they fussed over their wares.

Leota watched, impassive. "She could have ended it, if she'd wanted," she said.

"She can't," said Galhani, surprised by the heat in her own voice. "Not unless they break the rule. If she starts violence, the whole spell goes with it."

Leota looked at her, something like respect flickering in her eyes. "You knew that," she said, and Galhani realized she did.

"Jen's not just here for the rules," Vamir added, softly. "She's the keystone. The whole town's creed sits on her, whether she likes it or not."

They all stood at the window, watching as Jen crossed the square, her shoulders stiff but her stride unbroken. For a second, Galhani thought she saw the constable glance up, directly at their window, but the moment was gone before she could wave.

"She still believes in us," Galhani whispered, the words escaping before she knew she'd said them.

Leota heard, and smiled. "She's a fool, then. But that's what keeps the heart of a place beating."

For a long minute, none of them spoke.

Then Leota patted Galhani's back with more force than necessary, nearly knocking the wind from her lungs. "Well?" she said. "You going to sit up here and mope, or are you going to help the town remember what it's here for?"

Galhani looked at her friends—at the blue-stained light on Vamir's hands, at Finnian's calm determination, at Leota's sharp grin. She remembered Lara's thumb pressing into her palm, and the smell of new earth, and the unbroken, ridiculous hope that had brought them here in the first place.

She straightened, wiped the last of the tears from her cheeks, and squared her shoulders. "I'll try," she said. "But only if you're with me."

"Always," said Leota, as if it were the easiest thing in the world.

From outside, the low, angry hum of the wagon merchants drifted in, mixing with the sharper, brighter sounds of children on the green, and the slow, deliberate tick of Polyocular on the glass. The world outside had not changed, but for the first time in days, Galhani believed that maybe she could.

She stayed at the window, watching the life of the square. For now, that would be enough.

twelve

. . .

AFTERNOONS *at the Broken Claw were never supposed to be this crowded,* Galhani thought. She'd been here for each stage of the transformation: from the rare, cozy clatter of a baker's dozen regulars, to the slow, cancerous growth of the merchant crowd, to the current stampede that filled every bench and left the window ledges claimed by travelers who wouldn't have looked twice at this town a moon ago. Even the back step was crowded with children, ringed around the delivery hatch like wolves waiting for something to fall off the cart. There was no peace for anyone today, not even for a gnome who preferred her drama watered down and served at a safe distance.

Galhani sat at a corner table, her feet braced against the wobble in the floor, and tried to will herself invisible. She'd chosen the spot because it let her see both the bar and the main entrance, but now it was like sitting inside a bell, every crash and cuss echoing directly into her skull. The only consolation was that nobody was paying her any special attention; not when Sam was working the bar with murder in her eyes, not when the regulars were arming for the latest round in their ever-escalating grievance war.

Cole made his entrance with a slam, the door bouncing on its hinges. He hoisted his basket of produce like a trophy, but Galhani caught the way his arms trembled. He cut through the crowd, his elbows and voice clearing a path, until he reached the bar. He set the basket down with a showy thud, then raised his hands as if to summon silence.

It took a while for the room to notice him, but eventually the wave of noise shushed into a lopsided hush. Sam cocked her head, one hand still upended inside a mug.

Cole didn't bother with a greeting. "Who wants to see what the earth has given us this sennight?" He yanked a carrot from the pile and held it up, its tip leaking a slow, viscous ooze onto the counter. The color, instead of the usual vivid orange, was mottled and pale, like a root grown in darkness. He snapped it in half. Instead of the crisp crack everyone expected, the carrot bent, then split with a wet, hollow sound. The pieces fell to the bar and rolled, smearing themselves with shame.

He grinned, but the grin was a wound. "Best season I've had in years, they told me." He threw the halves into the basket, then fished out a tomato. It looked plump and perfect until he squeezed, and a thin jet of brine shot into the air, spattering the sleeve of the nearest traveler. "My compliments to the seed seller," Cole intoned, deadpan. "Anyone for a salad?"

A few people laughed. Most just stared, morbidly transfixed.

Sam flicked a rag over the tomato juice and said, "You could always pickle them, Cole. Might improve the taste."

Cole's laugh was too loud, too sharp. "That's what I tried! Cured in vinegar, salt, sugar, the whole recipe. After a day, the pickles dissolved. Nothing left but a jar of sad soup." He looked around, daring anyone to contradict him.

No one did. The crowd shuffled, then started to buzz again, everyone wanting to top the story. In the noise, Galhani lost track of the next few complaints—someone's bread went blue overnight, someone else's honey fermented into vinegar, another claimed her new cloth had lost its color and come out of the dye like unbleached linen. It was the same litany as every day, but louder, more desperate.

The door banged again. Lucy entered, carrying a burlap-wrapped bundle with both hands. She elbowed her way to the bar, planted the sack down, and untied the twine with fingers that shook.

"Sam," Lucy called, her voice ringing off the beams. "Can I show you something?" Sam didn't stop cleaning, but she looked up. "It's my work." She reached into the sack and pulled out a pottery vase—at least, it had started as a vase. The neck and rim had shattered in the kiln, and the base was riddled with fine, silvery cracks. She set it down gingerly, then tapped the side with a fingernail. Instead of the usual music of fired clay, the sound was flat, like tapping a shell made of ash.

"It's all like this now," Lucy said. "The color slips, the glaze peels. Sometimes the pieces just crumble in my hands. This one—" she brandished a smaller cup, its base already flaking— "this one turned to powder in the box. I thought it was the clay, but I got a new shipment from the north. Same thing. Dead in the kiln."

She looked at Sam, then at the rest of the bar, as if pleading with the world to give her back her skill. "What am I supposed to do? I can't sell this. I can't even break it apart to reuse the shards. It's all just —" She let the cup fall. It hit the floor and turned to dust, gray and lifeless.

Warren, who'd been brooding in the farthest corner, seized the moment. He held up a length of steel that should have been a sword blade but had pitted and dulled, its edge rippled like the margin of a dead leaf.

"Even the metal's gone bad," he grumbled. "You want to see something really sad?" He raised the blade, and it bent under its own weight, nearly folding in half before he caught it with his other hand. "I tried to fix it, but the fire just made it worse."

A voice piped up from the rear, thin and reedy: "My son's new shoes lasted two days. The soles peeled off, and the stitching unraveled."

Prudence, who'd managed to carve out a small, silent kingdom near the hearth, raised her hand, hesitant. "My dye's gone gray. Not just pale—gray. Every color I mix comes out the same." She looked down, as if ashamed to admit it.

The dam broke. Suddenly everyone had a story, a specimen, a

proof. The air thickened with the sense of a shared doom, an invisible current that pulled everyone along. Even the travelers joined in—one man claimed his coin purse had dissolved in the rain, another that his lucky amulet lost its luster the moment he crossed into town limits.

In the eye of the storm, Sam wiped the same glass, over and over, her knuckles white. Her voice was a thin wire, stretched to its breaking point. "Maybe it's just a bad moon. Or maybe you're all getting soft."

This got a few laughs, but nobody believed it. The mood was shifting, from self-pity to a kind of communal anger. The room was a powder keg; all it needed was a spark.

Galhani watched, every sense alert. She could feel the hunger in the room, the need for someone to blame or for some miracle to turn it all around. She wondered, not for the first time, if this was how a parasite did its work—not by draining a body all at once, but by hollowing out every hope and then waiting for the emptiness to fill itself with rage.

The din grew and grew, until it was no longer a conversation but a contest, each person trying to outdo the next in misery. The new shopkeepers—those who'd only arrived in the past few sennights—kept their heads down, unwilling or unable to join in. Galhani recalled that their wares, at least, looked as good as ever. The tins behind the bar still shone, the piles of pressed tea cakes were perfectly uniform, and the glass jars in the window gleamed.

She realized with a shock that even her own blends, the ones she'd considered failures, were better than this. At least they still had shape and weight, even if the flavor was gone.

There was a moment, a heartbeat of stillness, when everyone seemed to realize the same thing at once. The argument died, and the silence was so sudden that Galhani heard her own breath, shallow and fast.

Sam set the glass down, hard. The sound was sharp enough to make half the bar flinch.

"We're not dying," Sam said, voice low but carrying. "Not all at once. Not unless you let it."

Cole, never one to give up a good line, smirked. "So we go down fighting, then?"

Sam met his gaze. "Better than rolling over."

The regulars laughed, some genuine, most forced. But the energy had shifted. There was no miracle, no revelation, but in the gloom, a single, stubborn thread of will had been pulled taut.

Galhani watched the bar, the faces lined up like masks in a play. She saw Warren's grim smile, Lucy's set jaw, Prudence's hands clutched tight in her lap. She felt the weight of all their failures, and the weight was oddly familiar. It was the same ache that had carried her through the worst winters, through the first season in the shop, through the long, dark years before she'd met Lara.

She felt it now, sharper than ever, and knew—without knowing how—that this was the thing the parasite could never really understand. The hunger for hope, even when there was none.

She found herself standing, not sure when she'd risen. The crowd didn't notice, but Sam did. Their eyes met across the bar, and Sam's look was flat, unreadable. But she gave a tiny nod, the sort you'd miss if you weren't desperate for it.

Galhani sat, but the restlessness remained. She stared at her cup, at the half-dissolved dregs of what used to be a favorite blend. She felt the threads of the town—frayed, tangled, but still woven together. And for the first time in sennights, she believed that maybe, just maybe, it would hold.

Behind the bar, Sam poured herself a drink, hand steady now. She looked up at the room, at the regulars, at the strangers, and raised her glass.

"To the stubborn," she said.

The room answered with a ragged, tired cheer.

But the buzz didn't last. The cheers died to a murmur, then to an uneasy silence as everyone reached the bottom of their glass and remembered that stubbornness was not, on its own, a strategy.

The arguments started up again, but softer this time. Cole and Warren fell into a low-voiced debate about whether bad metal could poison a field. Lucy and Prudence squabbled in urgent, staccato whispers about the relative merits of fabric versus glaze. The travelers nursed their drinks, the regulars rehashed their complaints, and Sam went back to her methodical polishing, her hands moving as if they could restore order one glass at a time.

Galhani found herself drifting, half-listening to the room and half-remembering the words from Vamir's book. The parasite of dissonance, the anti-gift. It all sounded dramatic, but there was a truth to it that gnawed at the back of her mind, as if her own bones recognized the threat before her head could reason it out. She watched the bar, watched Sam's white-knuckle grip and the haunted way she looked at the bottles. She wondered if Sam ever dreamed about the old days, or if the present was too loud to let any other time through.

Then something happened.

It was not a crash, or a fight, or even a new voice. It was just Sam, in mid-wipe, freezing with her cloth inside a glass. Her whole body stiffened; her eyes flicked up and to the left, as if tracking a bird across the rafters. The room didn't notice at first, but Galhani saw it, the stillness in a sea of motion. She waited, holding her breath.

Above the front door hung a small, round, battered sign. Most people never looked twice at it. Galhani had never asked about it, but she'd seen Sam glance up at the clocklike sign whenever she was about to refuse a drink, or cut someone off, or send a regular home for their own good. Now the arrow was glowing, a faint, trembly light that was almost lost in the lantern-glow.

Sam's lips moved, but no sound came out. She set down the glass, wiped her hands on her apron, and looked straight at Galhani. Her voice, when it came, was small and scraping, but it carried to every ear.

"It's hollow," she said.

The word hung, unnatural. Sam frowned, then tried again, louder. "It's hollow. The pub says hollow."

Nobody laughed, not even Cole. Warren grunted. Lucy pressed both hands to her face, as if holding it together by will.

Galhani felt her heart skip, then restart on a new beat. "What does it mean?" she asked.

Sam shrugged, helpless. "It means—I think it means—there's nothing inside. Not just the food, or the crafts, but the—" She waved a hand, groping for the word. "—the magic, the thing that made any of it matter."

For a long time, no one spoke. Then a voice, thin and incredulous: "Is that what's killing us?"

Sam nodded. "It's not just draining us. It's replacing us. With something empty. With nothing."

Someone in the crowd snorted. "Who'd want that?"

Sam bared her teeth. "Some things don't want. Some things just eat."

The room was dead still.

It was Lucy who spoke next, her tone low and bitter. "Is it Silas? Or the new shops?" She glanced at the travelers, then back at Sam. "Are we just being replaced?"

Sam's gaze went distant, as if she was listening to something through a long tunnel. "Maybe," she said. "Maybe it's like Vamir said. A parasite. Or maybe just the world's way of saying it's tired of all of us."

Galhani sat back, the air suddenly cold. She remembered how she'd felt, for sennights, like her own hands were betraying her. She remembered every failed blend, every cup that tasted like nothing. She realized, with a pang so sharp it was almost joy, that she'd been right to be afraid. The problem wasn't her. It wasn't even the town. It was something bigger, something hungry and impersonal.

That should have been terrifying, but instead, she felt a relief so pure she wanted to laugh. She wasn't broken. The world was.

She saw the same realization flicker across other faces—the settling of a debt, the quiet thrill of knowing it wasn't just your fault. Even Cole, normally so quick to speak, looked down at his ruined basket with a strange, peaceful acceptance.

Sam wiped the bar, then poured herself another drink. Her hand didn't shake this time.

"It's not over," she said, not to anyone in particular. "We're still here. And if the hollow wants to take us, it's going to have to work for it."

The room didn't cheer, but it breathed. For the first time in what felt like forever, nobody had anything to prove. They just listened, and waited for the next word.

Galhani closed her eyes, just for a second, and let herself be part of the silence.

————

The cold met them at the door. It was sharp and immediate, a wet slap on the neck after the bar's feverish heat. Galhani breathed it in, felt it scrape clean the film of noise from her ears and tongue. The four of them fell into step without discussion: Sam, her pace heavy and bulldozing; Vamir, gliding with his hands clasped behind his back; Leota, silent, watching the street with eyes that didn't miss a thing; and Galhani herself, tucking her chin into her collar and letting the others set the path.

The square was only half as busy as the bar, but every shop front was alive. Where last sennight there'd been just the usual set—grocery, potter, smith, tailor—now there was a ragged line of newcomers: a cart selling hair tonics and scalp bracers; a glassed-in booth for "Traveling Taxes, Settled Instantly"; a crumbling stall stacked with nothing but used candle ends; and, most perplexing, a sandwich board advertising "Left-Handed Utensils, Right Price!" with a cartoon fork smirking out at the world.

Vamir wrinkled his nose. "A town built for exiles," he muttered, mostly to himself.

Leota pointed at the shop signs, her gesture small and efficient. "Notice anything?"

Galhani looked, then looked again. The old shops were as she remembered—each sign hand-carved, painted in careful, sometimes clashing colors, the letters imperfect but alive. The new ones were drab, stamped in tar or chalk, the kind of signs that would fade before the sennight was out. The windows on the old shops glowed with lamp and firelight; the new ones were already gathering dust, their glass clouded or smeared.

"Feels like they're already empty," Galhani said, more to herself than the group.

"Exactly," Leota replied. "The town isn't taking to them. It lets them in, but it doesn't let them settle."

They passed the left-handed utensils shop just as the owner emerged, scrawny and red-faced, a bundle of what looked like bent soup spoons cradled under one arm. He stopped halfway through the door, squinting up at the eaves, then swore and ducked back inside. A moment later, he reappeared on the roof, a makeshift ladder creaking under his weight. He hammered at a loose shingle, cursing every few blows.

Sam didn't slow down, but her voice was soft. "Doesn't even charge them rent. The town just... gives them space. Like it wants to see what they'll do."

They watched as the roof man slipped, caught himself, and then shouted down, "Damned if I'm not going to fix it—you realize they don't even charge rent for these spaces?" His voice was bright, a little desperate, the pitch of someone still convincing himself it was all a bargain.

The four exchanged looks, a quick round of wordless math. It wasn't just that the town had lost its magic, or its taste for itself—it had lost its boundaries, too. Whatever was eating at them, it had loosened the rules just enough to let in the hollow things, but not enough to let them last.

Leota summed it up: "It's trying to spit them out, but the parasite's too strong. So it makes life uncomfortable instead."

Sam grunted approval. "Ought to make it more uncomfortable."

They turned onto the narrow walk that led to Galhani's shop. The world here felt a little softer, the light more forgiving. Maybe it was the memory of the place, or maybe just that it still smelled like herbs and sweet dust even from the street.

Nobody said a word until they reached the door. Galhani unlocked it, stepped inside, and turned to watch as the other three filed in behind her. They took their usual seats—Sam by the stove, Leota at the counter, Vamir near the window—and waited for Galhani to light the lamps.

She did, one by one, until the shop glowed in little pools of amber. The glass jars caught the light and fractured it, scattering odd shapes across the walls and floor. Galhani poured water into the kettle, then leaned back against the counter, feeling the weight of the day slip just enough to let her stand straight.

"We're all here," she said.

Leota gave a tight smile. "Let's fix what's broken."

Outside, the wind rattled the signboards. Inside, a plan was waiting to be made.

———

The lamps gave a richer light than Galhani expected, pooling on the workbench and warming the jars until even the empty ones looked half full. The air was thick with last year's mint and a trace of lavender from the drawer she never remembered to close. It was, for a few minutes, almost like the old days.

They gathered at the workbench—Sam, still vibrating with the effort of not breaking things; Vamir, spreading his notes with the clinical detachment of a surgeon laying out tools; Leota, a silhouette in the lamplight, arms crossed and eyes narrowed.

Galhani poured hot water into a round of mismatched mugs, one for each of them, and waited for the first voice to claim the room.

Leota claimed it. "We're up against something old," she said, flat and precise. "Vamir found references to it in the Westcroft volume, and I've seen echoes of the same parasite in a war-coven, once." She looked at Galhani, then Sam. "It's not a curse, or a single spell. It's a thing that feeds on contradiction and grows in places where the center breaks. The more you try to brute-force it, the more it multiplies."

Vamir cleared his throat, shuffling his papers. "It's called the anti-gift, in some texts. Or the hollowing. It doesn't just kill the magic of a place. It installs a new order—a fake community, built on repetition and emptiness, one that keeps going long after the spirit is gone." He set a battered book on the bench. "If you want to break it, you have to give the center something to hold."

Sam sipped her mug, made a face, and set it down. "The vision today—it wasn't just a word. I saw the tea," she said, looking at Galhani, "but not yours. It was Silas's stuff. Stacked, packed, all the same. I tasted it, and it was like drinking memory, but not a good memory—a memory that just reminded you what you'd lost." She shrugged, then looked at the floor. "When I woke up, I could feel it. Like a chill behind the eyes."

Vamir nodded. "That's the parasite. It wants to get you remembering, but not creating. That's the only thing that really starves it out—newness. Not just making what was, but making what could be."

Galhani listened, and let the words sort themselves. She thought of every blend she'd failed, every time she'd tried to brew the old recipe and found only dust. It wasn't enough to try harder; she'd have to try something else.

She looked at the three of them—Sam, who'd rather fight than talk; Vamir, who'd rather explain than fight; Leota, who'd seen all of this before and still had the scars. She wondered, not for the first time, why any of them had ever believed in North Pointe Common Towne, or in the brittle, dogged hope that a handful of misfits could make a town last.

Then she knew.

She said it out loud, and her voice was stronger than she expected. "So we make something new. Not just survive, not just patch up the old, but actually build something none of us have tried before."

Leota's mouth quirked. "That's the idea. Enough novelty, all at once, and the parasite loses its grip."

"Will the town even let us?" Sam asked.

Vamir shrugged. "Only one way to find out."

Galhani closed her hand around the mug, feeling the heat settle in her palm. She'd been empty for sennights, maybe longer, but now the emptiness felt like a space to fill, not a defeat.

"We'll need everyone," she said. "Even the ones who've already given up."

Sam gave a rare, real smile. "I'll drag them here by the ear if I have to."

Leota relaxed her arms, uncrossing them for the first time all night. "Good. Because this isn't a job for four."

The kettle hissed, a small, insistent sound. Galhani refilled the mugs, and the new brew caught the light—amber, bright, not the ghost brown of the last batch. She poured for each of them, her hands steady, and this time nobody complained about the taste.

Outside, the town creaked and shifted, the signboards rattling in the dark. But inside, the four of them sat shoulder to shoulder, a new plan forming in the heat and the hope and the shared stubbornness.

When they left, it would be as a team, not as a set of losses. And maybe, if they were lucky, the town would remember how to fight back, too.

thirteen

. . .

GALHANI WOKE with a hard knot at the base of her neck and the sour taste of dread crawling up the back of her tongue. She'd slept in her clothes again, arms wrapped around her pillow as if it could shield her from the day ahead. For a moment, she considered pretending to be sick—staying in bed while the world outside made decisions for itself. But she could already hear the commotion on the street, and she knew the time for hiding was done.

She shambled to the window and pressed her forehead against the cold glass, peering down at the square. At the far end, not twenty steps from the gate, Silas's wagon was already open for business. The sides of the cart folded outward, revealing racks of tin canisters, all identical, their labels stamped with a logo so dull it hurt the eye to look at it. Silas himself stood behind a makeshift counter, slicing the paper seals on a new shipment, his hands moving with the impassive regularity of a wind-up doll.

She spotted the others assembling below, and felt a complicated pulse of pride, fear, and what might have been envy. Jen arrived first, moving at a pace that was deliberate but not slow, her boots biting the frozen mud and leaving perfect prints. Cole followed, a canvas sack slung over his shoulder, expression set somewhere between consternation and defeat. Lucy was last, her coat dusted with clay and her lips already compressed into a line that boded ill for anyone on the receiving end.

And then there was Sam. She moved like an argument waiting for a fight, every step a dare to the world to try her. The four of them converged just outside the wagon's shadow, and for a moment, they looked like nothing so much as a jury preparing to hand down sentence.

Galhani tried to count how many times she'd watched a drama like this unfold from her window. Too many, and never enough.

The group didn't wait for introductions. Sam took point, planting herself in the dead center of the wagon's path and fixing Silas with a look that would have sent lesser men running.

"Morning, Silas," she said, voice low but carrying. "You've drawn quite the crowd this sennight."

Silas didn't look up at first. He finished slicing the seals, stacked the tins, then finally regarded them with an expression just polite enough to be an insult. "I provide a needed service," he said. "People want variety. They want options. The trade road's open to all, or so I was told when I arrived."

Jen's hand hovered near her sword bracelet, but she kept it in check. "Nobody's saying you can't sell. Just seems like you're selling more than just tea."

Silas cocked his head, genuinely puzzled. "What else am I selling, then?"

Sam's mouth twitched. "You know what we mean. Since you set up shop, things have gone strange. Shops losing their knack. Recipes turning to ash. You can't tell me you haven't noticed."

Silas shrugged. "Seems like you all have a case of bad luck. Maybe it's the weather. Maybe it's just the way of things."

Lucy exploded before anyone could stop her. "You call this luck?" She yanked a pottery mug from her satchel and slammed it onto the counter. The glaze was patchy, the blue faded to the color of old bruises. "This was perfect yesterday. I made it myself, fired it with my own hands. Today it's trash. I can't sell trash."

Silas inspected the mug with a clinical eye, turning it this way and that. "Looks fine to me," he said. "People don't need perfect. They need affordable."

Lucy turned red, her hands curling into claws. "You don't get to decide what people need!"

Cole stepped in, as he always did, voice measured and even. "Let's not fight," he said. "Silas, you know as well as we do that this town's got rules. Not written down, maybe, but understood. We make what we're proud of, and we share it. We don't undercut. We don't sabotage. And we don't poach regulars with cheap tricks."

Silas's face went perfectly blank. "I'm not poaching anyone. They come to me because I sell what they want. If they don't like your goods, maybe the problem's not with me."

Sam leaned in, her hand drifting closer to her sword hilt. "You're draining us. The magic. The town. Whatever you want to call it. You're pulling it out of the air and pouring it into these—" She gestured at the rows of tins, "—these little dead boxes."

Silas finally let his irritation show. "You're all mad. This is business. You think anyone in the next town over cares about your 'magic'?" He made air quotes with both hands. "They care about price, and convenience, and whether the tea actually tastes like tea."

Lucy, still trembling, barked a humorless laugh. "If that's what they want, why are they even here?"

Silas's reply was a cold, hard smile. "Because they can't get it anywhere else."

Jen, who had been silent until now, raised both hands and stepped between Sam and Silas. "We're not going to solve this by shouting," she said, voice pitched low and dangerous. "You want to do business, you do it outside the gate."

Silas folded his arms. "Not what I was told. You said as long as I didn't cause trouble, I could set up wherever I wanted."

"Things change," Sam spat.

Jen rounded on her, and for a second, Galhani thought she'd have to separate them. "The rules are the rules, Sam," Jen snapped. "If we start making exceptions, we're no better than any other town on the road."

Sam glared, but let her hand fall away from her weapon.

Silas watched the whole thing with the air of a man who'd already won. "You can't stop me," he said, voice flat. "And I'm not moving. If you want me gone, you'll have to do better than threats."

Cole tried again. "We're not threatening you, Silas. We're asking. Please. This isn't about you, it's about the way things have always been."

Silas looked him up and down, then shook his head. "Tradition's just a cage. Sooner or later, everyone wants out."

There was a silence, thick and brittle.

Jen finally nodded, as if coming to a decision. "You've made your point," she said. "We'll be watching. Don't give us a reason to make this official."

Silas's smile returned, thin and bloodless. "You do what you have to. I'll do the same."

Sam spat on the ground, then turned on her heel and stormed away. Lucy followed, still muttering under her breath. Cole lingered, gave Silas a long, searching look, then trudged after the others. Jen stayed a moment longer, her eyes never leaving Silas's face.

When she finally left, Silas exhaled, wiped his hands on his apron, and began to arrange the tins in neat, geometric rows.

From her window, Galhani watched it all, heart pounding. She'd seen fights before, but never one where the winner felt so much like the loser.

She closed the curtain, and the world shrank to the size of her small, cluttered room. For the first time since arriving in North Pointe Common Towne, she wondered if the town could actually die.

She didn't like the answer her gut gave her.

———

She went downstairs, feet cold on the bare boards, and stared at her shop. The shelves looked more pathetic than ever, rows of jars half-filled, labels curling at the corners. She ran her finger along the glass, leaving a streak in the dust.

If she were honest, she'd stopped trying. Stopped hoping. Stopped even pretending to care about the future of her little shop. All her energy had gone into resenting the world for making her a loser, then resenting herself for not being strong enough to fight back.

Well. Now she had to.

She grabbed the first jar in reach, unscrewed the lid, and took a deep breath of the contents. Nothing. Not even the faintest trace of mint, or anise, or the rarefied herbs she'd once risked everything to import. She tried another, then another, growing more desperate with each failure.

At last, she found a tin at the back, something she'd blended years ago for a customer who'd moved away. She sniffed, expecting nothing —and was stunned by a bright, sharp note of green, a memory of early spring and hope. It made her dizzy, the way the best flavors always had.

She laughed, a rough, amazed sound.

Maybe it wasn't gone. Not all of it.

She dumped the blend into her mortar, crushed it fine, and set water to boil. She worked without thinking, hands moving the way they always had. By the time the kettle screamed, her shoulders had relaxed and her hands were steady.

She poured, steeped, and waited. The cup was small, a gnome-sized thimble of pale gold. She lifted it, sipped, and felt the flavor bloom across her tongue, alive and a little dangerous.

She smiled.

For the first time in sennights, she believed she could do it. Not alone, but with the others. With Sam, and Lucy, and even Jen, who lived and died by the rules.

She finished the cup, savoring the last, stubborn hint of sweetness.

She spent the next candlemark of morning still in her nightshirt, curled up on the window ledge with a blanket around her shoulders and her toes tucked under a basket of drying peppermint. The glass fogged at every exhale. Outside, the market square was in full swing, but inside her shop the silence was so complete that it made her own heart sound amplified, like the ticking of a clock left in a bare room.

The tea shop was supposed to be a sanctuary—she'd designed every shelf, every painted nook and jar, to offer some secret thrill to anyone who entered. But today, as she looked around at the dusty rows of tins and the brittle bouquets of old herbs, she realized how little she'd done in the last moon except try not to fall apart. The air, once scented with cinnamon and wild mint, now tasted only of dust and the sharp metallic note of regret.

She pushed herself up on her elbows, careful not to tip the pot of basil that had gone leggy and pale, and leaned closer to the glass. The others were still out there—Sam, Jen, Cole, and Lucy—clustered near the wagon like birds at a feeder, pecking and darting and every so often bursting into a flutter of movement. Even from here, she could see the tension in Sam's posture, the way she always squared her shoulders before speaking. She could see Cole's hands, palms up and out, always trying to settle the others. Lucy gestured in great, sweeping arcs, as if she could will her argument into being with the force of her arms alone.

Galhani rubbed the heel of her palm against her chest. The ache there wasn't hunger, not exactly, but something more akin to thirst—a desperate, dry need to be in the world again. To have a part in things, even if it meant being angry or afraid.

She watched as Sam said something, chin jutting, then as Lucy took a step forward and planted herself beside her. There was a brief exchange, the kind where everyone spoke at once, and then Jen stepped in with both hands raised, and the group stilled, their attention tightening like a knot. For a moment, they all turned toward the wagon's owner, and the energy shifted—less confrontation, more calculation.

She pressed her forehead to the cool glass and tried to imagine what it would be like to stand down there, to face the others and admit how much she'd missed them. Her hands balled into fists so small and tight she barely noticed the nails digging into her skin.

A customer wandered by the shop's front door, glanced in, and kept walking. Galhani couldn't blame them. There were better places to buy tea now, she supposed, and certainly more cheerful ones. She'd spent so long walling herself off from the town—every disappointment another stone in the barricade—that she'd forgotten how to invite people back in. Maybe she'd even wanted it this way, she thought, with a bitter flicker of self-contempt. Maybe it was easier to nurse her failures in private than to risk adding public shame to the pile.

The memory of the taste from earlier, the bright jolt of possibility in that single cup, made her shoulders tense. If it wasn't gone—if it was just hiding—then what the hell was she doing, sitting up here like a ghost?

A sound outside brought her back. Across the square, Leota was walking toward the group, black dress slicing through the colors of the market like an ink stain on parchment. She moved with her usual precision, the lines of her body so controlled they almost looked artificial. But today, there was something different—a hesitation, maybe, or a carefulness, as if she was navigating a space that might break underfoot.

Galhani watched as Leota joined the others, her arrival instantly recalibrating the group. Jen stepped back, deferential; Cole gave a brief, nervous bow; Lucy's hands stilled mid-gesture. Even Sam, who never took orders from anyone, let her arms fall to her sides.

She couldn't hear their words, but she could read the rhythm of the conversation in their posture, the way the tension first thickened, then slowly began to soften. Leota did most of the talking, her hands unmoving except for a single, repeated tap on her own forearm. The others listened, faces grave and unsure, and when she finished, even Sam had nothing to add.

It struck Galhani then—not in the mind, but in the gut, as physical and inescapable as a punch—that she'd let her grief turn her into a bystander. While the town fought for its life, she'd stayed inside, tending to a failure that was less about tea and more about her own cowardice.

For a few seconds, she just breathed, letting the realization hurt her. She let it fill her head with heat and shame until it boiled over, and then she stood, grabbing the nearest jar and clutching it to her chest like a talisman.

She looked around the shop, taking in the silent shelves and the abandoned stacks of order slips she'd never bothered to fill. She looked at the dust on the countertop, the cobweb in the far corner, the way the sign outside her door hung crooked, one end weighted with a little sack of dried lavender that now smelled of nothing.

All the things she'd built, left to rot because she was too afraid to lose them for real.

She unlatched the window, letting in a rush of air cold enough to make her eyes water. The voices from outside came clearer, not words but the sound of people arguing, people alive.

She set the jar on the sill, straightened the sign with both hands, and for the first time in sennights, let herself be seen.

Across the square, Leota was looking right at her.

Galhani felt the urge to duck, to hide behind the herbs and pretend she hadn't noticed. Instead, she raised her hand and waved.

Leota inclined her head in reply, then turned back to the others, voice rising just enough for Galhani to catch the shape of her words: "She's still here. She just needs time."

The knot in Galhani's chest loosened. Maybe it was true. Maybe she just needed time. Or maybe, she thought, she needed to stop waiting and make herself useful.

Her hands trembled, but she didn't let go of the jar. Instead, she carried it down the stairs, each step a little less tentative than the last. She set the kettle on the fire, swept the dust from the countertop, and waited for the water to boil.

It was a small thing, but it was something.

As she poured the first cup, she imagined the taste again: sharp, hopeful, and alive. She could almost hear the others in the market, their voices raised, their arguments loud and stubborn and filled with love.

And this time, when the wind rattled the window, she let it in.

———

The first thing Galhani heard, as she opened her shop's door, was the nervous, jittering tap of Leota's heel on the packed earth. She'd always liked that about the witch: even when the world was ending, Leota's body gave her away. The woman stood next to Silas's wagon with arms folded, dress as black as the rumor of midnight, and surveyed the assembled crowd like a mathematician calculating the shortest path to disaster.

Silas was there, of course, and behind him the towers of his product, every tin stamped with that impossible-to-forget logo. The man wore the same blandly pleasant expression as before, but Galhani noticed a twitch at the corner of his mouth—a hairline fracture in the mask. The others clustered nearby: Jen with her wrists tensed and her badge half-visible, Cole with hands at his hips and a growing flush in his cheeks, Lucy hunched over a crate, as if the whole thing might collapse if she stood too straight.

Vamir hovered at the edge, pale as a cloud, his familiar perched on his shoulder, eyes blinking in staggered synchrony. At the edge of the commotion, Finnian leaned against a post, cleaning his nails with a gear pick and watching everything with the careful detachment of a man who's seen far too many breakdowns.

Leota started in a voice so soft that Galhani had to strain to catch the words. "You believe this is just commerce," she said to Silas, "but the effect is deeper. The more you push these—" she gestured at the canisters, "—the more the soul of the place erodes."

Silas affected a sigh, the kind that said he'd endured this lecture many times before. "With all respect, madam, nobody here is forced to buy. If my tea is so dreadful, why do I have a line every morning?"

Lucy snorted, "Because it's all that's left! You poison the well, then sell bottles of water to the thirsty." Her voice caught, cracked, and she turned away before anyone could see her face.

Jen moved to cut the tension. "Nobody's here to fight, Silas. We just need you to see the bigger picture."

He looked at her with a smile, wide and toothless. "And what picture is that?"

Leota's reply was immediate: "A parasite is at work, and it's feeding off the sameness. The lack of care. The lack of risk. The less you put in, the more it takes out."

The crowd murmured at this—many of the regulars, and a few of the new faces, drifting in closer. Galhani realized the entire market was watching, everyone at a standstill.

Silas spread his hands, the gesture open, generous. "Let's pretend that's true. What exactly do you expect me to do? Sell less? Sell worse?"

"No," Jen said, voice clipped. "Just stop selling here. Go a day's ride either way, do your business in the places that can absorb it. Let this town have a chance to recover."

Silas looked at Jen with an odd, almost affectionate tilt of his head. "I have mouths to feed, too. I'm not the enemy here." He glanced at the crowd for support, and a few nodded, but most looked away.

At that moment, Galhani felt something in her chest break loose—a bubble, rising so fast it made her dizzy. She left the threshold of her shop and crossed the square, ignoring the stares as she closed the distance between herself and Silas.

"It's not tea," she said, breathless. "It's not even about the taste."

Silas looked down, startled. "What?"

"It's not about what you sell," she said, louder now. "It's about what the tea is supposed to do. People don't drink it just to drink. They want hope, or comfort, or a chance to start over. It's supposed to mean something. And all you're selling is—" She struggled for the word, her hands fluttering at her sides, "—is air, dressed up like the real thing."

A silence fell over the market. Galhani could feel every heartbeat in her fingertips.

She pushed on: "It's not the tea. It's what the tea represents. Just like it's not the coats Prudence makes, it's the warmth and the dignity they give you. It's not Lucy's pots, it's the meals people share, or the way a child keeps a pebble in one for luck. You can't mass-produce that. And you're not even trying."

Silas's expression flickered, something like uncertainty creeping into the lines around his mouth. "If that's true, why do people still buy it?"

Galhani shook her head. "Because it's all they have left. You took away the real thing, so now the substitute is the only thing left standing."

A sharp, nervous laugh erupted from the edge of the crowd. Finnian, who had drifted closer, stepped forward and held up a brass contraption, small enough to fit in the palm of his hand. "Would you like a demonstration?" he asked, his voice mild.

The crowd leaned in, uncertain but curious. Finnian turned to Lucy. "Do you have one of your old mugs? The ones from before the parasite?"

Lucy, caught off guard, fished in her satchel and handed over a battered cup, glazed blue and still bright under the grime.

Finnian set his device on top of the cup. At first, nothing happened. Then, the gears inside whirred to life, spinning faster and faster until the crystal at the center lit up with a clear, strong blue. The device emitted a high, clean note, like a bell struck in an empty church.

Next, Finnian took one of Silas's tins from the wagon—with a quick, sheepish glance for permission—and set the device atop it. The gears spun once—then stopped. The crystal went dark. The device fell silent, as dead as a stone.

The demonstration was simple, but effective. Even Silas stared, speechless.

Finnian looked at him, gentle but unflinching. "Your product is empty," he said. "It serves a function, but it contains nothing of the spirit that made the original worth copying."

Silas opened his mouth, then closed it. He took the tin, turned it in his hands, and frowned at the label as if seeing it for the first time.

Vamir spoke up from the crowd, his voice a dry wind. "It's not just you, Silas. There are hundreds, maybe thousands, like you. But North Pointe was supposed to be better."

Silas's reply was almost a whisper: "I'm just making a living."

Leota stepped in, her tone both kind and sharp. "You can do that without taking the living out of everything else."

Silas's gaze dropped to the ground. "So what would you have me do?"

"Leave," said Jen, but not unkindly. "Or change. Make something that matters, and then come back."

He nodded, slow and dazed. "Maybe," he said, "I will."

Nobody cheered, but the tension in the square dissolved, a long-held breath let out at last.

The crowd broke apart, drifting back to their shops and stalls, but everyone moved a little slower, as if each was turning over what they'd just seen.

Finnian packed away his device and offered Lucy her cup with a tiny bow. "I can make one for you, if you like."

Lucy smiled, small but true. "I'd like that," she said, and the two of them walked off together, talking softly.

Jen lingered for a while, then tipped her hat at Silas and wandered toward the grocer's.

Leota stood for a moment, watching Silas, then turned to Galhani and offered a nod of approval. "Well said," she murmured. "Maybe we have a chance after all."

Galhani's legs felt rubbery, but she managed a smile. "Maybe," she said, "if we work together."

She returned to her shop, heart thudding with the aftershock of what she'd done. She had no idea if things would improve, or if the parasite could ever be truly starved. But she did know that the next cup she brewed would not be for herself alone.

She filled the kettle, measured out the leaves, and set the table for four.

Outside, the square was brighter than before, and the wind through the open window carried a note of wild mint—so faint, you had to really listen for it.

Galhani listened, and for the first time in a long while, believed the flavor would come back.

fourteen

. . .

GALHANI HAD NEVER TRULY BELIEVED in the power of
morning, not the way the poets or the bakery signs did. But today, as
the first gold found its way through the shop's mottled windows and
set every jar aglow, she felt something close to conversion. Or maybe
she was just desperate for any small reason to believe.

She was already in motion. She'd been in motion for candlemarks,
actually—her sleep had lasted only until the second crow's call, after
which she'd lain staring at the ceiling, limbs tensed and mind twisting
through Finnian's metaphors and Vamir's reminders, replaying every
line until they blurred together like the labels on her oldest tea jars. So
when the blue half-light started climbing the wall, she was out of bed
and into the shop, a blur of small hands and bare feet and nervous,
kinetic energy.

On the workbench, she was assembling the day's offerings with the
speed and precision of a mouse setting traps for a cat. The teapots
were first: she lined them up in ascending order, tallest to smallest, a
parade of cracked-glaze and mismatched spouts. The cups came next
—none of them matched, of course, but that was the point, wasn't it? It
was supposed to look intentional. It was supposed to mean something

about the town, or about herself, or about the way that even when nothing fit together, you could still make a table out of the pieces.

Lara drifted in, hair tangled from sleep, eyes blinking against the sharpness of the dawn. She stopped in the doorway, arms crossed, and regarded the chaos with a familiar blend of fondness and worry.

"You're up early," Lara said, voice a rasp. "Or did you never sleep?"

Galhani grinned, though she knew it looked more like a grimace. "What is sleep to a woman of destiny?"

Lara picked her way through the teapots, careful not to tip any over. "And what destiny is that, exactly? The one where you exhaust yourself before the guests even arrive?"

"No guests," Galhani said. "It's a bazaar today. A proper one. Everyone is bringing something."

Lara reached for a cup, then thought better of it and began straightening the stack of saucers instead. "We just had a gathering. Last sennight. Remember? Half the town left early, the other half left angry."

"This isn't a meeting," Galhani replied, voice tight. "It's something else." She fiddled with a bundle of dried honeycomb, trying to make the wax catch the light the way it used to. "We're going to try the new plan."

Lara's eyebrows rose, but she didn't interrupt.

"I've been thinking," Galhani continued, stacking jars as she talked. "Maybe it's not about fixing the old thing. Maybe we just... make a new thing. Something that isn't what the parasite wants. Something it's never tasted before."

Lara made a soft, skeptical sound, but her hands kept moving. She plucked the dying flowers from yesterday's vase and replaced them with sprigs of purpled sage. "So the plan is to... what? Trick the parasite into leaving us alone?"

"No," Galhani said. "Just confuse it long enough that it gives up. Or changes its mind. Or maybe it learns to live with us, instead of feeding off us." She paused, letting the words hang in the steam. "Finnian said clocks are ruined by the first misaligned gear, but you can still get them running again if you improvise. If you let them run weird for a while."

"That's a terrible metaphor," Lara said, but she was smiling.

Galhani's mood lifted a little. "We have to show the town it can be more than what's being drained away."

Lara circled the table, collecting stray teaspoons. "And you're sure this is what people want?"

"No," Galhani said, honest. "But I want it. And I think maybe they do, too, even if they're afraid to say so." She was stacking napkins, but her hands were trembling, and after a moment she set them down and pressed her palms flat to the table, as if to steady the whole building.

Lara watched, then reached out and covered Galhani's hands with her own. "Tell me what to do," she said, soft as a moth's wing.

Galhani exhaled. "Help me hang the signs?"

They worked together, one at either end of a length of twine, threading it through the hooks above the shop's front window. The sign was a sheet of thick paper, hand-lettered last night in the uncertain light of a tallow candle. Galhani's handwriting was not the best, and the letters were slightly slanted, but she'd added little flourishes: leaves curling from the serifs, a tiny mouse in the tail of a Q. "Bizarre Bazaar: Bring One Thing You've Never Made Before" it read, though the word "Bizarre" had ended up twice as large as the rest, as if the paper itself had decided to shout.

Next, they placed hand-painted placards on the outer stoop and in the square, wedging them between the flagstones and brushing away the mud. The early sun caught the paint, made the words shimmer. Galhani's heart lurched with every step, as if she was walking a tightrope above the whole town.

When they returned to the shop, Lara set to work arranging the window display. She fetched out the special teaware—two porcelain cups with hairline cracks, a chipped sugar bowl with a bluebird on the lid, a battered tray that had belonged to Galhani's mother. She dusted each item, polished the glass, and set them in a little tableau, like a museum exhibit of a vanished world. Her movements were methodical, almost reverent.

Galhani watched her, the swell of gratitude mixing with something that felt like fear. If this didn't work, she wasn't sure what would be left of her.

She turned her attention to the herbs. The last of the mint, the dried lemon peel, the precious sprigs of night-bloom. She lined them up on the counter, fussing over the order, then rearranged them again. It had to be right. It had to look effortless, but not careless. It had to look like the kind of thing people would want to be a part of, even if they were too proud to say so.

When the time came to open the doors, Galhani did so with both hands, throwing them wide and letting the cold morning air sweep through the room. She stood in the doorway, blinking at the sudden light, and watched as the square below began to stir.

Children were the first to notice the signs, of course. They darted from stoop to stoop, reading the placards aloud and laughing at the word "Bizarre." Soon after, the first adults appeared: Dardrad, coat dusted with sawdust; Cole, arms loaded with mysterious baskets; Makota and her kits, trailing crumbs and argument. They paused at the signs, conferred in low voices, then set off for their own shops, urgency in their step.

Galhani felt a flicker of hope, sharp and fast.

She turned to Lara, who was arranging a basket of scones on the front table. "Do you think it will work?"

Lara looked up, her smile gentle but tired. "If it doesn't, we'll just try again. Or something else. That's what we do, isn't it?"

Galhani nodded. "That's what we do."

She stepped out into the square, feet bare against the frosted stones, and watched as the town began to remake itself, one small, stubborn act at a time.

By the time the shadows had shrunk to puddles beneath the benches, the entire green hummed with a kind of bright, tentative madness.

Makota had arrived first among the shopkeepers, setting up a display table covered in cloth the color of overripe plums. She'd brought only three pastries, but each was a marvel: a swirl of dough dusted with what looked like gold, a croissant topped with a blue glaze that seemed to refract the sun, and a dense, round bun studded with something iridescent. The first customer, a red-cheeked girl, reached for the bun, and Makota's paw batted her hand away. "Careful!" she chided. "They're not just food." She sliced the bun in half, revealing a spiral of fruit and cream inside. The moment the girl bit in, her eyes went wide—and then, for a second, her whole body glimmered, as if a veil had been dropped and she could see the next ten minutes of her own life. She shrieked with delight, then ran to tell her friends.

Galhani watched this from her tea station, her heart pounding. It was working. It was really working. Even if the magic was a little sideways, a little rough-edged, it was back.

Warren clattered into the square next, hauling his portable anvil and a crate of raw iron. He set up with a showman's flair, stripping off his coat to reveal a linen shirt bulging at every seam. He lifted a hammer in greeting to the crowd, then set to work—not on tools, or weapons, but on the tiniest, most ridiculous horseshoes anyone had ever seen. He hammered each one into a new and even less plausible shape: a star, a spiral, one that looked like it belonged on a beetle. "No horse could wear these!" someone called, and Warren bellowed back, "Good! Horses are tired of being shod, anyway." The crowd laughed, and he winked at Galhani as if to say, See? Even useless things can be worth the making.

Lucy followed, bearing only a single bowl. At first glance, it looked ordinary, but up close, the rim was clearly, intentionally lopsided, the glaze swirled in a way that made the inside seem to lean toward the person who held it. She placed it at the center of the table, patted it fondly, and then ignored it for the rest of the morning. "It's meant to be used," she explained to a curious neighbor. "But you have to figure out for what. I'm not the expert anymore."

Next came Cole, balancing a tray of roasted squash—some sweet, some savory, all from a peculiar batch of seeds he'd been saving for a day that needed brightening. He invited everyone to try, and most did, coming back for seconds and thirds. When asked the secret, he shrugged. "Didn't use a recipe. Just followed the shape of the seed." Someone made a joke about the shape, and he laughed so loud it drew half the children in the square over to see what was so funny.

Alred the grocer surprised everyone by setting up a table not of food, but of origami. He'd folded hundreds of tiny squares from old grain packets and painted them in jewel tones. The shapes themselves were odd—a bird with three wings, a fish with no tail, a flower with the petals arranged in perfect squares. "They're all mistakes," he said, but when a child picked one up and tried to unfold it, it snapped open with a tiny pop, revealing a perfectly wrapped piece of dried fruit inside.

Dardrad, never one for subtlety, had prepared sausages in patterns —braided, knotted, looped into little pretzel shapes. Each was marked with an herbal ink that, when sliced, revealed a message or a joke, some of them rude enough that the parents had to shield their children's eyes. "Can't say it if you can't spell it," Dardrad grunted, but he grinned as he handed out samples.

Even the fisherman, Calder, contributed: he had created a mosaic on an old wooden board, using nothing but fish bones and colored river pebbles. He propped it up against a crate, said nothing, and nodded if anyone complimented it.

The effect was cumulative. The longer people wandered the bazaar, the more their laughter brightened, the more voices rose. At some point, the awkwardness fell away, and what remained was the shared joy of making something for its own sake, of seeing your neighbor try and fail and then try again.

It was in this haze of motion and noise that Prudence made her entrance.

She wore a dress so vibrant, so absolutely at odds with her usual black, that it took several people a moment to recognize her. The pattern was a riot of yellows and reds, stitched into tight geometric whorls. Her hair was unpinned and loose, and she'd strung the handle of her toddler's pram with ribbons in every shade of the rainbow. The baby sat in the pram and giggled, one fist buried in a twist of Makota's bread.

Every conversation seemed to pause as Prudence made her slow circuit around the green. She did not meet any gaze directly, but she moved with a steadiness that dared anyone to challenge her. When she reached Galhani's table, she stopped.

"I'm here for the tea," she said, her voice the same clipped precision as always. "May I?"

Galhani poured a cup and handed it across, careful to keep her own hands from shaking. "Of course."

Prudence sipped. "Not your usual?"

"No," Galhani said. "Something new."

Prudence nodded once, then moved away, her dress a beacon in the crowd. The onlookers, freed from their surprise, drifted back into conversation. But there was a new note—a kind of awe, or perhaps relief.

Galhani felt the magic first as a prickle on her skin, then as a warmth behind her ribs. It pulsed through the green, subtle but unmistakable. The town, she realized, was hungry for this. For change. For proof that the world could be different than it was yesterday.

She looked at Lara, who stood at the edge of the square, hands clasped and eyes bright with a pride she never allowed herself to show. They shared a long look, and in it was the sum of a hundred tiny mornings, every failure and every hope, bound up in the fact that they were still here.

From her place at the tea table, Galhani watched the people. She watched the children chasing each other with folded paper birds; the old men competing to see whose sausage slice told the filthiest joke; the townsfolk sampling, swapping, laughing, calling out to each other across the green.

She watched, and she believed—not only in the morning, but in the whole, wild possibility of what the day might become.

The crowd around Galhani's tea table grew with every passing minute. At first, it was just the regulars—Cole, Makota, a handful of children sniffing the air for something sweet—but soon even the travelers edged closer, their faces cautiously open, as if testing the waters before deciding whether to join the game.

Galhani felt the eyes on her, and for once, it didn't fill her with dread. Instead, she drew herself taller, planted her feet on the stepladder behind the counter, and began the work of making her Renewal Brew.

She started with the water, boiled over a flame brought in from the bakery next door. She scooped it with the green-glazed kettle, poured it through the air so that the steam caught the morning sun and made a brief, brilliant column between her and the audience. She measured the leaves and herbs not by the spoon, but by sight and feel, trusting her hands to remember what her mind still doubted. A pinch of night-bloom, a dash of dried apple skin, a single slice of honeycomb to dissolve as it steeped.

People in the crowd began to nudge one another, pointing at the way she moved. Even the children grew quiet, their play dissolving into a hush that gathered around the table like a silk cloth.

She set the pot to rest, draping a square of linen over the top. The next part was the most important, and she could feel the anticipation in the air. A silence pressed in, broken only by the distant clatter of Warren's hammer and the far-off laughter at Dardrad's sausage stand.

Galhani placed her hands around the pot and closed her eyes. She tried to recall the words her mother had used, the secret litany passed down through the women of her line. It wasn't real magic, not in the way the world measured such things, but it was theirs, and it had once worked. She spoke the words, soft and careful, and at the end she breathed out and lifted the linen.

Nothing happened.

The aroma should have rolled out like a living thing, curling through the crowd and settling a warm hand on every shoulder. Instead, the steam was thin, the color of the tea inside pale and dull as gray dishwater.

Galhani's hands trembled, just once, but she forced a smile. She poured the first cup and held it up for all to see. The liquid was almost clear. She sipped, hoping for something—anything—but the taste was flat. Not even bitter, just absent.

The crowd didn't mock or jeer. But the silence sharpened. Someone coughed. A child asked, "Is that all?" in a voice so innocent it made Galhani's chest tighten. She tried to make a joke, to play it off, but her tongue failed her.

She set the pot down with more force than necessary. The cups rattled. She wanted to crawl under the table, to vanish into the wood, to take every risk she'd just made and stuff it back in the box where it belonged.

And then Lara was there.

She appeared at Galhani's side, not with a flourish or a speech, but with the simple, steady weight of her hand on Galhani's back. She didn't try to hide the support, or the fear she felt for her mate. Instead, she leaned in and whispered, "You felt it, didn't you? The way the magic was back, even if only for a moment?"

Galhani nodded, her eyes swimming. "I thought it would work. I thought—"

Lara squeezed her shoulder. "It did work. Look at them."

And Galhani did. The crowd hadn't dispersed, not really. Instead, they stood in awkward, shifting groups, each person holding their cup of nearly flavorless tea, talking quietly and glancing back at her. It wasn't disappointment, not exactly. It was something else—something that looked a little like hope, battered but alive.

"I can't do it alone," Galhani whispered, the words scraping her throat.

"Who said you had to?" said Lara.

At that moment, Finnian appeared, holding something cupped in his hands. He set it down gently on the table in front of Galhani—a bird, carved from wood so thin the wings were almost translucent. It had a whittled beak and tiny inlaid eyes, and every feather was marked with a line of silver paint. Finnian tapped the table twice, and the bird opened its mouth.

From inside, a single, perfect note emerged—a sound so clear it vibrated in Galhani's teeth, and in the teeth of everyone within thirty yards. It was not loud, but it was absolute: a line of music drawn straight through the heart of the square, pinning every conversation in place. People turned, stunned. The children stopped moving. Even the hammering and laughter seemed to hush, giving space for the song.

The note lasted three breaths, then the bird closed its beak and the sound faded, leaving behind a silence that felt charged, ready to spark.

Finnian met Galhani's eyes. "Even one note, if played just right, can change a whole symphony," he said. "Doesn't matter if the rest of the orchestra is out of tune."

Galhani looked at the bird, at the crowd, at the motley of her neighbors and their impossible crafts. She saw the truth of it then—not the magic of old, not the lost flavors, but the new thing they'd made together, even if they'd made it by mistake.

She looked at Lara, and Lara smiled through her own tears. "You did this," she said. "You got them to try."

Galhani wiped her face and stood a little taller. She raised her cup, and this time, the crowd raised theirs as well. Someone—Makota, probably—started a slow, lopsided clap. It spread, uneven and awkward, but it spread. Soon the whole green was filled with the sound of people applauding not for a triumph, but for the stubborn refusal to give up.

And as Galhani drank her bland, colorless tea, she realized it wasn't about the taste, or the magic. It was about the attempt. The togetherness. The refusal to go quietly.

She would try again tomorrow, and the next day, and the day after that. So would everyone else. And maybe, if they kept doing it, the real magic would return—or maybe they would discover something better.

She looked at the carved bird, and at Finnian, and at her friends scattered across the square...

And then walked inside her shop to think.

fifteen

・ ・ ・

THE SHOP HAD NEVER FELT SO hollow, nor so silent—nor so full of possibility. After the last of the crowd had straggled off, with paper cups and leftover pastries in their pockets, Galhani lingered in the aftermath, arms folded, bare feet pressed to the cold floorboards as if by sheer pressure she could force them to remember how it felt to be alive. The windows rattled against the night breeze. On the work-bench, the display of teapots and cups looked like a failed museum, an exhibit closed for lack of interest.

She let herself lean against the counter. The bazaar had come and gone, and for all its noise and cheer, it had not fixed the problem. The town still felt as if a layer of gauze had been laid over it, blunting every flavor and every sound. Even the laughter at Dardrad's stand had been the wrong pitch: too bright, too brittle, a light bouncing off glass instead of seeping into the bone.

There were signs of the party everywhere: paper plates sagging with the weight of uneaten food, a blue-glazed mug abandoned and ringed with fingerprints, a spill of sweet syrup on the windowsill already crawling with ants. She'd gone back out and helped clean for a candlemark, moving from task to task with the sluggish compulsion of someone halfway through a fever. The jars of tea—her pride, once—

were now ghosts of themselves, lining the shelves in quiet judgment. She could almost see the disappointment gathering on the labels like dust.

She stood there, staring at nothing, until her eyes ached. Then, with a suddenness that surprised her, she shut them and let her head fall forward. It would be so easy to give up. It would be so easy to let the shop fail and return to whatever cities or caves gnomes like her were supposed to vanish into, trailing rumors and regrets.

But she didn't want easy, not anymore.

She drew in a breath. The air tasted like failed honey and a faint, sour residue. She reached for a mug, the nearest one, and poured the dregs of the last blend into it. She drank, even though she knew it would be flat. It was.

She set the mug down and closed her eyes again, pressing her palms hard into her eye sockets until she saw points of light. In that small, self-inflicted darkness, a memory surfaced. Not of the day, but of years ago—a sliver of childhood, bright and sharp as a sliver under the skin.

Her grandmother's hands, knotted and blue, working a mortar over a bowl of earth. The old woman's voice, low and measured, saying: "Magic is not a thing, it's a line between things. When you forget what it's for, you forget how to use it." She remembered the gnarled finger tracing a circle on the wood, the way the dust gathered in the lines.

She remembered the old gnomish ritual—a tea ceremony, but not for show. It was about remembering how the earth and the leaf and the hand that prepared it all needed each other, or else the whole thing was only flavor and steam. It was so simple. She'd spent half her life running from it, trying to make things more complicated so she could be special, or at least necessary. But the answer had always been there, in a patch of sun on the floor, in a story told over an empty cup.

It wasn't about magic. It was about connection. The parasite, the hollowing, whatever it was—they were only symptoms. The real sickness was forgetting why anyone bothered to come together in the first place.

The bazaar had been a trick, a beautiful one, but it was always going to be fleeting. A party was not a cure. You could not force meaning with volume or with sugar. You had to grow it, and feed it, and protect it, every day. The magic was the line, not the show.

Galhani opened her eyes. Her hands were trembling—not from exhaustion, but from the strange, searing certainty that, for the first time in sennights, she actually knew what to do.

She pushed away from the counter and went to the back of the shop, past the jars of wilted mint and the sacks of stale bark. She pulled out the low bench from beneath the shelving and stood on tiptoe, stretching for the very highest cabinet. Her fingers found the latch. It opened with a crack, the wood warped from years of humidity and neglect.

Inside was a box, old gnome wood, carved with circles and dots in a spiral pattern. She hadn't opened it since leaving home. She'd brought it mostly out of guilt, and then let it collect dust at the back of every shop she'd worked in since. It felt heavier than it should, but maybe that was just the weight of inheritance.

She set the box on the table and ran her finger around the lid. Her hands shook worse than before. She was afraid to look inside. She was afraid it would be empty.

She was still there, holding the box and staring at it like a scrying bowl, when Lara came in through the back door. She must have seen the light in the window; she moved quietly, her steps careful, as if not wanting to spook a wild animal.

Lara looked at her, at the box, at her face. "You're still up," she said, voice soft and familiar.

Galhani nodded. "I figured something out."

Lara didn't smile, not quite. But her eyes warmed. "Is it about the tea, or about you?"

Galhani huffed, too tired to pretend. "Both, I think."

Lara came closer, until they were side by side at the table. She looked down at the box. "I've never seen you open that."

"I haven't. Not since I left." Galhani pressed her palm to the lid, then lifted it. The hinges creaked, and the scent of old, dried herbs spilled out—rich, sharp, and immediately familiar. It was the blend her grandmother had made for rituals, for remembering. Beneath the herbs was a folded scrap of cloth, and beneath that, a slip of paper covered in dense, spidery script.

She took out the paper and set it flat. The words were in Gnomish, and reading them was like drinking from a well she hadn't visited in a long time.

"Can I see?" Lara asked, gesturing at the box.

Galhani pushed it toward her. "It's from my grandmother. She said the recipe would only work if I didn't try to improve it."

Lara's smile broke through, small but real. "Maybe you should try that, just this once."

Galhani traced the line of the recipe. It was simple—barely six ingredients, most of them weeds. But the point wasn't the flavor, or even the magic. It was the act of making, the act of sharing, the act of seeing each other across the table.

She felt the whole of her earlier despair empty out, replaced by a kind of wild, nervous energy. "I think this could work," she said. "Not just for me. For everyone. If we do it together."

Lara's face softened, the lines of worry smoothing a little. "Tell me what you need."

"We'll have to gather a few things. Some from the foothills. Some from the gardens here." Galhani glanced at the shelves, the jars. "I can't do it alone, Lara. Not this time."

Lara squeezed her shoulder, steady and warm. "You're not alone."

They stood in the quiet of the shop, the old blend filling the air with a hint of memory. Galhani grabbed a pencil and began to sketch out the plan, notes piling up in tiny, precise handwriting. She would need help—maybe from Vamir, maybe from Leota. Maybe even from Sam, if she could get the woman to sit still for five minutes.

Lara watched her work, arms crossed and a fondness in her gaze. "You're sure this isn't just another bazaar? Another attempt to outdo yourself?"

Galhani shook her head. "No more outdoing. This is about putting things back together. One line at a time."

Lara nodded. "Then I'll help you find what you need."

They worked into the night, planning the journey, the gathering, the ritual itself. Galhani felt alive, not with magic, but with the knowledge that every part of her—every loss, every stubborn hope—could still matter.

Outside, the wind rattled the windows, but inside, the lines were being drawn anew.

———

They left before the sun had burned the mist off the common, Lara in her old boots and a scarf wrapped twice round her neck, Galhani with her satchel and the battered wooden basket that had belonged to her grandmother and, so the family insisted, to a dozen stubborn women before her.

The road out of town was still empty this early, save for a single dog nosing through the leavings of the bazaar, but even from a distance the world beyond the walls looked different. Where the town's colors seemed faded, the foothills shimmered with a kind of reckless energy. Wildflowers—blue, orange, a yellow so sharp it hurt—splattered the edges of the track, pushing up through gravel and in between the crushed, gray grasses of last year. A scatter of birds argued in the hedges, their calls high and constant, and every step sent up a perfume of dew, earth, and sweet decay.

Lara walked ahead at first, shoulders hunched, eyes on the path. She'd always preferred to be outside the boundaries of the green, and Galhani sometimes wondered if the wild felt more like home to her than any four walls could. They didn't talk for the first mile, and that was fine. The world did enough talking for them.

They found the first patch just past the ridge—a sprawl of sage, silvered by the morning. Galhani crouched to harvest, her fingers careful but sure. "Not for taste," she said, more to herself than Lara. "For clarity."

Lara glanced back, one eyebrow raised. "Do you want the stems or just the leaves?"

"Leaves are best," Galhani said, "but keep a few flowers if they're bright." She worked with slow precision, trying not to damage the next year's shoots. Every time she pinched a leaf, the smell followed her hand back up to her nose, and she couldn't help but breathe it in deep.

They went on, following the curve of the hillside. The next find was thyme, creeping through the rocks. Galhani's hands were too small for the whole job, but Lara's could lever out the roots with a twist, and together they picked a small clutch for the basket.

"This one?" Galhani asked, holding up the tangled herb.

"Remembrance," said Lara, with a small, crooked smile. "I do listen, sometimes."

Galhani let herself laugh. It came out as a hiccup, sudden and sharp, and echoed back off the stone. For a second she remembered being a child, and the way laughter could make anything possible.

Next came yarrow, clustered at the foot of a split boulder. It was a weed, really, but the flowers were creamy white and perfect for binding. Galhani reached for the tallest stem and snipped it low.

"Binding?" Lara guessed.

"For luck," Galhani said, and then, "and for stubbornness." She didn't say it, but the yarrow reminded her of Warren, the way he always stood up straight even when he wanted to bend.

By the time the sun cleared the highest branch, the basket was half full, and Galhani's fingers were stained green. They found two more—sweetflag, which grew in the damp cracks near the creek, and the dark, dusty berries of night-wort, which Lara had to climb for. Each time Galhani added something to the basket, she named it: "For patience," "for mending," "for sleep, when it finally comes."

Lara said, "You really think any of it works, if you name it out loud like that?"

"I think," said Galhani, "that if you name it, it becomes a little more real. Even if only for a moment."

Lara considered this, then shrugged. "There are worse ways to spend a morning."

They worked in rhythm, moving from patch to patch, neither of them saying what needed to be said: that the town was dying, or that Galhani had staked everything on one last try, or that even if the magic never came back, the memory of it would be enough to get them through. Instead, they filled the basket, one leaf and stem at a time, until it overflowed.

When there was no more room, they sat on a slab of stone, side by side, and looked back at the town. From the ridge, the green was a perfect circle, its shops and homes clustered tight, the new stalls at the edge like a row of mismatched teeth. The sun had caught the roof of the bakery and the glass in the bookshop windows, and the whole place shimmered as if under a spell.

Galhani closed her eyes and let the scent of the basket fill her head. She'd been so afraid the day would be a waste, but now, with her hands raw and her heart racing, she felt as if she could do anything. She opened her eyes and turned to Lara, who was already looking at her.

"You're smiling," Lara said, surprised.

"It feels good," Galhani said, not caring how it sounded. "It feels like I haven't in forever."

Lara grinned. "Let's see if it lasts."

They picked their way down the slope, every step lighter than the last. When they reached the bottom, Galhani stopped, and for the first time in sennights, she let herself hope that maybe—just maybe—the world could change back, or forward, or wherever it needed to go.

They walked home together, the basket between them.

———

The Claw was almost unrecognizable in its quiet. After the sennights of squabbling and complaint, the silence that filled the pub felt deliberate—like a collective decision not to let the world in for one more round. Only three tables were occupied, and even there the talk was soft, careful, the words dying before they reached the rafters.

Sam was tending bar, but her usual edge had dulled. She wiped the same spot with the same rag, even after the counter was as clean as it would ever be. Every so often, she looked up at the window, as if expecting something to crash through it. The regulars sat in their usual corners, but the energy had shifted. Instead of the old arguments, they passed the time in long stretches of silence, eyes on their drinks or the dull glow of the lamps.

Galhani arrived just as the evening light angled through the warped glass, making the dust in the air visible. She'd braided her hair with the same blue string she'd used as a child, and Lara had made her wear the good vest, the one with the subtle embroidery along the seams. The basket of herbs sat in her arms, wrapped in a damp towel to keep the scent fresh.

She scanned the room. Leota, Vamir, and Finnian already waited at the usual spot, near the stove. Lucy trailed in a few minutes later, hands in her coat pockets, face drawn and tired, with a dusting of glaze still visible under her fingernails.

Sam nodded at Galhani when she entered, and her eyes flicked to the basket. "You find what you needed?"

Galhani nodded back. "And a little more."

Sam grunted. "Good. Maybe you'll do better than my latest batch." She held up a mug. "Even the ale's got nothing to say."

Galhani smiled, a real one, and crossed to the table where the others had gathered.

Leota wore black, as ever, but tonight the dress was so matte it seemed to suck in the light. Her hair was slicked flat, and her hands were folded in her lap. She greeted Galhani with a nod, eyes sharp and searching.

Vamir looked even more tired than Lucy, though his face was set in a gentle, patient line. Polyocular perched on his shoulder, blinking its three blue eyes in rotation. Finnian was the only one who seemed at ease. He leaned back in his chair, turning a gear between his fingers.

Lucy took a seat at the end, settling her hands around a mug but not drinking from it. She seemed half-present, her gaze darting around the room, never quite meeting anyone else's.

Galhani unpacked the basket and spread the herbs on the table, careful to arrange them by color and shape. The aroma was immediate, a thick, green perfume that drifted out and softened the edges of the room. For a moment, even Sam looked up from her cleaning, the lines at her mouth loosening.

"Looks good," Finnian said. "What's the plan?"

Galhani laid out her notes, the pages still damp with sweat from her hands. She took a breath and began.

"It's not a spell," she said. "Not really. It's a ceremony—a way to remember why we're here, and what it's supposed to feel like to be a part of something." She looked at each of them in turn. "The parasite feeds on contradiction, on isolation. The only thing that's ever stopped it, in any of the old texts, is a moment of real connection. Not just doing the same thing, but actually meaning it."

Vamir nodded, eyes heavy. "The art of the blend. The moment when everything—"

"—snaps into place," finished Galhani, surprised at her own certainty. "It doesn't matter if the magic is gone. If we act as if it's there, and we do it together, it's enough. At least for one note." She glanced at Finnian. "That's all it takes, right?"

Finnian's face split in a grin. "One note, hit just right."

Leota tapped the table, the sound as sharp as a dropped pin. "There is precedent for this. In the coven, we called it a circle of belonging. It's not a matter of strength; it's a matter of... alignment." She paused, then added, "I can reinforce the boundary, if needed. Make it stick.

Galhani nodded. "That would help." She hesitated, then said, "It has to be all of us. Not just the people here, but the town. If even one person refuses, it won't work."

Lucy's hands trembled on her mug. "Most people are tired," she said, voice thin. "They won't want to try again."

Galhani reached across and squeezed Lucy's wrist. "Then we make them want it. Or at least, we let them see what they're missing." She pulled her hand back, then looked around. "We'll need a big pot, enough to serve the whole square. Sam—?"

Sam, who'd been eavesdropping from behind the bar, called out: "There's a copper kettle in the back. I'll haul it up. But you really think a tea party will fix this?"

"It's not about the tea," said Galhani, her voice firm. "It's about what we share through it."

Polyocular chirped, low and approving. Vamir scratched it under the chin, and it purred.

Leota's gaze went distant. "I'll need a few moments to draw the boundary. I can do it with chalk, or salt, or blood if it comes to it."

Finnian shrugged. "Chalk's good enough for me."

Lara, who'd stayed quiet until now, cleared her throat. "When?"

Galhani looked at the clock above the bar. "Tonight, at sunset." Then she looked doubtful. "Maybe. It should be brighter, maybe."

Vamir flipped through a small, battered book, then nodded. "The equinox is two days away. That's good, yes?"

Galhani smiled. "Perfect."

They spent the next candlemark assigning tasks. Finnian would help Sam prepare the fire and the pot. Vamir would write the words for the announcement, and Polyocular would deliver them around town. Leota would draw the circle at dawn, and Lara would help Galhani with the final blend, making sure every leaf and root was exactly right.

Lucy offered to bring bowls and cups, enough for everyone, though her hands shook as she wrote the list.

When the meeting broke up, Sam called Galhani over. "You really think this will work?" she asked, her eyes heavy.

"I don't know," said Galhani, honest. "But I have to believe it can."

Sam snorted. "Then I'll believe, too. For a day, anyway."

Galhani smiled, then turned to leave, but Sam caught her by the arm. "Hey," she said, her grip fierce. "I'm proud of you, you know. Even if it fails."

Galhani blinked, startled, then hugged Sam, the first time she'd ever done so. Sam stood stiff as a fence post, then patted her awkwardly on the back.

Outside, the night was deepening, the last light draining from the sky. Galhani and Lara walked home together, the basket of herbs tucked between them. For the first time in moons, Galhani felt not just hope, but certainty.

———

By the time the sun crested the roofs and scattered the morning chill, the town square was already half full. The word had gone out in the night—on chalked signs, in soft knocks at every door, through Polyocular's silent, eerie flits from window to window. Even the travelers, who'd learned by now to be wary of anything that looked like a town-wide event, gathered at the edges, clutching mugs and waiting for the catch.

Galhani and Lara arrived together, the basket of herbs between them. Sam met them at the center of the green, where the ashes of last night's fire still smoldered. She wore her sword at her belt and a scowl to match, but her hands were gentle as she showed them where to set the copper kettle. "Make it good," she muttered. "If I have to drink this stuff, it better work."

They built the fire with Warren's help. He'd brought the wood, split and stacked with care, and showed up early to make sure it burned just right. His arms were bare to the elbow, green skin stippled with old scars and new, the muscles bunching as he fed the fire.

Lara tended the kettle, filling it from buckets hauled in from the well. Galhani measured the first herbs, pinching them between her fingers and holding them to her nose before adding them to the pot. When the water rolled to a boil, the first sharp scent of sage and thyme pushed out across the green. Heads turned, faces lifting from their muffled conversations.

A few of the townsfolk formed a small circle at the fire. Sam, Warren, Cole, Lucy, Prudence, and Makota. Dardrad and Calder and the rest of the old guard, each with a cup in hand, each wary but unwilling to be left out. Leota came last, in her black robes, moving with a slow, deliberate pace as she marked the perimeter of the gathering. From beneath her sleeve, she drew a small bag of chalk and walked the ring, sprinkling down a single, unbroken line on the grass. As she finished, the chalk shimmered briefly, then faded, but Galhani swore she saw a pale, silvery thread that lingered in the grass, connecting the ground beneath every foot.

The rest of the crowd—new shopkeepers, wagon-vendors, and the travelers—clustered behind, forming a loose crescent at the outer rim. Some wore faces of open curiosity; others kept their eyes low and their bodies ready to bolt at the first sign of trouble.

Galhani moved to the center and began the work. She called out the names of each herb as she added it, letting the words hang in the air before stirring them into the roiling, fragrant steam. "For clarity," she said, as she scattered the sage. "For remembrance," as she crumbled the thyme. "For patience, for luck, for stubbornness, for rest."

Lara handed her the last of the sweetflag, and Galhani let it float atop the brew. The pot frothed, and for a moment, the whole square filled with the warm, green scent of the hillside.

Leota approached, arms folded. "It's ready," she said, eyes on the kettle.

Sam raised her cup. "Let's get on with it."

"A story first," Galhani insisted. "Why you're here. Why you stay." She passed Sam an empty cup.

Sam snorted, but after a moment, she said, "I came here with nothing. Just a sword and too many nightmares. I drank in this bar until I forgot how to care." She paused, eyes on the fire. "This town gave me a job, and then a reason to keep showing up. Even when it's all gone gray, I still want to be here."

Warren, next in line, grunted. "I never thought I'd have a family. Not the kind that would keep me, anyway. I thought I'd work the forge until it killed me, then go down to mud. But my wife, my boy—this place gave me a reason to change. To dream." He wiped his mouth with the back of his hand. "Even when the steel's gone soft, it matters who you're making it for."

Cole spoke in a rush, as if afraid the words would dry up if he waited. "My kids were born here. I remember when Ivy walked across this green for the first time, yelling at the crows. I remember the first spring I made bread that didn't turn to rock." He grinned, sheepish. "I want my children to have a better life than I did. And I want them to have it here."

Lucy's hands trembled when she took the cup. She sipped, then spoke, voice hoarse. "I lost my shop once. Back home. I thought I could never start over. But the people here—they bought my pots, even when they were ugly. They brought me clay when the road froze." She looked up, her eyes raw. "I need this place. Even broken, I need it."

The cup made its way around, each person adding a word or a

memory or a wish, no matter how small. Even Dardrad, who'd sworn never to talk about feelings in public, muttered something about "missing the days when the river stank of fish, and you could tell the seasons by the way your nose froze."

When it was Galhani's turn, she hesitated. She looked at Lara, then at the faces in the crowd. For the first time, she realized she wasn't afraid anymore.

"I don't want to leave," she said. "I've never belonged anywhere, not really. But I want to belong here. I want to see what this town can be, when we're not afraid."

Leota stepped forward. Her voice was quiet, but it carried. "The circle is set. The memory is shared."

"Now we begin," Galhani said softly.

sixteen

. . .

THE SILENCE that followed "Now we begin," was not empty, but waiting—a tight, expectant hush that pressed down on every person in the circle, from the stoic old regulars to the children huddled at their parents' knees. The air above the town green had settled into a bruised, lavender dusk, the color deepening behind the outline of the steeple and the black-armed signposts. The fire beneath the kettle popped and shifted, sending little pulses of heat that barely reached the outmost ring of bodies. Galhani could feel every pair of eyes on her, each weighted with something different: hope, fear, skepticism, a hunger that was not for tea but for proof that the world could be put back together again.

The perimeter of the circle was sharp as a drawn blade. Leota's line of chalk, white as bone, had not faded as expected but glimmered faintly, especially where the cold dew began to gather on the grass. Some of the children were staring at it instead of the fire, mesmerized by how the chalk dust refused to run or dissolve.

Galhani's hands trembled as she lifted the wooden scoop over the pot, the way her grandmother's had before her. The kettle was an antique—tin hammered to a shine, big as a baby's head, its spout curved like a sleeping animal's tail. It had belonged to the town long before any of them, and she'd seen it at every festival, every harvest, every funeral she could remember. The sound of boiling water was a hush and a threat: it would steam away to nothing if she waited too long.

Lara was there, a quiet presence at Galhani's left elbow, radiating a warmth that steadied her more than anything the fire could offer. She didn't say anything—she didn't need to. The look in her eyes was permission and challenge, both at once. Galhani let herself lean a fraction closer, just for a second, and felt her heartbeat slow.

She added the first herbs. Sage for clarity—bright, almost peppery, it gave off a cloud of scent that leapt over the rim and instantly settled on everyone's skin. The crowd inhaled as one, a shiver moving through them like a ripple across a pond. Next, the thyme, cut small to keep the stems from tangling in the mesh. The bundle of sweetflag, dried almost to nothing, broke when she pressed it between her fingers; the little dust motes of spice caught the firelight and hung there, glittering like pollen.

Then the yarrow—she hesitated before dropping it in. It was a stubborn, bitter weed, and she knew from experience that even a few leaves could overwhelm a whole batch. But this wasn't about taste. It was about binding, and luck, and all the stubbornness she could summon. She pressed the yarrow into the mix, and the water hissed, a sound that felt like the exhale of the town itself.

Finally, she took the night-wort berries from Lara's palm. They were sticky, dark, and smelled faintly of almonds and rain. She rolled them between her thumb and forefinger, letting the juice bleed out before dropping them in. The color spread instantly, a purple-black swirl that fought the other scents for dominance. Galhani stirred with the wooden spoon, slow and careful, counting each turn: three one way, three back, then a tap on the rim for luck. The spoon, like the kettle, belonged to everyone and no one.

She dipped the ladle, poured the first cup, and set it on the upturned crate that served as their altar. The cup was old, chipped at the rim, and it was said to have survived more feasts and arguments than anyone alive. It steamed quietly, the surface already flecked with green and gold from the herbs.

Leota was first. She stepped forward with her usual precision, the black hem of her dress almost brushing the chalk line. Her hair caught the firelight, giving her a strange halo, but her face was grave. She took the cup in both hands, held it beneath her nose, and closed her eyes. When she drank, it was slow, deliberate, as if the taste could be memorized and dissected in real time. She set the cup back down without comment, but when she returned to the circle, her cheeks were flushed—a high, bright color that had not been there moments before.

Next was Warren. He looked as if he'd been holding his breath since dawn. The cup was tiny in his hand, but he cradled it as if it were made of gold. He sniffed, grunted approval, and downed the contents in a single, practiced motion. He clapped the cup back down and gave a short nod to Galhani, the kind of gesture usually reserved for finishing a particularly difficult horseshoe. The light on his face was not just from the fire, but from something brighter, and for the first time since the troubles began, he looked younger than his years.

Makota and her two kits were next, moving together as if still joined by invisible thread. She sipped, then passed the cup to Kene, who licked the rim and giggled, ears flicking with pleasure. Sora, the smaller of the two, sniffed, made a face, but drank anyway. The Felis trio retreated, eyes gleaming with a wet, reflective shine that caught every movement of the flames.

Cole stepped up, hands already trembling from nerves or cold, Galhani couldn't tell which. His wife Caitlin waited just behind him, her arms wrapped tight around their youngest. Cole looked at the cup for a long time before he drank, then smiled wide and handed it to Caitlin, who took the briefest sip but held onto the warmth of the cup as if it might burn through her skin to her heart. When Cole stepped away, his back was a little straighter, and he pulled his children in close, whispering something that made them all laugh.

Minnie, from the inn, made her way to the crate with a quick, apologetic smile. She wore her best apron, even though it was now stained in three places and the sash had frayed at the knot. She sipped, eyes darting to Galhani and then to the crowd, and whispered, "That's strong stuff." But she did not let go of the cup until she'd drained every drop, not even after Dexter, the town's doctor, gave a pointed cough and tapped his wrist in a silent reminder of the line behind her.

Dexter took his portion with a surgeon's precision, eyes flicking over the rim as if expecting to find a flaw in the blend. He drank, then tilted the cup to catch the last of the herbs before handing it off to the next in line. Galhani caught his gaze as he stepped back—there was a tightness in his face, but also a satisfaction, the look of a man whose worst suspicion had not come true.

Lucy, the potter, was next. She was still dressed in her work clothes, clay smudged up to her elbows, but her hands were clean and her nails filed flat. She sipped, smiled, and nodded, then set the cup down with a care that spoke of years spent handling fragile things. When she rejoined the circle, her eyes were damp, and she did not bother to wipe them.

Prudence, the tailor, took her turn in silence, her child asleep in a sling at her chest. The baby's fist was wrapped around a shred of blue fabric, and every so often Prudence would stroke the child's hair with a gentleness at odds with the severity of her own expression. She drank, then passed the cup down without comment, but Galhani could see the way her shoulders relaxed, just a fraction.

Vamir, the bookshop keeper, took the cup last of the shopkeepers. He sniffed it first, then took a delicate sip, eyes half-lidded as if searching for a hidden meaning in the flavor. His familiar, Polyocular, perched on his shoulder, and the moment he set the cup down, it let out a three-noted trill that made every head in the circle turn. Vamir bowed to Galhani, a formal, almost theatrical gesture, then resumed his place beside Finnian, who was already sketching the ritual in the margins of a battered ledger.

Now came the moment for the town's legends—the ones who lived at the edges of things, rarely seen except when absolutely necessary. Knodalon was first among these, a figure so old and bent he looked like a scrap of bark in a worn robe. He hobbled forward on his cane, eyes clouded but alive with interest. When he reached the crate, he paused, lifted the cup, and sniffed. His smile was slow, but it grew and grew, until Galhani could see all his teeth, bright and sharp as a new moon. He drank, sighed, and set the cup down. When he turned, the crowd parted for him, and Galhani could swear she heard the faint whistle of wind, even though the air was still.

The last to drink was a child. Not the youngest, not even one Galhani could name, but a boy who'd hovered at the back of the circle all evening, face smudged and eyes too big for his head. He stepped forward, looked at the adults, then at the kettle, and then at Galhani herself. She nodded, and he took the cup, both hands shaking so hard it sloshed over the rim. He drank, sputtered, and wiped his mouth with the back of his sleeve. The crowd laughed, and the sound was the first unforced laughter Galhani had heard in sennights.

As the cup completed its journey, Galhani reached for the kettle and poured the rest of the brew into the communal bowl, the one that always ended up full of coins and notes at every town gathering. She set the bowl on the crate, and the aroma—earthy, bright, and under-pinned by the sharp tang of night-wort—rose up and spread out over the whole assembly.

At first, nothing happened. The crowd waited, breathing in the steam, but the world remained stubbornly the same: the air was cold, the town square was ringed by shadows, and the shops that made the icosagon stood silent, their signs unmoving in the wind.

Then, slowly, a change. It began at the margins, where the shop lights should have been the weakest. The faded letters on the bakery sign brightened, as if someone had come by with a fresh coat of paint. The windows of the potter's shop caught the firelight and refracted it, throwing gold shapes onto the square. Even the black, matte surface of the smithy's sign seemed to drink in the glow and reflect it back with a stubborn luster.

The change swept inward, gathering momentum. The color returned to the faces of the crowd—cheeks flushed, eyes bright, even the hair of the Felis kits shone with a livelier sheen. The chalk line around the circle, which had looked thin and tentative at dusk, now blazed with a cold, lunar blue.

But the real magic was in the air itself. It vibrated—subtle at first, like the aftershock of a distant bell, but growing into a hum that pressed against Galhani's skin. It tingled at her scalp, ran in waves up her arms, made the tips of her fingers ache with energy. She could see

Lara shiver, could see Warren's thick hands tremble as he gripped his wife's shoulder, could see even Leota's composure falter for a second as the new magic settled over them.

Now, as one, the shopkeepers stepped into the inner ring, closer to the fire. They took their places as if it had all been rehearsed: Warren at true north, Makota to the east, Cole to the south, Lucy to the west. Vamir and Leota stood at opposing points, anchoring the circle with the weight of their histories.

Each spoke in turn, adding their intention to the brew.

Warren went first, his voice a low rumble. "For honest work," he said, "and the pride of a job well done." He reached into the pouch at his belt and dropped a blackened nail into the communal bowl. The liquid inside shimmered, then cleared.

Makota followed, her voice quick and light. "For nourishment, and the hunger that makes it worth the making." She plucked a single hair from her forearm, dropped it in, and the tea frothed, sending up a cloud of steam that smelled like sugar and sun.

Cole, hands steady now, added, "For plenty, for the table that never runs empty, and for the laughter that fills the empty spaces." He tore a crust of bread from his pocket, crumbled it into the bowl. The surface sparkled with gold.

Lucy spoke last, her words soft but unyielding. "For beauty, even if it's never perfect. For the hands that make it, and for the home it finds." She dropped a chip of glaze, blue as the evening, into the liquid, and it dissolved, sending ripples across the surface.

Each addition made the bowl brighter, the scent sharper, the hum in the air louder. The tea, which had begun as a muddy, dubious brown, now glowed with a gold so pure it hurt to look at directly. The light bounced from face to face, reflected in every eye, and for a moment Galhani could not tell where the magic ended and the people began.

At last, it was done. The circle held. The town green, ringed by fire and chalk and human hope, was brighter than Galhani had ever seen it. The colors were too sharp, the shadows too deep, but the feeling in the air was unmistakable: something had been mended, if only for a little while.

The crowd stood, not speaking, just breathing in the magic and letting it settle inside them. The children clung to their parents. The regulars looked at each other, and at Galhani, with something like awe. Even the newcomers, the travelers and merchants on the edge of the square, stared in with a longing that was almost painful.

Galhani looked down at her hands, which no longer shook. She looked at Lara, whose smile was small and proud, and at Leota, who mouthed a single word—"Well?"—as if daring Galhani to believe what she'd done.

Galhani exhaled. Everything tasted sweet and alive.

The hum in the air had just begun to settle into something like music—higher and higher, until it felt as if the whole town would lift off the ground—when the first cold knot hit Galhani square in the chest.

It was as if someone had dropped a lump of ice into her heart, and the chill spread in an instant, radiating up her neck and out to the tips of her fingers. She tried to ignore it, to will the ritual forward by force of memory and will, but the cold fought back with a vengeance. Her jaw locked. The next breath she took was sharp as broken glass, and it made her teeth ache.

The air shimmered, and for a heartbeat everything was doubled. She looked down at the bowl, expecting it to glow brighter, but the gold was already dimming, draining away as if sucked through a hole in the bottom. The chalk line around the circle flickered, then pulsed once—a desperate, uneven throb—before fading to a dull, grayish blur.

She heard a sound, too—almost a static, like the click of beetles in a bone-dry field. It filled her ears, drowned out the low voices of the crowd, and made her scalp crawl. The first sign that something was wrong was in the color of Makota's apron: what had been a vibrant green only moments before was now a washed-out, sickly gray, as if all the pigment had been drained by a single, greedy mouth.

A child whimpered.

Galhani's eyes snapped to the far side of the square, where the children had been chasing each other, bright kites in hand. One of the kites —a brilliant red triangle, stitched by Prudence's own hand—had turned the color of old linen. The child holding it tugged desperately on the string, but the kite didn't respond, just sagged and wilted in the air before finally tumbling to earth.

A gasp moved through the crowd, then a mutter, then a rising panic as other details shifted and dulled. The painted trim on the bakery shed flickered from plum to ash in a blink. The fire beneath the kettle, once so confident, sputtered and cracked, its orange and yellow paling to the color of cheap wax.

Galhani's mouth filled with a sudden, awful bitterness. She coughed, almost retched, and looked to the bowl. The tea inside was no longer gold, or even brown, but a bilious, green-black sludge. The scent—once sharp and invigorating—had become acrid, like burned hair and vinegar. She felt a wave of nausea and dread.

She looked around in frantic desperation, seeking help, a hint, a way out. Leota stood motionless, lips pressed white, eyes furious but helpless. Warren's big hands clutched the rim of the crate so hard that the wood began to splinter. Cole was shaking, his arm around his family, as if he could shield them with body alone. Even Polyocular was silent, the three blue eyes glassy and blank.

The crowd began to edge backward, some drawing the children away, others murmuring darkly about curses and reversals. Lucy was weeping, hands cupped over her mouth. Prudence was rocking her baby, face twisted with anxiety.

Galhani tried to stir the brew, tried to bring back the rhythm, the intention, the purpose—but with every stroke of the spoon, the liquid grew murkier, the smell more foul. Her hands shook so badly she almost dropped the ladle. She heard the voices now—not from the crowd, but inside her own mind. They hissed and clicked, a thousand tiny knives, each one finding a soft spot to stab.

Your magic is broken.

You've made it worse.

They see you now, and they know.

You've failed them all.

She wanted to scream. She wanted to run. But her feet were locked to the ground, the weight of expectation heavier than ever. She felt the hope bleed out of the circle and into the ground, where it pooled in cold, oily darkness.

The world shrank to a pinpoint of sensation: the rotten stink of ruined tea, the cold on her skin, the grinding sound in her ears. The hum was gone. The laughter and the light—all gone. In its place, a raw and bottomless hunger. She remembered the line from Vamir's book: *It is not alive, not as the world understands it, but it is hungry, and it will not rest until it eats itself to sleep or is starved by purpose restored.*

Galhani tried to fight it, to recall the morning's hope, but the voice in her head was louder than anything she could muster:

You are not enough.

You never were.

A hand gripped her shoulder—Lara, steady and solid, but the warmth was gone, replaced by a distant, numbing pressure that might as well have belonged to a stranger. Galhani wanted to lean into the touch, but the chill was too deep.

The murmurs in the crowd grew louder. Someone shouted, "Stop! You're making it worse!" and the words lashed across her skin. A wave of fear swept through the circle. The travelers and new arrivals were already leaving, grabbing their bags, their children, hurrying for the safety of closed doors and old habits.

In her ears, the static built to a deafening shriek. The world dimmed, and the last thing she saw before her vision narrowed to black was the tea, bubbling and roiling in its bowl, the surface broken by little bursts of steam that stank of failure.

Galhani closed her eyes. She had nothing left.

She floated for a while in the darkness, the static droning to a distant thrum. The crowd's voices faded, replaced by the old, familiar ache of loneliness. It was the same emptiness that had haunted her since before she learned to read, before she knew what it meant to want something so badly that it hurt.

You are not enough.

You never were.

But the voice—so sharp, so certain at first—grew thin, lost its edge, became a sullen whine as it echoed around the empty space inside her head. It was like listening to a distant argument in a language she no longer cared to understand. It repeated itself, but each time, the words grew less real.

She reached back, beyond the tea, beyond the circle, beyond even the town itself. She remembered her father's kitchen, remembered the first time he let her measure the water, the way his huge, rough hands guided hers, steady but never forceful. He'd said, "Don't rush it. It's not about the boiling, it's about the waiting." She'd hated waiting, had always thought the world could be fixed by moving faster, by thinking harder, by being the first to finish.

The next memory was Sam, not long after Galhani had come to town, sitting in the Claw, pouring a drink slow and deliberate. "The strongest magic isn't always the loudest," Sam had said, "and it's rarely the prettiest." She'd laughed after, as if it was a joke, but the words stuck.

She let the static hiss, let it break apart and fade into nothing.

She opened her eyes, and the world had not changed, not really. The fire was nearly out, the crowd in shambles. The tea was still a cloudy mess, the air sour and cold. But she was still here. She hadn't left.

She set the ladle down, and instead picked up the spoon, the old wooden one with the burned mark at the tip where her mother had once left it too close to the hearth. She gave the pot a single, steady stir, not to fix it but to remember how it felt. She let her hands move slow, the way her father had shown her, the way every gnome in her line had moved when the stakes were highest and the odds the worst.

She heard a sound—soft, but real. Lara's breath, close and even, not afraid. Galhani looked up, and Lara's eyes were waiting for her, calm and open.

"You're still here," Lara said, and the words were a lifeline.

"So are you," Galhani replied. She reached for the kettle, drew a shallow cup, and this time, instead of tossing it back or sharing it with the crowd, she sipped. The first taste was awful, but she held it in her mouth, let the flavors settle. Beneath the bitterness, there was a ghost of sweetness, a trace of what it had been.

She remembered the next part, the part from her grandmother's stories: When all else fails, serve with both hands.

She poured another cup, handed it to Lara. Lara smiled, drank, and grimaced—but swallowed anyway.

Galhani looked to the crowd, which had thinned to a ring of the most stubborn: Warren and Susan, Makota and her two, Lucy and Vamir, Leota, Cole, even Dexter and Minnie, huddled together at the edge of the line. The rest hovered farther back, watching, waiting, afraid but not gone.

She poured a cup for Warren, who took it in his huge hand and sniffed. He sipped, made a face, but then let out a laugh that was so sudden and bright it shocked the night. "I've made worse," he boomed, and set the cup down with a thunk.

Makota was next. She sipped, ears flicking, and then handed the cup to her kits. They tasted, and one sneezed, but then started to purr —a sound low and strange, but undeniably pleased.

Lucy took hers and drank. Her face, still red from crying, softened. She did not speak, but she nodded once, a gesture of acceptance.

It spread from there, person to person, each one passing the cup, each one finding something—however faint—to hold onto.

As the cups moved, so did the air. The static receded, replaced by a softer hum. The fire, nearly gone, caught on a stubborn ember and sprang up, just enough to throw shadows back onto the circle. The color did not return all at once, but slowly—first in the ribbon of a girl's braid, then in the gold of the bakery sign, then in the deep blue of the sky, newly visible between the clouds.

Galhani felt a pulse—not of power, but of something better. She looked around at the faces, at the hands passing cups, at the way the circle was holding, not by force but by the small, repeated act of sharing. She realized then that the magic wasn't the tea, or the chalk, or even the words. It was the simple, stupid act of not giving up. Of serving, even when there was nothing left to serve.

She set the kettle down and looked past the circle, to where the travelers and wagon-vendors stood at the edge of the green, watching, not with hope but with hunger. They had not been invited. The rules of the ritual, as old as any in the town, said it was only for those who belonged.

But that was the parasite's trick, wasn't it? To make you believe you had to protect what was left, when the only thing that had ever worked was letting it go.

She stood, her legs wobbly but steady enough. She called out, loud enough for the whole square to hear: "This is for all! It's not ours alone! If you're here, you're part of it. Come share. Come drink! *We serve all!*"

There was a moment of silence, then a stirring at the edge. The travelers, the new shopkeepers, even the ones who'd only been in town a sennight or less—one by one, they moved in. Some hung back, suspicious, but others pressed forward, drawn by the scent, the light, the possibility that maybe, just maybe, they could belong, too.

Galhani poured more cups, passed them around. The townsfolk made space, widened the circle, extended hands.

The parasite hissed in her mind, but its voice was thin now, all teeth and no jaw. It faded as the circle grew.

The kettle steamed, and the color inside was gold again—not as bright as before, maybe, but true. The taste, when she tried it, was nothing special. But it was enough.

They drank together, old and new, broken and stubborn, and the circle held.

It always had.

The fire blazed up so suddenly that it startled even the old-timers, those who had watched a hundred bonfires climb into the night sky and come back down as ash. The logs caught with a roar, licking gold and blue high above the kettle, illuminating every line and edge in the square. For the first time all night, the air was properly warm—a shock of comfort after so much chill.

The change in the tea was immediate. What had been a scum of bitterness on the surface cracked and fell away, sinking to the bottom as the liquid above cleared to a pure, amber brightness. The scent rolled out in a wave, sharper than any before: citrus and honey, a hint of mint, and under it all the slow, sweet gravity of a perfect summer day. The steam curled into the air, catching the firelight and refracting it in a hundred directions.

As the cups were passed again, this time to anyone who would take one, Galhani watched the faces change. The first sip brought surprise, then delight, then laughter—real, loud, unselfconscious. Hands reached for seconds. The old jokes returned, and the regulars at the back of the circle started up a song, low and rough but rich with harmony.

Color flooded back into the world, not in a single sweep but in pulses. The bakery's sign, once faded and cracked, gleamed with a lacquered yellow that made the morning sun seem dull by comparison. The flower boxes beneath Lucy's windows threw out new blooms, the petals so bright they almost hurt to look at. Even the stone of the square's flagstones seemed to shed its grayness, showing veins of gold and quartz that hadn't been visible in years.

Galhani felt it in her bones: the moment the parasite broke. There was a sound—like glass shattering, but soft, somewhere in the distance—and then a surge of relief so strong it made her knees buckle. The static was gone, replaced by a low, even hum that settled in her chest. She looked at Lara, who was watching her with wet eyes and a smile so wide it looked dangerous.

People were talking, shouting, laughing. Cole and Caitlin danced a clumsy reel, lifting their children into the air and spinning them until the kids shrieked with joy. Makota's kits ran wild, chasing each other in circles and colliding with the legs of anyone who didn't dodge fast enough. Even Warren, who had sworn he'd never dance again, let Susan drag him into a slow, swaying orbit near the fire.

Galhani poured herself a cup, let it cool for a moment, then drank. The taste was—perfect. Not fancy, not magical in the way spells were, but exactly right, like the flavor of a memory you thought you'd lost forever.

Leota approached, arms folded, her dress catching every shadow the fire could throw. "Well done," she said.

Galhani laughed. "It wasn't me. It was all of us."

Leota nodded, then glanced over her shoulder at the edge of the square. "Have you noticed?" she whispered.

Galhani looked. The travelers, the wagon-vendors, even the shop-keepers who had only just arrived in the past moon—gone. Not a trace of the wagons or the sandwich boards or the pop-up shops remained. It was as if they had never existed, or had dissolved at the first hint of real magic. The green was empty now, save for the townsfolk and the lights and the last of the night birds fluttering through the fire's updraft.

"They left?" Galhani said, half to herself.

Leota shrugged. "Maybe the town let them go. Maybe they never really wanted to stay."

"Or maybe," said Lara, joining them, "this was always just a stop along the road for them. They took what they needed, and now it's our turn."

Galhani found her hand in Lara's, fingers interlaced, warm and sure. For a moment, she just stood and let the world happen around her. The music, the laughter, the pulse of community stronger than any magic she could have brewed on her own.

When the last cup had been poured, when even the ashes in the fire glowed contentedly, Galhani and Lara sat together on the old stone bench that overlooked the green. They watched the crowd dwindle, the families drifting back to homes and beds, the regulars lingering to trade stories and watch the embers die.

Galhani poured a final cup, split it with Lara, and toasted the night. The taste was even better than before, if only because it was the last.

They drank it slow. There was nothing left to rush.

Above, the sky was black and full of stars, each one a promise that tomorrow would come, and with it, a new day.

For the first time in a long time, Galhani believed it.

seventeen

. . .

THE MORNING LIGHT in North Pointe Common Towne was not gold but a milky, watery blue, the color of frost under glass. Galhani stood just inside the tea shop's door, bare toes curling on the worn wood, and watched the street as if it were a stage and she the only one in the audience. The town square was a hush of motion, not the awkward quiet of uncertainty but the soft, collective breath of something newly begun. She had not slept, not really, but had drifted in and out of dreams so closely tethered to memory that the two refused to be sorted.

She felt the old pull to get a head start—be the first to sweep the stoop, the first to set out chairs for the morning's regulars, the first to see if the flavor of the magic would hold. Instead, she lingered, watching the vendors who clustered along the trade road as they packed their wares into crates and trunks with a kind of gentle, methodical disappointment.

One of the wagon-mongers—a man with a long face and fingers perpetually ink-stained—hoisted a crate of "Inspiration Candles" onto his cart and caught sight of her. "Early as ever," he called, but it was not the jeer it might have been yesterday. "You hear about the scones?" He jerked his head toward the bakery.

Galhani squinted down the lane. Makota's kits had already set up a table outside the bakery, bright pastries stacked in a pyramid, and were engaged in a loud and deeply technical debate about whether the blue glaze on their new spiral bun was sufficiently blue. The younger of the two saw her, yipped, and pointed. Within seconds, both kits were waving vigorously, and Galhani waved back.

The vendor gave a shrug that nearly toppled his crate. "Supposedly the first one sold this morning made a grown woman weep," he said, "and I'm not even sure it was the Felis owner." His lips twitched. "Starting to feel like someone who came to a party under-dressed."

He was one of a dozen or so vendors packing up as if the road itself had suggested it was time to move along. Their wagons, with their hopeful banners and slogans—"Soap for Sore Spirits," "Coins Traded for Confidence"—had started the sennight jostling for space on the approach to the green. Now, as Galhani watched, they seemed to recede from the town, the weight of their own surplus dragging them home.

She watched another trader—this one purveyor of "Betterment Tablets," small chalky disks meant to make one's inner life more vivid —fold up a rickety sandwich board with care, then gently sweep up the unsold tablets into a muslin sack. He caught her looking and flashed a brittle smile. "Lost my edge, I guess," he said. "Might try again next spring, if you're still here."

The joke was gentle, but Galhani heard the smallness in it. "We'll be here," she said, "unless you can talk the mountain into moving."

He gave a tired laugh and tipped an imaginary hat.

Travelers came and went in twos and threes, but there was a difference now; they no longer passed through North Pointe with the harried hunger of the desperate or the practiced scorn of the bored. A cluster of young women, bundled in mismatched shawls, stopped in front of Galhani's shop and pointed at her window display. One of them pressed her nose to the glass and said, "This is the place I told you about—the one with the tea that makes you see in colors." The others snickered, but within moments all three were inside, the air behind them pulsing with the cold as they crowded up to the counter.

She served them without ceremony, measuring leaves with a

steady hand. The giddiness of the night's victory was still with her, and she felt no need to hurry. She heard the girls chatter as they sipped their cups—"It's really back!" one said, as if she hadn't expected it—while outside, the day arranged itself into lines and shapes she'd never noticed before. A man in a motley cloak crossed the street, pausing to break off a piece of Makota's new blue-glazed bun and pop it into his mouth; he staggered, then gave a whoop, and half the bakery's queue turned to see what could possibly justify that level of delight.

Galhani let herself savor it. The flavor of the morning was not just in the tea but in the air itself, tinged with the bright, peppery tang of renewal and the softer, richer bass note of relief. She watched the travelers, the vendors, the children playing at the edges of the square, and she found herself humming under her breath.

She passed the first of the shuttered shops. "Darning for Socks" had always been an odd fit—no one in town had ever seen the proprietor, and the interior looked as if a single pair of needles had been left to fend for themselves among a sea of thread. This morning, the window was papered over, and a modest pile of battered darning eggs lay in a crate on the stoop, a handwritten sign offering them "free to a better home." She took one, feeling its smoothness, and dropped it into her apron pocket. The absence of the shop felt not like loss, but like a cough clearing the throat.

Next door, "Tuning for Harps" was being emptied in quiet, efficient stages. The owner—a dour fellow who had once told Galhani she "lacked the wrist" for serious stringed work—was out front, wrapping the last of his tuning forks in a rag. He saw her, nodded, and did not bother with the usual warning about "the peril of slackening your strings." Instead, he said, "If you need a fork for the tea kettle, I have some left," and then, with a slight smile, "or perhaps you have everything tuned already."

"I think we're close," she said.

He seemed to approve, and she kept moving.

Some of the shops had not simply closed, but had vanished. A storefront that had previously been covered in garish, ever-changing chalk slogans ("Buy Your Next Self Here!") was now a blank wall, the seams between the stones smoother than they ought to be. Galhani ran her fingers across them, marveling at how thoroughly the building had let go of its former life.

Elsewhere, the doors and windows remained, but the interiors were hollow, shelves cleared and swept. She saw one woman—her face vaguely familiar, but perhaps only because she looked like half the women who'd ever sold lace or perfume on a trade road—sit on the stoop of her "Unmatched Buttons" emporium, feet dangling, and stare out at the sun rising over the hills. She wore a green cap and a faded dress, and the basket on her lap was empty. For a moment, Galhani considered stopping, but the woman seemed content with her silence.

The farther she walked, the more she saw it: the town's peculiar ability to slough off what did not belong, to heal itself by subtraction as much as by addition. It had not always been this way. There had been moons, even years, when North Pointe held onto every grudge, every slight, every failed experiment in trade or magic or love, storing them up like a squirrel with a grudge against winter. But now, after last night, the place felt lighter, the air inside the walls moving freely for the first time since the parasite's shadow had crept in.

She wove back toward the shop, her small frame dipping and darting among the carts and departing vendors. A trio of children nearly bowled her over, too busy chasing a wooden hoop to notice the gnome in their path. She stepped aside, let them pass, and grinned at their shrieks of apology—half genuine, half performative, all of it delightful.

At the edge of the green, just before the road turned toward the lake, a wagon loaded with "Efficiency Schedules" had jammed its wheel into a rut. The owner, red-faced and sweating, was cursing at the axle. Galhani approached, and offered a hand—not that she could help, really, but it seemed wrong to watch someone struggle with such a bad idea in broad daylight. He glanced at her, recognized the offer, and together they rocked the wagon loose. The vendor paused, looking up and down the street as if realizing for the first time how many of the other peddlers had already left.

"Not much market for this now, is there?" he said, with a wry smile.

She shrugged. "You never know. The world's always got a use for more time."

He nodded, and for a moment, Galhani thought he might start crying. Instead, he heaved himself onto the driver's seat, gave her a solemn little bow, and rolled off toward the gates.

She lingered at the intersection, watching as the last of the efficiency, the betterment, the inspiration, and the unmatched all made their way out of town. What remained was only the familiar: the bakery, the potter's, the smithy, the inn, and of course her own little corner of the world. It was not much, but it was everything she needed.

She felt a pang then—not of loss, but of curiosity. The town had done its part. Now it was her turn to see if the flavor held.

The first real test came at Warren's forge. The smithy was a squat, heavy-limbed building of blackened stone, its roof slung low like the brow of a boxer. Even from the street, Galhani could feel the pulse of heat from within, and as she drew near, the air took on the flavor of scorched iron and the sweet tang of burning oak.

Warren's shadow filled the doorway—a green mountain of a man, his sleeves rolled high, arms laced with veins like rope. The hammer he wielded looked as if it had been forged for a creature twice his size, but he swung it with the delicate, almost hesitant touch of a gardener tending seedlings.

Today, there was no trace of the tension that had haunted his movements during the long, cursed sennights. The blows were measured, each strike followed by a hum of satisfaction. The sound was so regular, so right, that for a moment Galhani thought she could feel the echoes in her chest cavity.

She let herself stand and watch, certain she would be noticed, and certain it would not matter if she was.

Warren finished his current run of strikes, then set the hammer down with a softness that belied its heft. He squinted through the steam, noticed her, and gave a lopsided smile. "Heard the parade passed you by," he said, voice like gravel rolled in honey. "Surprised you're not out in front, leading it."

Galhani grinned. "Had to see if the morning was real. The way people are acting, I half expected to find the green paved with gold."

Warren snorted, then beckoned her closer. "Better than gold," he said. "We got work again."

He took the bar of metal—still glowing at the tip, but losing heat by the second—and held it up for her inspection. It was not a horseshoe, nor a door hinge, but the beginnings of something long and narrow, with a twist at the base that made it seem almost alive. Galhani reached up (she had to stand on tiptoe to see) and looked at the shape. "Sword?" she guessed.

"Yours if you want it," Warren said, "but I think it's for someone coming soon. Had the dream last night. Clear as ever. Big fellow—could be human, could be something else—coming in from the north, pursued by three bandits. Makes it here just in time. Needs this to make it through."

He ran a finger along the blade's edge. "Used to be the dreams were muddy. Last moon, they were gone altogether. Today..." He trailed off, eyes gone distant. "It's like I remember what my own hands are for."

Galhani felt a spike of pride—not in herself, but in him, and in the town. "That's how it's supposed to be," she said.

He nodded, then reached for the tongs. "And you? You feel the magic come back?"

She considered. "It's there. Maybe stronger than before."

Warren rumbled with satisfaction. "Good. The world's been off-balance too long."

She watched him lay the metal on the anvil, lining it up with a practiced eye. "If the dream's right," she said, "he'll be here before supper. You think you can finish by then?"

He rolled his shoulders, the muscle and bone cracking audibly. "If not, I'll fake it and apologize later."

Across the street, a line of white linens fluttered from the inn's porch. Minnie—short, round, and as cheerful as a plum—was out front with her son Trevor, the boy barely visible under the armful of towels he carried. They moved together in a dance as old as hospitality itself, Minnie pinning one end while Trevor hopped and stretched to loop the other over the line.

A pair of travelers stood nearby, saddlebags in hand, their faces creased with the pale, almost reluctant joy of people who had woken up to a new world and weren't quite ready to trust it. One of them caught Galhani's eye and smiled shyly.

"Best night's sleep I've had since Dendria," the woman said, bowing her head a little. "Dreamt I was back home. Not back there, exactly, but—" she glanced at her partner, searching for the word, "— like home, but better. Brighter."

Trevor's head popped up over a towel. "Ma says the beds are magic now. Or maybe they always were and the magic just went hiding."

Minnie shooed him with a flick of her wrist. "Ignore him. Beds are only magic if you don't eat the pillows."

The travelers laughed, then wandered toward the bakery, voices trailing behind like banners. Galhani paused, watching as Minnie dropped a hand to Trevor's head, ruffling the boy's hair with an affection so casual it stung. For a moment, she thought of the home she'd left, the parents she missed, the way her father had always made morning seem like a promise.

She crossed to the inn, letting her feet crunch on the frost-bleached grass. Minnie grinned and waved her in.

"Is it true?" Minnie asked, eyes wide with the pleasure of a gossip well-earned. "They say you started it. That you made the fire burn right through the sickness."

Galhani flushed. "It was everyone. I just poured the tea."

Minnie raised an eyebrow. "Pouring the tea is the most important part."

She offered Galhani a seat on the front bench, and for a few minutes they sat together, talking about nothing and everything—the guests who'd left at dawn, the rumors of a new clockmaker in the next town over, the prospect of a proper party on the green once the weather turned. It was the first time in moons that conversation felt like a gift, not a duty.

Eventually, Galhani excused herself and walked the curve of the square to the Broken Claw. The pub was quiet, the door propped open to let the cold air clear the last of the smoke from last night's revelry. Sam stood behind the bar, her white hair falling in a sharp angle over the ragged scar that ran from her brow to her chin. She was cleaning glasses with a thoroughness bordering on violence, but her face was soft, almost lazy.

She looked up, saw Galhani, and let out a whistle. "If it isn't the town's new saint."

"I'm retired," Galhani replied.

Sam grinned, set the glass down, and poured herself a small measure of something from a new cask. The liquid caught the sun through the window, sparkling gold.

She sipped, rolled it on her tongue, and gave a tiny nod. "Back to proper," she said. "None of that sour edge it's had for sennights. You done good."

Galhani slid onto a stool. "Did you sleep?"

"Like a woman who just quit three wars at once," Sam said, and it sounded true.

They talked for a while. The morning crowd was thin—just two regulars and a thin man in traveler's garb, face hidden by a high collar —but the mood in the room was light, unburdened. Sam's movements were unhurried, her voice low and content. Even the scar seemed less severe in the new light, as if the night had given her permission to let it rest.

She poured Galhani a taste from the same cask. "You did more than you think, little one."

"I just followed the recipe."

Sam leaned on the bar, her eyes sharp but kind. "That's all anyone ever does. The trick is to know which recipe to follow."

Galhani drank, savoring the warmth and the slow, gentle burn.

At the far end of the green, the outfitters shop was already open, Tyran's booming voice echoing from the awning as he extolled the virtues of a newly-restocked pack or an "indestructible" tin canteen. He was demonstrating a pocketknife to a trio of travelers, the blade glinting in the morning sun, his hands moving with the exaggerated confidence of a man who had never doubted himself for a second.

Galhani watched as he closed the sale, shaking hands with all three travelers and then, when they were gone, turning to reorganize the display window. She approached, and he greeted her with a bear-like embrace that nearly lifted her off the ground.

"Did you see what happened?" Tyran said, voice loud enough to carry half a block. "Overnight, the shop put all the good stuff back up front. Real gear, none of that plastic rubbish." He gestured to a rack of boots, each pair perfectly matched and polished. "I swear the place just knows when the world's right again."

"Maybe it just follows your mood," Galhani said.

He roared with laughter, then lowered his voice. "No, it's you. You sang the green back to life last night."

Galhani tried to demur, but he cut her off. "Don't sell yourself short. Takes a special kind of person to get this town in line."

He squeezed her shoulder, then set about rearranging a row of hats that had apparently appeared overnight. They were all practical now —broad-brimmed, well-made, ready for rain or sun. None of the old fads, none of the desperation.

Galhani smiled, then took the long way back to her shop, weaving through the last of the carts and the first wave of new arrivals. She saw faces she hadn't seen in sennights—children walking to the schoolhouse, neighbors trading gossip, the butcher and the baker haggling over the price of eggs. Every movement, every gesture, seemed to shine.

She reached her door, put her hand on the worn brass knob, and paused for just a moment, letting the sounds of the town fill her head. It was not perfect. It would never be perfect. But it was whole, and it was home.

She stepped inside, ready to begin again.

———

The tea shop's bell jangled as Galhani pushed open the door, and she was greeted not by the musty quiet of the last few sennights, but by the soft thrum of anticipation—a queue of early risers, some in traveling cloaks, some in the patched, familiar coats of neighbors. The sun was only just breaking past the roofs of the square, but already the window was fogged with the breath of waiting customers.

She took her place behind the counter, the old ache in her wrists already replaced with the sharp, almost giddy thrill of competence. The line was not long—never more than four at a time—but the orders came quick, each request a small puzzle to solve. She found herself mixing leaves by memory, her hands moving in rhythm with the flow of the morning. Every now and then, a customer would pause to comment on the blend, and the compliments—never false, always measured—landed in her heart like drops of honey.

"New batch?" asked the baker, her mouth already dusted with flour. "Tastes like spring in the hills."

Galhani grinned. "That's where it's from. Picked it myself."

The baker sipped, then winked. "Keep doing it, then."

By the time the bell chimed for the tenth time, her shelves were lighter, her chest looser. She barely noticed the passage of time. The tea did not just taste good; it sang. The customers lingered, talking in low voices, and the sound in the shop was the closest thing to music she could remember.

When the last of the morning crowd drifted out, Galhani slumped against the counter, head tilted back, and closed her eyes. She heard Lara come in, heard the soft footfalls across the scuffed floor, and smiled before opening her eyes.

Lara's hair was pulled back, her cheeks pink from the cold. She moved behind the counter and set her hands on Galhani's shoulders, squeezing them with gentle pressure. "You did it," she said.

Galhani opened her mouth to argue, but the words wouldn't come. She let herself sag, just for a second, and let Lara hold her up.

"It's not all fixed," Galhani said, voice small. "But it's working."

Lara leaned in, her face so close that Galhani could see the fine lines at the corners of her eyes, the silvered lashes that never showed in daylight. "That's all we need. The rest we can figure out."

They stayed like that for a long moment, the quiet in the shop a comfort rather than an absence.

At noon, Finnian appeared in the doorway, his hands full of contraptions and a look on his face that could only be described as "scientific glee." He nearly tripped over the threshold, then righted himself, offering up a small brass disc.

"Watch," he said, and held it in his palm. The disc flickered, then spun, then projected a faint image above his hand—two young children chasing each other around the green, their laughter so clear Galhani could almost hear it.

She reached for it, and as soon as her fingers brushed the brass, the image shifted: now a pair of old men sharing a drink on a sunlit porch, the air full of the scent of bread and honey.

"See? It's working," Finnian said, eyes wide. "But only since this morning. Until now, it was just... nothing. I think the magic finally settled."

Galhani turned the disc in her hands, feeling the pulse of energy inside. "It's beautiful," she said, and meant it.

Finnian looked sheepish, then leaned in close. "I tested it on the baker—she saw herself finding a coin in a loaf, and five minutes later, she did." He beamed. "It's never been that precise before."

Lara glanced at the disc. "What happens if you use it on yourself?"

Finnian's ears turned red. "Nothing. It just shows me standing here, handing this to you." He shrugged. "Which is exactly where I want to be."

They laughed, and the sound filled the shop.

Later that afternoon, after the rush and the laughter had faded, Galhani stepped outside with Finnian, the two of them taking in the quiet that had returned to the square. It was not the brittle silence of uncertainty, but a slow, comfortable hush—the way the world sounded when it trusted itself again.

On the bench beneath the bakery's window, Lucy sat with Leota. The potter's hands were dusted with blue, and she was holding a mug of something steaming, her gaze on the middle distance. Leota, all in black, watched the street with her usual keen, predatory focus, but when she saw Galhani and Finnian, she waved them over.

Galhani settled onto the bench, legs swinging above the ground, and looked at Lucy. The other woman was quiet, her face softer than usual, the scars on her fingers almost pretty in the sun.

"I'm leaving," Lucy said, and there was no drama in it, just a plain statement of fact. "Not right away. But soon. South, maybe. There's a school for potters past the old line, and I think it's time."

Galhani felt something tighten in her chest. "Are you sure?"

Lucy nodded. "I never made anything that wasn't touched by the magic here. When it went away, I realized I needed to know if I could make things on my own." She smiled, the corners of her mouth trembling. "I want to try. I want to see if it's me, or just the town."

Leota sipped her drink. "She's not running," she said, as if reading the thought on Galhani's face. "She's testing herself."

Finnian fidgeted with the disc in his pocket. "You'll come back, though, right?"

Lucy reached over, squeezed his arm. "Of course. If only to see what new machines you've made."

They all laughed, and it was easy, unforced.

For a while, the four of them sat together, watching the people on the green. Sam ambled by, her arms folded and her stride easy. Warren and Susan paused to greet Minnie, who had a basket of sweet rolls for the guests leaving town. Across the street, Makota and her kits were painting a new sign for the bakery, the three of them arguing over the spelling of a single word.

The sun dipped behind the roofs, and the square glowed with the warmth of a day well lived.

Galhani looked around, taking in the faces, the sounds, the small pieces of a world she'd almost lost. She thought of the shops—the exact number, twenty, no more and no less. She thought of the way the magic moved, not as a flood but as a tide, gentle and persistent, shaping the shore over and over. She thought of Lucy, and Finnian, and even Leota, and how each of them had chosen to stay or go, not out of fear, but out of hope.

She looked at Lara, who stood just inside the shop, watching her with an affection so clear it made Galhani's heart ache.

For a long time, she had believed her worth was in what she could do, what she could fix. Now, for the first time, she understood that her value was in the trying, in the stubbornness, in the joy she brought to even the smallest parts of the day.

When the sky finally darkened and the lamps along the street flickered to life, Galhani stood, dusted off her skirt, and led the others back inside.

———

Lucy returned to the tea shop in the thin moments before sunset, arms full of odd-shaped bundles and a satchel slung heavy on her hip. She wore her best work shirt—the one with the indigo collar and the paint-stained cuffs—and her hair was pulled back so tight that it looked like a challenge to the world. Galhani heard her boots on the stoop and felt the urge to duck behind the counter, but she stayed put, hands wrapped around the warm pot on the stove.

Lara was stacking mugs, her back to the door, but she turned when Lucy entered and gave her a smile that was all welcome, no sorrow. Lucy grinned back and dropped the first of her bundles on the closest table. "Thought I'd see if you had any of that new blend left. Might be a while before I taste anything like it again."

"Plenty," Galhani said, and her voice sounded steadier than she felt. She filled a mug and slid it across, fingers brushing Lucy's for a blink. The silence in the room was good, thick with unspoken things, but none of them sharp.

Lucy took a sip and made a face, then grinned. "You ever think about how tea is just a way to slow time down?"

"Sometimes I hope it does," Galhani said, and that was the truth.

They sat together, Lara abandoning her tower of mugs to pull up a chair. Lucy worked at the satchel, unspooling lengths of twine and little parcels wrapped in linen. She laid them out one at a time on the table—mugs, a few bowls, the smallest pitcher Galhani had ever seen, all finished and glazed in colors so deep they looked alive. Each one had a flaw: a chip, or a run in the glaze, or an edge that didn't quite match the curve. Lucy arranged them in a row, her hands careful, as if she was saying goodbye to kittens.

"These are for you," she said, looking at the table instead of at

Galhani or Lara. "I made extras, for the shop. Thought maybe you could use them for the traveling crowd, next time they come through."

Galhani tried to find words, but her tongue stuck, so she reached for the closest mug and turned it over in her hands. The base was stamped with Lucy's mark, a tiny swirl set inside a circle. The blue was the color of early morning, and the rim was uneven in a way that felt deliberate.

"They're beautiful," Lara said. "No one else could have made these."

Lucy shrugged, but the tips of her ears went pink. "Maybe. I want to find out, though." She paused, then said, "I think I've been scared to try. Maybe I need to let myself fail, just to see what's left."

The quiet that followed was full of warmth. Galhani poured another round of tea and set the pot between them. She tried to fix the moment in her head: the slant of the light through the lace curtain, the steam rising in lazy spirals, the way Lara's hand rested just close enough that Galhani could reach it if she wanted.

Lucy finished her tea, then stood up and shouldered her satchel. "Time I was going, then." She paused, her eyes a bit moist. "Look in on Finnian, will you?"

"You two got close quickly," Galhani said softly. "Of course."

Lucy opened her mouth as if to say something, but quickly closed it and smiled. With a nod, she was out the door and on her way.

eighteen

· · ·

THE MORNINGS at Finnian's shop always started the same way: with the steady pulse of the wall clocks, a hint of lemon-oil polish in the air, and the faint memory of the forest outside town carried in by the draft beneath the door. Today, a wedge of light from the eastern window cut a pale path across his workbench, scattering gold over the battered surface and making every screw and gearhead gleam like treasure.

Finnian cradled the pocket watch in his palm, its case warm from his own skin. The hands on its tiny dial quivered in anticipation—a trick of the trembling spring, but also a reflection of his own nerves, which had not yet fully accepted that the world was back in order. He used his finest screwdriver to nudge the minute hand into place, feeling the soft give of the brass against the tool. Satisfying, and a little bit sad: once, he'd wanted all his repairs to be invisible. Now, he found comfort in the subtle marks he left behind.

He held the watch to his ear and listened. The tick was crisp, with just a hint of stutter at the top of each minute. He closed his eyes, letting the rhythm count off the seconds inside his skull. It was not perfect, but it was alive, and sometimes that was enough.

"Don't you ever get tired of the sound?" came a voice from the doorway.

He didn't have to turn to know it was Galhani. Her approach was always careful—never a sudden entrance, but a gradual reveal, as if she were testing the room for danger before letting herself in. She carried a mug in each hand, both steaming, and the look on her face was equal parts curiosity and concern.

"Good morning," Finnian said, setting the watch aside. "I thought you'd be busy with the morning rush."

She made a face. "The rush can wait. I wanted to see if you needed a refill."

He reached for the mug, the heat seeping into his chilled fingers. "Thanks. This is…?"

"Garden blend," she said. "It's mostly mint, but there's some of the wild yarrow from the ridge."

He sipped. The tea was sharp, invigorating. "It tastes like standing in a field."

"That's the idea." She perched on the edge of the counter, legs dangling, scanning the shelves with a kind of hungry restlessness. "You ever think about closing all these up, just for a candlemark? The noise must drive you mad."

He shrugged. "It's not really noise. I'd miss it, if it stopped."

Galhani nodded, looking unconvinced. "Maybe. Or maybe you'd find you like the quiet even more."

A creak at the door interrupted them, and a customer entered—a young woman, hair braided with copper wire, eyes darting between the displays with the greedy joy of someone who had never owned a clock in her life. Finnian recognized her as one of the new arrivals from last sennight, a traveler who had decided to stay a few nights.

She pointed at a glass dome on the shelf. "What's that one do?"

He set down his mug and retrieved the dome. Beneath the glass, a tiny brass bird perched atop a music box. When he turned the key, the bird bobbed its head, and a line of clear notes wound out, filling the shop with a tune so sweet it made Finnian's chest ache.

The woman clapped. "Is it magic?"

"Just mechanism," Finnian said, and for the first time in years he felt a pang of pride at the answer. "The trick is in the camshaft. It lifts the bird's beak exactly in time with the chime."

The woman watched, transfixed, as the bird pecked at an invisible seed and the song resolved into a delicate trill. "How much?" she asked.

He named a price, too low, but she grinned and handed over a small stack of coins from her pocket. As she left, cradling the dome like a lost child, the bell above the door gave a lazy jangle.

Galhani watched the exchange, then turned her gaze to Finnian. "You could sell a thousand of those if you wanted," she said.

He smiled. "But then I'd never see what happens to them. Or who takes them home." He set the tools aside, wiping his hands on a linen square. "Besides, I like having projects."

Galhani looked at him for a long moment, then asked, "Do you ever... I don't know. Make things just for yourself?"

Finnian thought of the drawer beneath his bench, where half-finished experiments and old failures lived side by side. "Sometimes," he said. "But it's easier to finish them when I know someone else is waiting."

Galhani seemed to understand. She set her mug down, and for a while they listened to the ticking, the silence thick but not uncomfortable.

After she left, Finnian opened the drawer and took out his current secret: a wooden flower, its petals sanded thin as tissue, each one painted with a thin wash of blue and gold. The flower was mounted on a stalk of polished walnut, and at its base was a complex array of gears and levers, so delicate he had needed three tries to get them to mesh correctly.

He placed the flower on the windowsill, where the sunbeam caught the tip of each petal. He wound the key at the back, slow and careful, then waited.

As the sunlight shifted, the petals quivered—just a little at first, then with more confidence. They began to open, each gear turning in slow harmony with the others, until the flower stood fully revealed, basking in the warmth.

Finnian let out a shaky laugh. For moons, he'd tried to make it work. The last time he'd attempted anything so ambitious, he'd nearly thrown the whole thing in the stove. But now, watching the motion play out, he felt a surge of relief, and then, quietly, a feeling of rightness.

He closed his eyes and listened to the town beyond the walls of his shop—the distant ring of the smithy, the children's calls in the square, the hiss of bread crusts breaking in the bakery oven. Everything in its place, every second accounted for.

He looked at the flower again. The gears caught the light, the petals luminous, and for a moment he imagined every house in North Pointe with one on its table, opening and closing with the day.

The thought made him smile. It was not the life he'd pictured for himself, back when he'd left home. But it was his, and it ticked on, steady and bright.

Finnian reached for his mug, savoring the taste and the moment. Then he turned back to his workbench, already plotting the next improvement.

Outside, the town's clocks chimed the time, and for the first time in years, the sound made him glad to be awake.

———

Galhani measured afternoons by the way the light shifted through her shop window. In early spring, the sun ducked behind clouds and rooftops by midmeal, but today, it lingered, filtering through the lace curtain and pooling on the counter in long, warm ribbons. She tidied the empty tables, pausing every so often to savor the sharp, clean perfume that wafted from the drying rack above her head. Even after so many years, she still caught herself surprised by how alive the place felt at this time: the faint simmer from the kettle, the creak of floorboards adjusting to the day's heat, and the soft rustle of leaves as the breeze carried news of the outside world inside.

She'd seen Finnian earlier, through the warped glass, and had watched him linger on the step before pushing open the door. He entered as he always did, careful, shoulders rounded as if to apologize for the space he occupied. He wore a shirt rolled to the elbows, his forearms streaked with brass polish and ink. In his hands, he cradled a box—a simple thing, but wrapped with a neatness that made it look more valuable than anything on the shelves.

"Right on time," Galhani called, and she saw the way his eyes brightened at the greeting.

He set the box on the counter. "I made something," he said, "but only if you want it. I mean, it's for you. If you want it." His voice had the awkward lilt of a person not yet convinced he belonged here, and Galhani felt a sharp pang of recognition.

"I always want things," she said, "especially if they're made by hand." She gestured for him to open it.

He slid the lid free, careful not to tear the paper. Inside was a flower, not quite life-size, but rendered in wood and lacquer with such fidelity that for a moment Galhani thought it might be a real wild-flower, frozen mid-bloom. The petals gleamed in bands of blue and gold, and the stalk had the gentle curve of a plant leaning toward the light.

Galhani lifted it from the box, turning it in her fingers. It was heavier than it looked, and the base was fitted with a tiny metal key. "It's beautiful," she breathed, not bothering to disguise her awe. "How did you—"

"Put it on the windowsill," Finnian interrupted, his words tumbling over each other. "It'll work better there."

She obeyed, clearing a space between two jars of lemon balm and placing the flower where the afternoon light was strongest. Finnian wound the key, three slow turns, and then stood back.

At first, nothing happened. Then, as the sunbeam crept up the stalk, the petals stirred—a delicate shudder, followed by a smooth, almost imperceptible unfurling. The blue arcs widened, catching the gold in their seams, until the whole blossom seemed to breathe.

Galhani stared, transfixed. "It opens with the sun."

Finnian grinned, more with relief than triumph. "And closes when it gets dark. There's a spring and a… well, it's complicated. But I wanted you to have something that never faded, even on the gray days."

She reached out and touched his arm, just above the wrist. "I've never seen anything like it," she said, and meant it.

For a while, they just watched the flower do its work, letting the silence settle around them. When the petals had reached their limit, Galhani poured two mugs from the fresh kettle and brought them to the table by the window.

They sat, the flower between them, and sipped in companionable quiet. The taste was a little wild, a little bitter, but it suited the day.

"Do you remember," Finnian began, "when I first came to town? I spent a sennight pretending I was just passing through." He laughed, a dry, self-deprecating sound. "I thought if I didn't linger, nobody would notice I didn't fit."

Galhani smiled. "You fit better than half the people born here. The clocks never lied about you."

He frowned, as if turning the phrase over in his mind. "You think the clocks have opinions?"

She shrugged. "They keep the rhythm. You keep them alive. That's a kind of conversation, isn't it?"

Finnian sipped, mulling it over. "Maybe. I used to think if I kept busy enough, I'd forget what it felt like to be out of place." He looked at the flower, then at Galhani. "But after the ritual, after the tea on the green, it's different. The whole town feels... easier, somehow."

"I know," Galhani said, her voice soft. "It's like we remembered how to breathe together."

Finnian's face relaxed, the last trace of tension smoothing away. "I wanted to thank you," he said. "For making it easier to stay. For treating me like I belonged, even before I did."

Galhani felt the compliment settle in her chest. "I just served the tea," she said, but she knew he meant it.

They finished their cups, trading stories about the day: the customer with the music box, the baker's new honey cake, the rumor that Dardrad was teaching his youngest how to drive a cart. Galhani noticed that Finnian spoke more easily now, his hands expressive, his laughter bright and open. He told a story about a gear gone wrong and nearly slicing the tip of his finger off; she countered with one about Lara's attempt to brew dandelion wine, and how it nearly melted the stopper from the bottle.

When the tea was gone, they sat for a time in the companionable hush, watching the play of light through the window. The flower's petals shifted, closing just a fraction as a passing cloud muted the sun. They both watched, amused by the timing.

"It even knows when to rest," Galhani said, turning the phrase over in her mind.

Finnian nodded. "I wish I did."

She smiled, the motion easy and real. "Maybe it can teach us both."

He looked at her, then at the flower, and for a moment, Galhani thought she could see the shape of the future—slow, bright, and full of unexpected warmth.

They parted with a promise to meet again tomorrow. Galhani stayed behind, tidying the mugs and watching as the cloud passed, the petals resuming their steady opening. She thought of the way Finnian had looked at her, the way his careful hands had made something so unnecessary and so perfect.

In that moment, she felt lighter than she had in years.

Outside, the afternoon lengthened, and the shop filled with the patient, expectant quiet of a place that knew it would be full again soon.

———

By the time the sky over North Pointe had softened to a plum-dark wash, the Broken Claw had filled with the purposeful noise of a town making up for lost time. The pub's lamps burned with an oily warmth, lending the whole room a glow that made even the oldest scars—on faces, tables, or the very bones of the building—look like badges of pride. Finnian arrived to find the front tables already claimed by a shifting population of regulars and travelers, all jostling for position at the crossroads of rumor and hospitality.

He scanned the crowd for a familiar face, felt a moment's doubt that he'd ever be more than a quiet fixture on the edge of things, then caught Galhani's wave from a table near the center. She had staked out two seats, one for herself and the other—he realized with a strange, full-hearted rush—for him.

"Over here!" she called, as if the room itself required instructions.

Finnian threaded his way through the crowd, pausing to dodge a pair of children waging a war with bread crusts. He slid onto the bench beside Galhani, feeling the press of warmth on either side as the table filled with the other shopkeepers: Warren, with his arms folded like logs across his chest; Leota, her dress even darker under the candlelight; Sam, never still, weaving between tables with a pitcher in one hand and a battered mug in the other.

"What's the occasion?" Finnian asked, as Galhani slid a cup toward him.

She shrugged, but the smile gave her away. "Does there need to be one? It's a good night. The clocks all rang true, the bakery didn't explode, and nobody's tried to buy a 'fortnight's worth of betterment tablets' since Tuesday. I'd say that's worth celebrating."

Sam dropped off a round of drinks, the foam sloshing over the rim of Warren's pint. "Tell him the real reason," she said, and then to Finnian, "It's because you're here, new leaf."

Finnian flushed, unable to meet her gaze. "I've been here for moons."

"Yeah," Sam said, "but now you actually show up." She rapped the table for emphasis and disappeared into the crowd, leaving only the aftershock of her grin.

Warren leaned in, voice pitched low. "We're all just glad you didn't turn out like the last clockmaker. That one sold me a 'self-winding carriage watch' and it nearly took my finger off."

Leota sniffed. "I always suspected it was a curse. Finnian's clocks, at least, only tell time."

"That's the secret," Finnian said, unable to help himself. "They tell time, but they never gossip about it later."

The laughter at the table was immediate and genuine. Galhani beamed, and even Leota's lips curved in reluctant approval.

Soon enough, the conversation turned to stories—old fights, new rumors, the endless petty wars of who owed who a drink or a favor. Someone (Finnian couldn't tell if it was Cole or one of the travelers) asked him about the clock on the green, the one that always ran fast, and whether he'd ever figured out the cause.

Finnian spun the tale with a confidence he hadn't known he possessed. "It's said that a famous explorer once left town and promised to return before sunset. The mayor, not wanting to be caught unprepared, instructed the old clockmaker to set the time ahead, just a little, so the homecoming would look more impressive. But the trick is, once you start running fast, it's hard to slow down."

He mimed the wobbly gait of the clock hands, and the table erupted in laughter. Warren slapped the wood so hard the mugs rattled.

Leota, serious as always, interrupted: "But how did you fix it?"

Finnian grinned. "I didn't. I just tuned it so the difference is always exactly the same. That way, the people who trust it are never late, and the people who know better just ignore it. There's a lesson in there, I think."

A few of the children from the bread-crust melee drifted closer, drawn by the promise of story and spectacle. Finnian let them crowd around the edge of the table, then produced a battered pocket watch from his vest. He opened the back, revealing a swirl of gears and springs, and let them peer inside.

"Careful," he said. "It bites."

One of the braver kids reached out, only to yelp in mock horror when the cover snapped shut. The whole cluster dissolved into giggles, and Finnian felt something settle in his chest—a warmth he hadn't realized he was missing.

The evening spun forward, rounds of drinks passing with clock-work regularity. More townsfolk joined the table: Dardrad, gruff and red-nosed, who traded jokes about dwarven timepieces ("They only go off at mealtime, and even then they're late"); Makota, who brought a plate of pastries and threatened to dock Galhani's tea privileges if she didn't try at least three.

Every so often, a neighbor would stop by, clapping Finnian on the back or offering some small token—a strip of cured meat, a bundle of odd screws, a folded slip of paper promising "one free favor, within reason." Vamir appeared at one point, cheeks flushed with pleasure, and pressed a worn pamphlet into Finnian's hands. "You might find this useful," he said. "It's an old treatise on gear harmonics. From the forest libraries. There's a bit about music boxes, too."

Finnian accepted it, almost speechless, and for the rest of the night kept the pamphlet tucked against his heart.

Somewhere between the pie course and the first round of closing songs, Leota drew him into a quiet aside. "You've done well," she said, voice low enough that the others couldn't overhear. "Not just with the clocks. You fit. You balance things."

Finnian didn't know how to answer, so he just nodded.

She regarded him with a piercing, witch's look. "That's not easy, you know. Most people—" She waved a hand, encompassing the whole room, "—never get the balance right. They try to push, or to run away, or to remake the place in their own image."

He thought of the clock shop, and the way he'd once tried to keep himself wound too tight, afraid that anything less than perfection would get him exiled from the green. "I think I'm learning," he said.

Leota sipped her drink. "You are." She returned to the table, and the night moved on.

As the crowd thinned, Finnian found himself in the center of a calm, familiar orbit. The laughter was less raucous now, more content, and even the fire in the hearth had settled to a slow, comfortable burn. He looked around, at the friends and strangers who had become—almost without his noticing—his people.

Galhani caught his gaze and raised her mug in silent salute.

Finnian smiled, and the smile lingered long after the final round, long after the lights dimmed and the regulars shuffled out into the cool, forgiving dark.

He walked home alone, the stars crisp above, and every step felt lighter than the one before.

When he reached his shop, he paused on the threshold, listening to the steady tick from within. It was the most welcoming sound in the world.

———

The shop, after dark, belonged to Galhani alone. The benches gleamed with a memory of polish, and the shelves glowed in the soft blue of a single enchanted lamp. All around her, jars and crocks stood in patient attention, their labels crowded with the names of plants and roots that, until this year, had mostly gathered dust.

She worked at the main table, sleeves pushed to her elbows, eyes narrowed in concentration. In the hush, she could hear the faintest crackle of the brazier's embers, the slow cooling of the day's last pot, and—far above—the wind combing through the roof's thatch. It was as peaceful as a church, but with none of the pressure to believe in anything but her own two hands.

Galhani's movements were efficient, even graceful. She didn't measure; she trusted the weight of her palms, the curl of her fingers, the way a handful of petals felt against the skin. She pinched mountain sage into a bowl, followed it with a scatter of honey crystals, and then hesitated, eyes landing on a jar that had never once been opened.

The blue flower was called moon's tear, though nobody in town could agree on whether it was poisonous or merely inconvenient. The dried petals crumbled at a touch, and Galhani let them dissolve into the mix, watching as the color bled instantly into the honey and sage.

She inhaled, caught a note of something new—smoke, sweetness, and the faint, medicinal tang that always meant a risk. Her grandmother's voice, deep in memory, said: "If it can't kill you, it can cure you." She smiled, set the bowl aside, and started on the next blend.

The bell over the door jingled, sharp and quick. Galhani glanced up, surprised at the interruption, but found it was only Lara, hair wild from the wind and arms loaded with a basket of fresh leaves.

"Did you forget the time?" Lara asked, setting the basket on the table. "It's nearly midnight. You know what they say about witching time."

Galhani grinned, unbothered. "I say it's the best time. Nobody else in the world to bother you." She reached for a sprig of something in the basket—lemon balm, soft and fragrant, still wet from the dew. "This is perfect. Did you pick it from the riverbank?"

Lara nodded, shedding her coat. "It's coming in thick, this year. I thought you'd want the first of it." She eyed the bowl. "What's this?"

"Experiment," Galhani said. "I want something for strength. Not just to keep people awake, but to help them recover." She measured a spoonful of the blue-streaked powder into a fresh cup, poured water from the kettle, and watched as the infusion bloomed to a gold edged in violet.

Lara sniffed. "Smells… lively. Maybe a little dangerous."

"Isn't that the point?" Galhani asked. She let the cup steep, then handed it across.

Lara sipped, eyebrows rising. "Oh. That's—" She searched for the word. "It's good. Makes my teeth tingle."

Galhani laughed. "You'll live."

The next customer was a traveler, lean and stooped, with the look of someone who'd spent the last moon sleeping in ditches and hollowed-out haystacks. He hovered in the doorway, uncertain, until Galhani waved him in.

"Looking for anything special?" she asked, though she already knew what he'd say.

"Something to keep me walking," he muttered, voice rough. "Just another day or two."

She nodded, fetched down the fresh jar. "Try this," she said, pouring him a cup. "It's new."

He watched her, wary, then lifted the cup with both hands. The first sip made him blink; the second, he drained in one go. Galhani saw his posture straighten, the pallor fade a little from his face.

"It works," he said, surprised. "I can feel it in my bones. Like summer sun."

She smiled, not with relief but with the quiet certainty of a craftsman. "Take some for the road," she said, packing a small satchel. "It'll get you through the worst of it."

The traveler hesitated, looked as though he wanted to ask the price, then shrugged. "I'll pay it forward," he said, and left the coin on the counter.

When the door closed, Galhani and Lara shared a moment in the deep, easy silence.

"I think you're getting better at this," Lara said, voice low. "Not just the blends. The rest of it, too."

Galhani wiped her hands, leaned against the counter. "It's easier, now. Like I remember why I started."

Lara drew close, breath warm on Galhani's cheek. "You did save the town."

"Not alone," Galhani replied, but the words had lost their protest. "And it's not saved. It's just—" She trailed off, unsure.

"It's in good hands," Lara finished.

Galhani smiled, let the comfort of the words settle in. She reached for the recipe book, flipped to a blank page, and began to write: Notations on Moon's Tear. Best when combined with honey or lemon. Strengthens the heart. Cures what can be cured.

Outside, the town was deep in sleep, but the shop was alive with the memory of every customer, every shared cup, every experiment that had gone right or wrong or somewhere in between.

Galhani finished her notes, tucked the book away, and poured two more cups—one for herself, one for Lara. They drank in companionable quiet, letting the new magic work its way through their veins.

She had never believed in happy endings. But this, she thought, was close enough.

epilogue

. . .

SCENE 1 - FROM VIEWPOINT CHARACTER: GALHANI)'S point of view

Galhani measured mornings by the way the sunlight caught the jars along her highest shelf. Today, the beams came in clean and low, slicing through the front window in perfect, measured increments—one for every candlemark she'd managed to sleep. The air in the shop was still crisp, holding just a little of the night's chill despite the stove's quiet efforts. It was a good morning for new work.

She moved among the benches barefoot, her toes making damp prints on the scrubbed planks. With every step she took, she felt the rightness of the place settle a bit deeper into her chest: the close, rich perfume of steeped mountain sage; the dry dust of honey crystals ground fine and stored in tight-lidded crocks; the hanging bundles of wild sweetflag, their yellowed stalks crackling faintly as she brushed past. The herbs she needed today were the ones for her new project—a strengthening tea, meant to bolster the body and the will, and maybe, if she was lucky, the spirit too.

Galhani set out her tools: a mortar and pestle, a big mixing bowl, a strainer so fine it could catch dreams. She began with a measured handful of dried nettle, tossing the leaves into the bowl and bruising them with a wooden pestle. The sound was a dry, friendly hiss, like the rustle of paper under a cat's paws. Next came the bright green tips of wild mint, snipped fresh from the rack by the stove. She pinched off the smallest leaves and rolled them between her fingers, savoring their sharp, green scent.

The shop was quiet, the only customers a trio of travelers clustered at the back table. They'd arrived just after first light, shedding the mud and wind of the trade road in a noisy spill at her threshold. Now, cleaned up and fed, they kept their heads together, talking in a low, urgent way that didn't quite fit the room. Galhani tried not to listen, but their voices leaked into her work whether she wanted them or not.

"…not just one banner, but three. All the same sigil." That was the youngest, a boy with a pale scar across one eyebrow. His voice held a note of awe, but also fear.

"They say he took the valley at Bellos with hardly a fight," said the second, older, his hair gone at the temples. "Two days, maybe three. The farmers left with nothing but the shirts on their backs."

"It's not like before," the third traveler said, her tone cautious. "This is different. I heard they're calling it a kingdom, now. Not just raids. They're building towns. Roads."

Galhani's hand paused mid-measure, the next pinch of honey crystals poised above her bowl. She kept her face steady and let the crystals fall, watching as they disappeared into the dark, green tangle below. She'd heard the rumors, of course—everyone in North Pointe had, though most chose to ignore them. The idea of a true goblin kingdom, with laws and borders, was the kind of talk that usually brought a scolding from the town's elders, or at the very least, a hasty change of subject. But now, in the hush of her own shop, the words landed with a weight that surprised her.

She continued to blend the tea, but her mind drifted to the maps behind the bar at the Broken Claw. For generations, the western forests had been a problem for travelers, but never more than that—a source of danger, yes, but also of stories and wild fruit and the occasional lost sheep. Now, if the stories were true, there were armies out there, and a king to command them. Galhani wondered what that would mean for a town like hers.

The travelers' voices faded for a time, and she finished her work in the comfort of her own silence. She mixed the blend, then spooned it into a tin marked with a fresh label: "For Courage." She doubted the label would help, but it felt right to try.

At midmorning, she brought out the tray of test cups and set them by the window, hoping the first sunlight would coax a little more color from the brew. She poured herself a cup, then let it cool as she returned to the counter to take stock.

She was half lost in counting her stock of dried yarrow when the travelers' conversation spiked, urgent and unguarded.

"...but what if it works?" the boy asked. "What if it's not just a warlord, but a real kingdom? It would change everything."

"It already has," the older man replied. "The border towns are empty. Saw it with my own eyes—storefronts boarded up, stables burned, even the church bell gone. They're moving east, some of them. Here, maybe. Or farther."

Galhani looked at her hands and saw that they'd gone still. She set the jar down, careful not to chip the glaze, and breathed deep until the feeling passed.

She knew, in the old days, she'd have felt a jolt of fear so strong it would have driven her under the counter, or at least into a corner behind the stacked casks of night-wort. But now, after the crisis—after the parasite, the circle on the green, the night when she'd watched the town bend and nearly break—her nerves were different. The old panic didn't have the same grip. In its place was something slower, heavier, but maybe a little wiser.

She crossed to the travelers, carrying their refill on a small round tray. She poured for each of them, then set out a plate of oat cakes, just pulled from the warming rack. The older man looked up at her with the eyes of someone used to being disappointed, then blinked in surprise at the extra treat.

"Thank you," he said, and meant it.

Galhani smiled. "You'll want something stronger, if you're heading west again. I've a new blend, for strength."

The woman sipped first, then set her cup down with a thoughtful sound. "You always have the right thing for the road," she said. "It's why we stop here."

Galhani inclined her head. "It's easy, when the road always comes back."

The boy, emboldened by the comfort of hot tea and a real chair, spoke up. "Do you think it's true? About the goblin king?" His question came out too quickly, and he flushed as if already sorry for asking.

Galhani set her hands flat on the table, feeling the grain of the wood against her palms. "I don't know," she said, honest. "But I think the stories are more dangerous when you try not to believe them."

The woman's face softened. "You have family here?"

"Just me," Galhani said. "And the shop."

The travelers nodded, as if this made perfect sense.

She watched them eat and drink, and wondered how many more would come, and how many might not make it past the forests if the rumors held true. She wondered what the world would look like, in a year or two, if the goblins really did build a kingdom.

She gathered the tray and returned to her place behind the counter. She watched the light as it crawled across the floor, measured the time by the dust motes and the distant sounds of the green. She felt the warmth of the restored magic running through the bones of the shop, and took comfort in the steadiness of it.

Outside, the day went on. More travelers arrived, some for tea, some for word of the road ahead. The morning slipped by in a quiet, constant rhythm, each cup served a small act of defiance against the uncertainty waiting just beyond the hills.

When the sun climbed past the highest roof and the shop filled with gold, Galhani poured herself another cup of the new blend. She drank slow, savoring the taste, and thought of what was coming. She let herself feel a little fear, just enough to keep her sharp, then set it aside for later.

There was work to do, and it was a good morning for new work.

Scene 2 - from Viewpoint Character: Galhani)'s point of view

The evening found the Broken Claw running warm, every lamp above the bar shrouded in amber and every bench occupied by someone determined to drink their share of the daylight's end.

Galhani arrived late, her coat damp from a brief spell of mist, her hair twisted up and still clinging to the smell of mint and honey from the shop. She slipped inside with the ease of habit, nodding to Sam, who polished a row of mugs with the proprietary air of a woman who owned her world one glass at a time.

Sam didn't need to ask her order. She set a heavy-lipped mug on the counter, poured a generous finger of something sharp and bright, and slid it across. "You look like a woman in need of bad news," Sam said, not unkindly.

Galhani snorted and sipped, the warmth tracing a familiar path down her throat. "Heard any?"

"Only the usual." Sam leaned on her elbows, eyeing the tables. "Every traveler west of the lake has a new story. Most of 'em about the Goblin King."

Galhani took in the room. At the long table near the hearth sat the familiar faces: Warren, his bulk nearly tipping the bench; Leota in black, eyes luminous in the firelight; Vamir, who was bent over a map that curled at the edges from age and candle wax; Finnian, who looked more at ease here than anywhere else, his hands folded with practiced stillness. A few locals clustered at other tables—Cole from the bakery, Lucy the potter, a couple of younger shopkeepers—but all eyes drifted to the big table whenever the talk rose above a murmur.

Galhani joined them, squeezing onto the bench beside Finnian. The table was cluttered with tankards, crumbs, and a plate of pickles that had been picked over to nothing but brine.

Warren greeted her with a deep nod, the scars on his knuckles catching the firelight. "We saved you a seat," he said, as if there had ever been any question.

"Vamir brought a new map," Finnian offered, tapping the parchment with one blunt finger.

Vamir looked up, his eyes bright behind the fog of his glasses. "It's from a merchant. Passed through two days ago, claimed the old northern highway is closed now. All traffic's being diverted east."

He pointed to a fat, red line drawn through a cluster of hills. "They say the Goblin King controls everything from here to the pass. More than a hundred miles, if you believe the rumors."

Leota arched an eyebrow. "I don't believe anything until I've seen it. Or smelled it." She sniffed, as if expecting goblin musk to be wafting in from the trade road.

Warren drained his mug, then set it down with a gentle thud. "It's not like the old days," he said. "Used to be you could tell a raid by the smell of burned oats and the noise. But this—" He gestured at the map. "This is something else. No chaos, no fire. Just…banners, and rules."

Galhani looked at the map, and then at the faces of her friends. There was a steadiness here she envied, a way of accepting bad news without letting it root in the bones. "People are running," she said. "Every day, more of them show up at the shop. They're scared, but mostly they're tired."

Finnian poured a measure from the shared pitcher. "It's not just the goblins. The road is worse than ever—bandits, scams, even the old waystations shutting down. They say the King's taxes are steep, but the toll is the only thing keeping the worst of them away."

Leota scoffed. "A protection racket, dressed in royal trappings."

"Still a racket," Warren agreed, "but at least you know who's in charge."

Galhani turned to Sam, who hovered nearby, drying her hands on a square of linen. "What do you think?" she asked, voice low.

Sam shrugged. "Makes no difference to the Claw. Travelers come, travelers go. If the King keeps the roads safer, maybe it'll be good for business."

"But it's not just business," Leota interjected, her eyes on Galhani. "It's about what comes next. If the King wants a real kingdom, he'll want more than roads and taxes. He'll want the towns. He'll want us."

A hush fell over the table, broken only by the snap of the fire and the rattle of ice in the bottom of Finnian's glass.

Vamir traced a slow line on the map. "The question is, do we change the way we live, or do we wait for the change to find us?"

Warren grunted, a deep, chesty sound. "I'll tell you this: if the King wants a fight, he'll find one. But I don't think that's what he's after. I think he wants to prove he can do it—to build something that lasts."

Galhani thought of the shop, the tidy rows of jars, the comfort of routine. She thought of the parasite, and how it had nearly hollowed the town from the inside out. "Sometimes," she said, "change comes whether you're ready or not. The trick is surviving it, and finding what's still yours when it's over."

Leota raised her mug in a small salute. "Spoken like a woman who's seen the other side."

They drank to that, each in their own rhythm.

Sam returned, carrying a tray of cider mugs that steamed in the cool draft from the door. She set them down with a practiced sweep, then perched on the edge of the bench, wiping a stray droplet from her wrist. "We're not going to be the heroes of this story," she said, matter-of-fact. "That's not what towns like this are for. Our job is to hold the line, help the ones passing through, and keep each other fed and whole." Her smile was a little tired, but it held. "If the world wants to change, let it. Just don't let it change you so much you forget who you are."

Galhani nodded, her chest tight with something like relief. For all the talk of kingdoms and kings, the real work would always be here, among the people who remembered your birthday and your favorite tea and the way you liked your bread cut.

The talk drifted, then, into easier topics—rumors about the next festival, bets on when the snow would come, the old joke about the potter who tried to make cups out of eggshells. The fire sank lower, and the regulars drifted home one by one, until only the core group remained.

Leota pulled her coat on, glancing at the map one last time. "If the King's men come, I'll see them before they cross the old line. I'll send word."

Warren cracked his knuckles, then reached for his hat. "I've got a backlog of blades to finish. I'd rather not think of who'll use them next."

Finnian gathered the empty glasses with the care of a man who'd been a waiter once, and Vamir tucked the map into his coat, the corners peeking out like a secret.

Galhani stood with the rest, stretching the ache from her shoulders. She lingered at the door, watching as Sam doused the lamps and set the bar to rights. Outside, the street was blue with evening, the mist heavy enough to muffle even the rowdiest songs from the lakeside.

She stepped out and let the air settle over her. The town was quieter than she'd ever known it, every window aglow, every hearth alive with the warmth of people stubborn enough to stay. She walked slow, hands in her pockets, feeling the strength of the new blend coursing through her—courage, yes, but also caution. A sense that the world was always waiting for the next storm, and that the only defense was to keep the lamps burning, and the doors open, and the tea hot.

She turned the corner toward home, and for a moment, she almost missed the old feeling of dread, the certainty that nothing good ever lasted. But it wasn't like that anymore.

She knew what to do, and she knew she wouldn't have to do it alone.

Inside the shop, she found Lara asleep on the couch, a book fallen to her chest and her hair spread out like a banner of dark silk. Galhani paused to watch her breathe, the slow rise and fall a comfort in the hush. She poured herself a final cup, drank it at the window, and watched as the last of the lamps on the green winked out, one by one.

The night settled, but she was not afraid.

Outside, beyond the ring of magic and memory, the world could do what it liked.

Here, for now, was enough.

award-winning fiction

Daniel Scratch: a story of witchkind

- Kirkus Starred Review
- Winner, American Fiction Awards—Best Fantasy (2023)
- Finalist, American legacy Book Awards—Best Fantasy (2024)

———

Clara Thorn, the witch that was found

- Winner, American Fiction Awards—Best Young Adult (2023)
- Runner-Up, American Fiction Awards—Best Fantasy (2023)
- Finalist, American Legacy Book Awards—Best Fantasy (2024)
- Finalist, American Legacy Book Awards—Best Young Adult (2024)

———

Find these books and more at DonJones.com

about the author

Don Jones spent two decades writing tech books before he finally penned his first sci-fi novella, *A History of the Galactic War*. His well-reviewed and award-winning novels span fantasy and science fiction, with a focus on world building and relatable characters.

Connect, get free novels and short stories, and learn about upcoming releases by visiting Don's author website at DonJones.com.